I0563317

A Precarious Homecoming

Arabella Stewart Historical Mysteries, Volume 1

D.S. Lang

Published by D.S. Lang, 2022.

This is a work of fiction. Similarities to real people, places, or events are entirely coincidental.

A PRECARIOUS HOMECOMING

First edition. April 11, 2022.

Copyright © 2022 D.S. Lang.

ISBN: 978-1736838563

Written by D.S. Lang.

Also by D.S. Lang

Arabella Stewart Historical Mysteries
A Precarious Homecoming
A Lingering Shadow
A Lethal Arrogance
A Baffling Absence
A Fatal Reunion
A Surreptitious Undertaking
A Treacherous Accusation
An Uncertain Ceremony
Arabella Stewart Historical Mysteries Books 1-4
Arabella Stewart Historical Mysteries-Books 5-8

Doro Banyon Historical Mysteries
The Catalogued Corpse
The Murdered Matron
The Jammed Judges
The Problem Professor
The Bottled Bootlegger
The Doomed Doctor

The Hounded Hoopster
The Surly Secretary
The Doro Banyon Mysteries Books 1-3

Watch for more at https://www.dslangbooks.com.

Chapter One

Ohio—December 1919

Arabella Stewart pressed her gloved hand to the window, wiped away the steam fogging its surface, and gazed out into the dawning light. Cold penetrated the glass and her gloves, but the real chill was inside her. Outside barren fields stretched to the horizon. Coming home should have been a cause for celebration but now, like thousands of others, she had little to celebrate.

As the train slowed before entering her hometown, she strained to see the Methodist church marking the outskirts of Moreley. The familiar spire was barely visible against the pale gray sky and swirling snow, as was the cemetery in its shadow. Gravestones—dark silhouettes in the faint light—rose in silent testimony to those now at rest. Bella didn't have to count the markers to know many more had been added since she had left home almost two years earlier.

Hot moisture pricked her eyes, and she blinked hastily to clear it away. Bella didn't want to greet Mac with red-rimmed eyes and tear-stained cheeks. Although the hour was early, he would be at the station to greet her. For that, Bella was grateful. Her family was gone, but she still had Mac, and they still had Ballantyne, the resort founded by him and her Grandfather Stewart four decades earlier.

By the time she stepped off the train, kit in hand, Bella gained a semblance of control. No longer on the verge of tears, she scanned the station, but there was no sign of Mac, or anyone else for that matter. The place was vacant.

"Here, miss," the conductor, a tall man in his early forties, said. He laid her other bag on the platform under the station roof's overhang. He looked around before glancing back at her. "Is someone coming to collect you?"

"Yes, a family friend will be here." Once again, she noted the silence. Bella had been in the station many times, but never had it been so quiet, so empty. When Bella had left to join the Army Signal Corps, the train stopped at the Moreley station three times every day during the winter months and more often during the summer season. Three years ago, at this same time, the station would have been decked out in its holiday finery with visitors arriving to spend Christmas in town or at the resort. Now, not even a sprig of holly was visible.

"Why isn't the station open?"

The man frowned. "You're just getting home from France, aren't you?" he asked, acknowledging their exchange about her uniform as she boarded the train in Sandusky. "Since you're from here, you must know this area was hit hard by the Spanish flu. That affected business at the nearby resort and in town. Between losing some of their boys in France and other people with the pandemic, Moreley isn't the same as it used to be."

Bella fought to maintain her composure. "I know," she murmured. "Mac MacLendon, our family friend, has been in touch with me. He said there was only one train south out of Sandusky weekdays now, but I didn't realize the station was closed." Bella made a closer study of the place. Not only was it barren, the building's paint was chipped and faded while the arrival and departure board was blank. Cobwebs, filling every corner and crevice, projected an overall atmosphere of neglect and abandonment.

"The ticket office will open shortly for a couple of hours," he told her. "Geneve may be running late because he is usually here by now."

"Is he the only employee these days?" Edgar Geneve had been the station master as long as Bella could remember, but there had been other workers. A number of others. As Ballantyne had grown in popularity, Moreley had prospered from overflow visitors.

"Yes. The line still goes from Sandusky to Columbus, but as I said, we don't stop here nearly as often these days."

"I see."

The conductor looked past Bella. "Your friend is here," he said with a smile. "I'll leave you in his hands. A Merry Christmas to you, miss."

"Merry Christmas." Her reply, an automatic one, went to his retreating back. Despite the gloom of the station, Bella felt a smile curving her lips as she turned to greet Mac, but it quickly died because Mac wasn't walking toward her, Jackson Hastings was.

Tall and lean, Jax was a familiar figure and, for a moment, Bella was again swept back in time—back to Christmas three years earlier when he had also been the one to collect her. She had been returning from school and not only had the station been bustling and festive, Jax had welcomed her with a wide smile and a warm hug. Now, no smile lit his handsome face and no hug was forthcoming, either. Not that she expected or wanted one. Not anymore. Not from him.

Jax stopped a few feet from Bella. With his constable's cap pulled down, his grass green eyes were barely visible but the hard set of his square jaw was clear. "Good morning, Bella, and welcome home."

His deep baritone sounded slightly rough, and no trace of warmth was evident. As far as welcomes went, it wasn't much. "Good morning," she replied, keeping her own voice and expression as devoid of emotion as his was. Bella looked past him. "Mac will be here to pick me up any minute."

"No, he won't. Doc called and asked me to get you. Mac caught a bad cold and needs to stay in bed for a couple of days."

"A bad cold? Are they sure it's not influenza?" Panic gripped Bella, and she knew it was in her voice and expression, but she didn't care. Nothing could happen to Mac. She couldn't bear to lose him, too.

"Absolutely sure." His voice lost some of the chill. "Doc has been out to check on him every day. Carl is staying in the inn, so he's there if Mac needs anything. It's simply a precaution that he stays home, especially in this weather."

The snow wasn't heavy, but the wind was harsh and icy. "Of course." She tamped down her fear and looked at Jax again. His expression had lost any trace of warmth or softness. She sighed. "I'm sorry they had to bother you."

He bit his lower lip and glanced away. When Jax met her gaze again, some emotion clouded his eyes but Bella couldn't identify it. Nor could she identify the tenor of his tone when he responded. "It isn't any trouble."

For long moments, they stood looking at one another, yet, as close as they were, Bella was very aware of an invisible barrier between them. His cold rejection and clear disinterest after her brother—his best friend—died was still inexplicable to her. A shiver ran through Bella as she recalled that day in France when Jax had offered a brief condolence before turning away from her and to a pretty, young French nurse. If he had slapped her, Bella couldn't have felt more rejected. She had fought to forget the moment, but it rose in her mind's eye now, and a shiver ripped through her.

"You need to get out of the snow and cold," he said when she made no reply. "These bags are yours?" Jax picked up her kit bag and portmanteau. "I'm parked just outside the station."

"I can carry my kit," Bella said as he started toward the station exit. Jax turned back with a frown. Once again, she remembered December 1916 when she'd gladly allowed him to carry her luggage. But that was a different time, and they'd had a different relationship. Her chin lifted a fraction. "In France, I always carried it myself."

He inhaled sharply, but said nothing. Instead, Jax handed the kit bag to her and, once again, headed away.

When they got to the car, Jax stored both bags and moved to the driver's side. Once they were settled in the Chevrolet Chummy, he glanced at Bella, who was looking straight ahead. Unsure what to say, he studied her for several moments. Up close, the mauve shadows beneath her dark eyes were obvious. So was the fact she was reed slim. Not for the first time, he wondered why Bella had been among the last of s the Army Signal Corps operators to come home. Only a handful had stayed in Europe after the expeditionary force left. Why had she been one of them? Since asking might put a chink in the wall he'd built between them, Jax made a milder inquiry. "Do you need anything while you're in town? The drug store should be open."

Briefly, she met his gaze before glancing away. "No, I spent a few days with Ida and her family in the Cleveland area and picked up some items there."

Jax knew her best friend, Ida Byington, had stayed in Europe with Bella. He merely nodded, pulled away from the curb, and headed down Main Street into the business district. Since no other vehicles were on the road, Jax shifted into a higher gear. Within moments, Bella put one hand on top of her uniform cap. At the same time, he saw the ends of her bob being whipped by the cold wind. Since the Chummy, a sporty two-door, had no side curtains or isinglass, a breeze was inevitable. Jax never paid much attention, but he rarely had any passengers and never any females. "Sorry," he said, shifting into a lower gear. "I should have brought a blanket for you."

"I'm fine," Bella murmured, but her attention was on the passing buildings. "The hotel, theater, bookstore, and emporium are all closed. Is it just for the winter?"

Jax followed her gaze and remembered his own reaction upon returning home eight months earlier. Over the years, Moreley had turned into a resort town of sorts, mostly due to Ballantyne's proximity. The resort, on a river downstream from Lake Erie, had grown as people had more leisure time and wanted to escape the city. Since accommodations at Ballantyne were limited, many visitors had once stayed at the Moreley hotel. Jax imagined Bella was picturing how things had been when businesses flourished. Back then, shops of various kinds would normally be opening at this hour, but little activity was apparent. "I'm afraid not. Didn't Mac mention how things have changed?"

"Yes, of course, he told me. It's just seeing the place and hearing about it aren't the same. I knew he and Dad cancelled most of the summer events in 1917 since I hadn't left for France yet, and Mac let me know he couldn't keep the inn and cottages open last year. It was too much for him to do alone."

Jax took a sidelong glance at Bella. Reluctantly, he filled out the story, but only a little. "Very few people came last summer, so I doubt if opening the inn and cottages would have been profitable. That's why the hotel in town closed. Not enough visitors to make keeping it open worthwhile." He scanned both sides of the street. A faded, battered sign was the only remnant of the small dress shop where his mother had purchased all of her ready-made clothes. The same was true for the furniture store. As he glanced around, Jax considered how Bella must feel at the sights.

"Mac never said how bad it was."

A moment passed before Jax spoke again. "You had enough to handle, so I'm sure he wanted to spare you. And I'm sure he hoped the town and Ballantyne would be back to normal before you got home."

"But they aren't." It was a statement, not a question.

"No, unfortunately, they aren't. After the war, there was a slowdown everywhere. Things improved last spring. Other places. Not here."

"At this time of year, it used to be busy in town and at the resort. Ice skating and sledding were popular. The theater showed moving pictures every night," she said as they drove past the building's boarded doors. "And all of the shops had special window displays for Christmas. Everything was bustling and busy."

The note of nostalgia in her voice opened a door in his mind. "Moreley prospered after your Grandfather Stewart and Mac opened Ballantyne. A golf course and inn on the river were a big draw for city people with more leisure time." He heard a heavy sigh escape her.

"People must still have time and means to escape the cities. If they don't come here, where do they go?"

"Cedar Point is very popular. So are Crystal Beach, Port Clinton, and Catawba." Out of the corner of his eye, Jax saw Bella nod.

"Grampa Stew and Mac opened Ballantyne because Cedar Point was a big tourist attraction. Even though Ballantyne isn't on the lake, the golf course was something other area resorts didn't have."

"It didn't hurt that both of them had been golf professionals in Cleveland," Jax said. "They knew a lot of people who came to Ballantyne for golf and spread the word about how great the course is." Golf has gained in popularity over the years. It still was. "Adding the tennis courts helped, and so did making boats available so folks could enjoy the river."

"Yes, they were smart to add activities beyond golf. That helped the town, too."

Bella continued to gaze out at the town. "Now, it's filled with empty stores and empty houses." She turned back to Jax. "How bad is the resort?"

"Needless to say, no golf or tennis is being played now. Some golfers from the area played last summer, and a few folks came from Toledo. Mac let the tennis courts go, but they can be brought back in shape quickly. The boats are safely stored away, so they could be used again with no problem. Nolen and I take turns running out there a couple of times per week, and the property looks fine."

"Nolen?" Bella echoed. "Nolen Rogers?"

"Yes, he's my part-time deputy."

"I still think of him as a boy, but I know he was your platoon sergeant during the last few weeks of the war. Why only part-time?"

Jax's hands tightened on the steering wheel. "For the first few months after I took the position, I didn't have a deputy at all. With the population down, the mayor and council thought I could do the job alone."

"And now they don't?" She turned to study his profile, but his attention had moved to something on the sidewalk. Bella followed his gaze and frowned when she saw a small group of men gathered—their voices loud enough to carry well—in front of the café. Almost simultaneously, Jax slowed the car and muttered under his breath.

"I need to intercede before things get out of hand." He pulled into a parking place, killed the engine, and glanced at Bella. "Stay here."

Chapter Two

The words were an unwelcome order, but she had no chance to object because Jax was quickly out of the car and on the sidewalk. Bella watched the exchange with rapt attention. The biggest man—a muscular blonde in his mid-forties—turned to Jax with a furious expression on his weathered face. For a moment, Bella wondered who he was. Finally, his name came to her—Gustav Schwarz, a farmer who lived outside Moreley. Bella knew him primarily by reputation, a bad reputation as a bully. His current demeanor reinforced that view. Trepidation rippled through her and, despite Jax's admonition, she got out of the vehicle and moved to stand behind him.

"Gus, step back," Jax said.

The big man's eyes flashed with blue fire. "Why don't you tell your men to step back? Taking up for them, as usual. To you, they can't do nothing wrong—set my livestock loose, burn my sheds, and do the same to Meyers."

Jax's nostrils flared with a sharp intake of breath. "Gus, you know we've investigated all the crimes, and we haven't found the guilty party yet. We're still trying. Right now, I'm telling all of you," he said as his gaze went from the farmer to two younger men clad in army overcoats, "to step back. Owen and Curt, what's going on here?"

Bella turned her attention to the veterans. Although she hadn't seen either of them in France, Owen Carlson and Curt Molitor had been in her brother's platoon. From what she knew, both had been with Matt when he died. She swallowed hard over the lump of grief that still rose so easily. With effort, Bella fought to stay grounded in the present and focused on what was happening in front of her. Gus Schwarz—fists clenched and jaw set—looked enraged while Owen and Curt appeared uneasy. Curt shifted from one foot to the other as he put one hand on Owen's shoulder. She studied their pale faces and shadowed eyes. The war had exacted a heavy toll on soldiers and civilians alike.

Curt plucked at his army coat, which hung loosely on his lean frame. "Schwarz don't like our attire."

"The war is over," Gus said in a hard, harsh tone. "You need to forget it."

"I don't have no other coat, lieutenant." Owen's voice was barely audible.

"Even if you did," Curt put in, "you can wear what you want. Gus has got no say over you."

"I think it's best if everyone goes on about his own business." Jax glanced at another man who stood a few feet back from the trio. "Mr. Smith, are you involved?"

The short, square man shook his head. "No, constable. I left the café as they started to argue. Not involved at all and, since I need to open the post office, I will be on my way."

Jax nodded, and the older man hurried off.

Once he was gone, Schwarz's attention went to Bella. "You living in the past, too?" the farmer asked in a contemptuous tone as his gaze went from her cap to her service boots.

Resentment flared within her. As a Signal Corps operator, Bella had been limited in what she could take to France, which meant she'd had little extra space in her bags, and none for civilian attire. Once back at Ballantyne, she planned to tuck her uniforms away and return to regular clothes, but that was none of this man's business. She was about to say so when Jax spoke.

"Miss Stewart is just returning home, and she can wear whatever she wants. Now, I suggest you move along, Gus."

For a moment, Bella thought Schwarz might strike Jax. Instead, he snorted derisively before looking back at Owen and Curt. "The constable let you off, but I better not catch either of you on my land or I'll be after you. Mark my words." He turned on his heel and stalked away.

"Don't take the law into your own hands, Gus," Jax said to the retreating figure. Curt started after the farmer, but Jax caught his sleeve. "Let him go."

Curt released a long, low breath. "I'm fed up with him and Meyers getting after us for wearing our uniforms."

"I know," Jax replied as he released the other man. "Gus is set on taking offense, but try to ignore him. The same with Meyers."

"I'll try," Curt said, but his tone was not convincing.

Jax turned to the other man. "Owen?"

"I can't afford new clothes, lieutenant. Haven't been able to hold a job, neither." Once again, tremors rippled through him. "Schwarz don't understand and don't care."

A look of genuine anxiety softened Jax's expression. "I know it's been hard for you, Owen. Just look after yourself and let me worry about Gus."

Owen's heavily shadowed and red-rimmed eyes met Jax's steady gaze. "Yes, sir, but it's hard to take."

"Let's go," Curt said to Owen before looking at Bella. "Not a very nice welcome, but it's good to see you again."

"And you two, as well," she said with a forced smile.

Once Curt and Owen left, Jax turned to Bella with a forbidding frown. "Didn't I tell you to stay in the car?"

His expression and tone telegraphed deep disapproval which annoyed Bella. He had no right to rebuke her. "I don't have to follow your orders, Jax."

He ground his teeth until a muscle jumped in his jaw. "When a law officer says not to do something, you'd be wise to follow the advice. This could have turned into a physical fight, and I didn't want or need you in the middle of it."

Concern replaced censure which made Bella wonder about what she'd heard in the exchange. "What was Gus talking about when he mentioned his animals being set loose and his buildings being burned?"

With one hand, Jax rubbed his forehead. "Let's get in the car, and I'll tell you on the way to Ballantyne."

As they pulled away from the curb, Jax continued. "As Gus said, we've had some incidents. That's the main reason Nolen was hired. People want more protection than I could provide alone."

Alarm flickered through Bella as she shifted toward Jax. "What's been going on?"

When Jax replied, his voice telegraphed tension. "Schwarz had several chickens killed last spring. Around the same time, two of his sheds caught fire. This fall, his horses were found on the road and the gate was open although Gus swears he closed and locked it himself. Werner Meyers has also had livestock get loose—two cows and a goat—and one of his fields and a shed were set on fire. Both Meyers and Schwarz have had other more minor vandalism as far back as last spring." He paused briefly before continuing. "Unfortunately, news of the local trouble spread quickly, and it's played a big part in visitors not returning to the area. And in Mac not opening the inn or cottages."

Bella struggled to absorb the revelations. "I can hardly believe such things are happening around here. I know there were petty thefts occasionally, but vandalism, arson, bothering animals..." Her voice trailed off. Little wonder the tourist trade hadn't resumed. The war and influenza were behind them, but crime had evidently become a new challenge.

"It's troubling, especially since, as you say, this type of thing has never happened around Moreley until recently."

"Did the problems start during the war?"

Jax briefly turned his head to glance at her before looking back at the road. "No, they only began last spring after most of us got home from France. They've gotten worse over the past couple of months."

Niggling suspicion assailed Bella. "Gus and Werner are from German families. Their parents were immigrants. Curt mentioned their heritage, and Gus obviously dislikes seeing veterans in uniform. Do you think the crimes relate to that?" She hoped not, but the possibility could not be ignored.

"I don't know. I don't want to think it is. I've talked to almost everyone in town, and there were no problems during the war. At least none were obvious. If some held a grudge against German-Americans here, they hid it very well. Besides, others of German descent haven't been victims of any crimes." Frustration underscored the observations. "You heard Gus. He's said much the same to all of the soldiers over the past few months, and he started before the incidents began from what I know. In fact, he was mad about America getting into the conflict at all. I remember some of his ranting from before I was called up."

"Do you think that's why he was targeted?"

A sigh escaped Jax. "In the past two years, he and Meyers evidently took offense at anti-German sentiments common in other parts of the state and the country. Mrs. Meyers has relatives in Cincinnati, and the problems were especially bad there. Meyers has said, to me and to others, that his in-laws were harassed. As far as Gus, he's always been hot-headed, and I can see him taking offense even if he didn't experience hatred himself."

Bella studied his chiseled profile. "Do you know if any of the soldiers holds a grudge?"

Jax shrugged. "None of us loved being gassed or shot at, but I never heard anything hateful from any of the men. You could see Curt is angry. So are most of the others, and I can't blame them. They don't need to be berated for wearing their uniforms, and forgetting the war is impossible." His nostrils flared with a sharp intake of breath. "I want to find out who is behind the incidents and make sure the problems don't get worse. The town and the resort aren't likely to recover if crimes continue like they have."

Bella chewed on her lower lip as she considered the dilemma. "Has anyone who lost a son or brother in France been angry or upset?"

"Not that I know of and, like I said, I've spoken to almost everyone in town. I can't know how grieving folks feel inside but, if people hold a grudge, they've kept it to themselves. The worst part is this all started soon after we came back."

"Do people other than Gus Schwarz suspect them?" The possibility was as troubling as the incidents themselves. Bella knew every one of the men who had served in France, and she didn't want to think any of them were behind the recent crimes. She didn't want to think any of them could harbor so much hatred.

"It might be more correct to say that most are under suspicion. Curt Molitor is one of the main suspects to Schwarz and Meyers. He's been living out at Ballantyne with his brother Carl since he got home. Since their cabin is between the two farms, Gus and Werner say he has easy access to both places. I've told Mac about my concerns, but you need to know, too, especially after witnessing that confrontation. I don't think Gus would come after Curt at the resort, but I can't be sure."

Bella mulled over the observation. "I appreciate that, but I can't imagine Curt ever doing harm to anyone or anything, and I especially don't think he'd ever hurt an animal. He loves animals and always has." He had looked furious with Schwarz, but as Jax had said, who could blame him?

"I know, and I don't believe he's guilty, either, but he doesn't have an alibi for any of the incidents. Of course, neither do Owen Carlson, Fred Snyder, Harold Horton, or Warren Ritter."

"All of them are under suspicion?" Bella asked in dismay. Some had served in Jax's platoon and others in her brother's. The men had been in the same National Guard unit, so they were called up together.

"Schwarz and Meyers confronted Owen, Fred, and Warren before Nick stepped down as constable last May. When I took over, I spoke with them, Curt, and Harold. As the incidents have gotten worse, Nolen and I have talked to a number of people. We haven't learned anything helpful," he admitted on a sigh.

"Have Schwarz and Meyers done more than talk to the men? I never really knew either of them, but Mr. Schwarz seemed very angry."

"Yes, angry and mean. He's always been a bully. Since the latest incident, he's threatened more than once to take care of the problem if I can't. You heard him say the same thing a few minutes ago, so you can understand why I'm concerned. Werner may go along with him, which is another worry." Jax took a sidelong glance at Bella. "Mac didn't like Curt and Carl being in the cabin without a telephone since it's isolated. Week before last, he got them to move into the inn. Since Mac caught a bad cold, they've been a big help to him."

"I'm glad," Bella said, but her mind reeled with Jax's revelations.

Several moments of silence filled the confines of the car before Jax spoke again. "Curt isn't the same guy who left for France. I don't believe for one minute that he's dangerous but, as you could see, he's not himself. He helped Carl with the golf course last summer, and he's done odd jobs for Mac but he can't hold a regular job. Not yet anyhow. He's too unsteady."

For several moments, Bella absorbed the information. "He isn't the only soldier with those problems. Many left France with similar issues."

"No, he isn't. Most of the townspeople understand that war changes men." He paused briefly before continuing. "Curt and Owen may only need time. Or they may never be the same."

Sad remembrance filled Bella. "Curt was Matt's sergeant, so he'll always have a place at Ballantyne," she replied. Out of the corner of her eye, Bella saw Jax stiffen as if struck. Immediately, she swiveled to look at him. The color had drained from his face and tension was clear in the set of his square jaw. Bella wanted to say more, but Jax's voice kept her from doing so.

"I believe it's good for him to be with Carl and at Ballantyne. I just wanted you to know he isn't the same but, as I said, I don't think he's a danger to anyone." The coolness was back in his voice and in his manner.

Bella wanted to ask if the mention of Matt was upsetting to him, but Jax looked so cold and remote that she simply followed the new line of conversation. "What about Owen? He seemed very shaky, and he said he can't hold a job."

Jax sighed. "Owen is even worse off. The theater closed a year ago which was before he got home, so his old job was gone. He might have been able to do that since he wouldn't have been interacting with people as the projectionist, but he hasn't been able to find anything else. Even worse, his wife left him a few months ago. Since then, he's really struggled."

"I wish we could hire all of the veterans who need work," she murmured. A sigh escaped her. "Do you think Gus and Werner would attack any of the men?"

"I don't know. Curt has taken up for all of them, which might make him a bigger target. He's told Gus to leave the boys alone a few times that I know about. Like I said, I don't think Schwarz will come after him at the inn. Just be aware of the situation. If anything happens, let Nolen or me know. We're trying to get to the bottom of the problem since it seems to be worse and worse."

"Of course. If I see or hear anything, I'll call the office," Bella readily agreed, but this news disturbed her. Only a short time ago, her focus had been on helping Mac restore Ballantyne. Now, there was much, much more to consider.

Chapter Three

As they drew closer to the resort, Bella put the troubling revelations aside. At long last, she was home. Tears filled her eyes, and she quickly brushed them away as a host of emotions assailed her. This wasn't the homecoming that she had dreamed about when she left for France, but—despite everything—she was happy to be back.

Her heart twisted when the Ballantyne sign came into view and, as Jax turned on to the long drive, Bella's attention immediately went to the inn sitting in the distance. The large three-story Georgian home, white with black shutters, had been built in 1870 by an Ohio industrialist. When a big economic depression hit in the 1890s, he had been forced to sell his home and land at a low price. More than once, Mac and Grandfather Stew had stated that the man's misfortune had been their luck. They had started with a nine-hole golf course. Later, they'd added other amenities. Over the years, good fortune and hard work had helped them make Ballantyne into a fine and popular resort and, as Jax had observed, that success had spilled over into Moreley.

When the car stopped at the base of the porch steps, Bella climbed out and looked across the expanse of white spreading from the inn to the golf course. Once again, she thought of her last Christmas at home. Dozens of guests had filled the inn and cottages. Ice skating, sledding, and sleigh rides had added to the festive spirit. Her train had arrived later, one of several bringing people to Moreley, so the place had been alive with activity when she'd gotten to

Ballantyne. Both the resort and town had gone all out to welcome holiday guests in those days.

Had all progress been lost? Jax's disclosure about tourists staying away due to crime was disturbing.

"I'll put your bags in the foyer," Jax said, his voice breaking into her reverie.

Bella swallowed hard and turned to face him. "Thank you," she replied and followed him up the steps and on to the wide veranda. Adirondack chairs still sat on each side of the porch. On summer days, guests could watch the tennis courts, the golf course, or the river in the distance. She sighed. With luck, the seats would be filled in a few months. Hope and anxiety tangled inside her until she saw the front door. A large balsam wreath with a crimson bow, much like ones from years past, was a warm and welcoming touch. Mac's touch, no doubt. Some of the sadness left her. Not everything had changed.

Jax stopped beside Bella, following her gaze. "According to Carl, Mac insisted decorations be up when you got home." He opened the door for her and let her precede him.

"How lovely," she said before stepping into the inn's large lobby where another surprise waited. "Mac," she cried out as she saw the gray-haired man sitting next to the blazing fire. Bella hurried to his side, dropped to her knees, and hugged him. Tears came again but, this time, she let them fall.

Mac gently patted her back. "Lass, let me see ye," he said in his rich Scots brogue. Despite having left his homeland more than thirty years earlier, his accent hadn't disappeared.

Bella looked up at the man who was like a grandfather to her. His gray waves were still closely cropped, but new lines bracketed his mouth and radiated from his silver-gray eyes. He looked pale and wan. Fresh apprehension filled her. "Mac, you're sick. You should be in bed."

He shook his head. "The lads built up the fire, so I'm cozy and comfortable. Besides, I wanted to be out here to welcome ye home, lass. It's been too long."

She bit down on her trembling lip and wiped away the moisture streaking her cheeks. In an effort to gain more control, Bella scanned the wide foyer. "It looks like you've done more than simply sit here." A quick survey revealed a tall spruce tree standing next to the wide stone fireplace and greenery decorated the stair rails leading to the second floor. Mac had made sure everything was just as it had been for all of the holidays of her youth. Bella's heart swelled with gratitude.

"Carl and Curt did all of this," Mac said with a sweep of his broad, wrinkled hand. His gray eyes twinkled with pleasure. "Christmas is only two days away, and I dinna want ye working to deck the place out."

The observation caught Bella off-guard. She hadn't given a single thought to decorating until she'd seen the wreath on the front door. Suddenly, she was very aware of Jax's earlier words: *War changes men...* But it changed women, too. It had changed her. A tremulous breath left Bella. It wasn't only war that had changed her. It was loss and grief. Her attention moved to Jax, who had laid her bags at the base of the stairs before coming to stand by Mac's chair. Once again, his features looked as if they'd been carved out of granite. Despite his proximity, she felt as if they were as far apart as Heaven and Earth—and perhaps even farther.

"How are you feeling, Mac?" he asked.

"Much better now that our girl is home."

Bella felt more than saw Jax flinch. She had never been his girl. Not really. She'd hoped she might be some day, but that had been a different life. She had been a different person and so had he. As awkward silence filled the room, she got to her feet. "I'm glad to be home." Her comment and her attention were for Mac.

"I'm more than glad to have ye here, lass." Mac's deep voice was filled with emotion that resonated inside Bella.

Several moments of silence passed before Jax spoke. "I need to get back to town."

"Thank ye for picking her up, lad," Mac told him. A smile wreathed his weathered face.

"It was no trouble, Mac." Jax managed the semblance of a smile for the older man but, when he looked at Bella, it faltered. "Again, welcome home."

"Thank you for coming to the station," she managed, although her own voice lacked any real gratitude. The gulf between them was too great. Jax had shared a lot of information about the current issues in Moreley, but only because she had witnessed the confrontation in town—and because Curt lived at Ballantyne. Otherwise, Bella doubted if he would have revealed a single detail to her.

He nodded before turning toward the door and walking out into the swirling snow. Bella watched him go with mixed emotions. While Jax had provided information and a warning, his cold demeanor still stung. Not as badly as it had right after Matt died. Then, her heart had felt like it was caught in a steel vice. Now, it was more like it was gripped by an unseen fist. The worst part was that she had no idea why Jax acted so coldly toward her. Bella surmised it had something to do with the nurse, but she didn't plan to ask. Her focus now was Ballantyne.

Before taking the chair across from Mac, Bella put a smile on her face. "You really should go back to bed, but I can fix breakfast before you do."

"Carl already made toast and tea for me, lass. Let's just talk for a few minutes. Then, I'll go back to my room willingly."

Concern furrowed her brow. "I don't want you to wear yourself out."

"I'll nay do that, but it's been almost two years since I've seen ye and heard ye. Humor an old man and chat a bit."

"You'll never be old, Mac," Bella replied, although she was very aware that the weariness in his gray eyes was not only from a bad cold. More likely, it resulted from the losses and ensuing strains of the past sixteen months. A man nearing seventy should be relaxing. Instead, Mac had been left to handle the resort on his own. Regret filled Bella. "I'm sorry I didn't get home sooner."

"Ye were doing yer duty to our country, lass."

"But you were left to manage everything after..." Her voice broke as raw emotion again assailed her. Bella bit hard on her lower lip to control the rising tide of sorrow.

Mac reached across the space between them and patted her hands, now clasped in her lap. "By the time yer father left us, there was little left to manage," he said, his voice rough and ragged. "We'd already closed the tennis courts, inn, and cottages due to the Spanish flu. And we hadn't planned on holiday guests last year, either."

"What about last summer? You wrote about the course being open," she commented. "Jax told me about the area crimes. He thought people didn't return due to them."

"The lad is right. Some reservations were made before the trouble started. Most cancelled. Word spread that our boys were causing problems."

"That's terrible," Bella said. "I know all of them, and I can't believe they would have damaged property or harmed animals."

Mac shook his gray head in disgust. "Around here, mostly Schwarz and Meyers think so. They're both riled up, most especially toward Curt, but the other boys, as well."

"I know," she said before describing the confrontation she and Jax had witnessed.

"I'm sorry ye saw that yer first morning home," Mac said. "Gus knows how to stir folks up, and most of our boys are quick to react."

"Jax mentioned Curt always takes up for the others, and it certainly seemed so this morning. He also said both Curt and Owen are having problems since they got home," Bella said, unsure of how to characterize Curt's issues. "Jax wasn't very specific. Mostly, he said war changes men."

"That it does. As close as ye were to the front, ye saw for yerself, I'm sure." A troubled expression blanketed his weathered features.

Bella knew he was asking, as much as observing, and she offered what she hoped was a reassuring smile. "I was near the front for a few months, but I was in Paris, too. We were luckier than the boys in the trenches. They suffered terribly although they seldom complained."

"Harold Horton said ye went to visit him after he was wounded. Ye lifted his spirits, lass. And, from what I know, ye did the same for many of our other boys."

The pride shining in his eyes was a healing balm to Bella's wounded heart. "If I was close enough, I tried to see them in the field hospitals. Occasionally, I ran into a few when they came back from the line, if they were near my posting. I was as happy to see familiar faces as they were. At least, most were glad to see me." Once again, the image of Jax on the day after her brother's death—cold and hard and dismissive—came to her mind. With effort, she thrust it away.

Something flickered in Mac's gaze. "As Jax said, war changes men. Some can nay accept being seen as weak and debilitated, especially by someone close to them."

Bella sensed a message underlying the words, but she no longer felt close to Jax. He'd spoken at length on the way to Ballantyne, but as town constable, not as Matt's best friend. Not as her friend. "Yes, I'm sure that's true," she said without any real conviction. "Anyhow, I'm glad you asked Carl and Curt to stay in the inn. I think it's best for all of us. What rooms do they have?"

"They're in Julia's old suite off the kitchen. Since she wed, the space has been vacant. As I said, we did nay open the inn these last two seasons, so a cook-housekeeper was nay needed. Julia has been kind enough to come three days a week for light cleaning and to cook enough food to keep us going. We manage in-between."

"That's kind of her," Bella replied with a smile. "I'm glad Curt and Carl are here, though."

"I suggested a bigger suite on the second floor, but both lads preferred those rooms," he told her. "I s'pose it's a big change from the cabin, but a good one."

"I'm sure it is," she agreed. Mac's pallor and weakness were becoming more obvious, so Bella got to her feet. "I think you belong in bed. Once I have breakfast, I may lie down myself. I slept a bit on the train, but a nap would not go amiss."

Chapter Four

Carl and Curt came to help Mac back to bed and to take Bella's bags to her third-floor suite. When the brothers arrived in the kitchen a few minutes later, she thanked them and said, "I'm going to fix breakfast. I see there are plenty of eggs and some ham. I can make biscuits. How does that sound?"

"You're just home, Bella," Carl said. "You shouldn't be doing no chores." Slight and gaunt, the man was soft-spoken and shy. His hazel eyes, so much like his brother's, darted away from her.

"It's been a long time since I had a chance to cook a real meal. I'm making food for myself, so it's easy to make a little extra," she assured him. "I see you already started a fire in the stove."

A smile touched Carl's mouth. Despite his weathered face, earned from years of working in the sun and wind, at thirty-six, he looked almost boyish. "That sounds mighty good. How about you, Curt?"

When Bella looked at Carl's younger brother, she saw his eyes held the residual weariness and wariness common to those who had served in the trenches. She had noted the differences in him earlier, but only in passing.

His gaze flickered from Carl to Bella and back before settling on a spot on the floor. "I ate at the café. I gotta shovel snow and bring more wood in. We got some upstairs for you yesterday." His medium brown hair, also like his brother's, had not seen scissors in some time. That and the dark stubble on his face made him look rough. She hadn't noticed any of that earlier, but then her attention had mostly been on Gus Schwarz. Jax's observation about Curt being a different person resurfaced. Bella hoped the change was temporary.

"That can wait," she assured him. "I made coffee, so why don't the two of you sit down? The rest will be ready soon. Besides, even if you ate, Curt, some fresh biscuits would be good with coffee, if I haven't lost my touch in making them." The last was meant to inject a casual note.

Curt's expression didn't lighten, but he acquiesced. "Sounds fine."

Bella served the meal in short order. Both men stood up as she joined them, and Curt pulled out a chair for her.

During the meal, Curt said nothing, but Carl, who had always been quiet and reserved, managed to keep the conversation going. Bella was glad to see it. In the past, Curt had been the one to look out for his big brother. Now, when he needed support, Carl was there for him. Bella was pleased, but it also made her yearn for her own brother.

Sorrow suddenly welled within her. In France, she hadn't felt Matt's loss so keenly since she had seldom seen him there, but here at home, his absence left a terrible hole. With her parents gone, too, the hole seemed like an abyss. A deep abyss that might swallow her whole, if she let it. Knowing the danger in being consumed by the past, Bella brought her thoughts back to the present. It was only when the meal was over and the men made to leave that Curt spoke again.

"Bella, I should have said something earlier..." He clasped his hands in front of him and studied them as if he could find the right words there. "It was the first I saw you since

Matt died. I was with him." His voice faltered briefly. "I'm sorry I couldn't save him. So very sorry."

When Bella saw moisture gather in Curt's hazel eyes, she laid her hands over his. His dark lashes fluttered down. "Thank you, Curt. Thank you for your kind words and for being with him. That means more to me than I can say." The memory of hearing about her brother's death filled her mind. Matt had been leading his men over the top and, only twenty yards out of the trenches, he'd been hit with gunfire from a sniper's nest. Bella could too easily imagine the awful scene and, when Curt's gaze returned to meet hers, Bella saw a world of devastation there.

"The lieutenant was very brave. A loyal friend, a good man, a fine officer. We all liked and respected him." Curt paused for a moment. "Doing the right thing shouldn't have ended his life."

The last words confused Bella. Doing the right thing didn't really describe Matt leading his men into battle, but she simply nodded. "He was a wonderful big brother, and I'm glad to know his men also held him in high esteem."

"The highest," Curt asserted. Although his voice remained rough and raspy, it rang with certitude.

Bella released his hands and glanced away. "Thank you." She cleared her voice. "Now, I should clean up the kitchen. Since I spent a lot of last night in the Sandusky station, I didn't get much sleep. I'll probably nap in my room until lunchtime, but I'll see the two of you then. If you'd check on Mac once, I'd appreciate it."

Carl assured her that they would before the pair went out to shovel snow and gather wood.

Weary in body and spirit, Bella finished cleaning up, banked the fire in the stove, and went to her room. Immediately, she realized the brothers had not only carried wood up yesterday, one of them had started a fire in the grate today. The warmth encompassed her and, exhausted, she took no more time to study her surroundings. Bella simply collapsed on to the bed with its familiar rose and pink quilt. As she was about to doze off, she wondered again what Curt had meant that Matt shouldn't have died doing the right thing. She didn't know all of the details surrounding his death, but he'd been leading his men as he had all during the war. Again, she decided Curt's confusion must have made him misspeak. Or maybe he simply meant Matt always did the right thing, but why say so? The question lingered as she fell asleep.

***

Jax found no such respite. During the short drive to town, his mind kept replaying the awkward scene at the train station and the troubling exchange in front of the café. If he was honest, going into the inn again was just as disturbing. While he drove out to Ballantyne every week or so, Jax never went inside the rambling old mansion or the cozy golf shop. Too many memories lurked in both places.

Tired and unsettled, he headed back to work. When he opened the door to the constable's office, he was immediately greeted by his deputy.

"I bet Bella is happy to be home," Nolen said. The younger man's smiling welcome and friendly observation did nothing to lift Jax's spirits. Neither did the dreary office. The scuffed floor and dingy walls were outward evidence of neglect by the town council, whose members refused to spend an extra penny on the space.

After dusting the snow off his cap and coat, Jax focused on his deputy's words. "Yes, I believe so."

Nolen's smile faded, and his freckled face took on a concerned look. "You believe she is. Didn't she seem happy?" For several moments, the younger man studied Jax. "She's planning to stay, isn't she?"

The last question made Jax start in surprise. He hadn't given a moment's thought to the possibility that Bella might leave again. With her parents and Matt gone, she and Mac were partners. She wouldn't desert him, would she? "I don't think so, but I don't really know. Bella and I only spoke briefly about Ballantyne. What makes you ask?"

"She left college to join the Signal Corps, so I thought maybe she'd go back. Didn't she want to teach?"

"Yes, she did," Jax agreed. Would she return to college and leave Mac alone? If she did, would Ballantyne survive? The resort was no longer part of his life, but it had been for years and Jax couldn't imagine the area without it. He couldn't imagine Ballantyne without Bella. "I don't know if she's going back or not."

Nolen's auburn brows rose as if in amazement. "You picked her up. Didn't you two talk?"

Jax sighed. "I got her because Mac was too sick to go, and Doc asked me to do it. Unfortunately, on the way home, we saw a confrontation involving Owen, Curt, and Schwarz in front of the café, and I stopped." Jax summarized the clash while mentally reviewing his time with Bella. They'd talked about the recent troubles on their way to Ballantyne, but nothing else. In fact, if he was honest, he had barely looked at Bella. Her pallor and slimness had been obvious, as had her fatigue, but Jax hadn't asked how she felt. He hadn't asked about her journey home. He hadn't asked about her future plans. He hadn't even offered his condolences on the loss of her parents who had died of influenza within weeks of each other. While not overtly rude, Jax had treated her with less concern than he would a stranger because he wanted to maintain distance between them. Unfortunately, doing so without being callous wasn't easy. Neither was keeping his attention away from her. Despite her weariness and sorrow, Bella's eyes—as dark as her bobbed hair—had still sparkled with pleasure when she saw her home and Mac. But not when she had looked at him. Chocolate ice had been in her gaze then.

Nolen's next observation broke into Jax's thoughts. "Not a very nice welcome for Bella to have Gus go after her for wearing a uniform."

"No, but I told her to stay in the car, and she didn't listen."

Nolen blinked as if in surprise. "Did you really expect her to?"

"I'm the constable, so, yes. I expected her to do what I said."

A low laugh left the deputy. "You know Bella a lot better than me, but I can't picture her being ordered around, except by a commanding officer."

The observation was certainly apt. Bella had never liked being told what to do. Jax need only remember her decision to join the Army Signal Corps, something that had worried her brother, her parents, and him. Bella had listened to their qualms and gone ahead with her plan. He cleared his throat. "Yes, well, she might consider heeding a law officer."

Nolen chuckled again. "She might, but she probably won't." His humor ebbed. "Did you tell her about the other incidents with Schwarz and Meyers?"

Jax nodded. "I did. And I asked her to let us know if she sees or hears anything. I doubt if Gus or Werner will go to the resort to confront Curt, but she needed to understand that he's one of Gus' targets."

"It's good Curt is living in the inn in case anything else happens," Nolen observed. "But he's only one of many who had run-ins with Schwarz, if not Meyers."

"That is certainly an issue," Jax agreed. "I just hope there aren't any more incidents." It was probably a futile hope which made him question his decision to take the job as constable.

"Maybe the holidays will be calm," Nolen said.

"Maybe so," Jax agreed, but he couldn't shake his uneasiness. Calm did not describe Gus Schwarz at all. But it didn't describe a lot of others in Moreley, either. Not anymore.

***

The next day after breakfast, Bella headed to town. Although she had a gift for Mac, she wanted to find presents for Carl and Curt since they would be sharing the holiday celebration.

Shivers rippled through her once she got on the main road. While the side curtains of the Model T helped, they didn't keep out all of the damp air. Yesterday's snow had started to melt overnight, leaving slush and puddles along the road. She shifted into a lower gear to lessen the breeze and avoid road spray. At least the trip to town was short.

As she drove along, Bella scanned the fields. Several small farms lay between Ballantyne and Moreley. Some of the homes were set on side lanes, but she was familiar with the buildings, if not with all of the farmers. They tended to do business in nearby Boxwood, where they sold their grain and corn. Some sent their children to school there, as well.

Bella downshifted again to navigate a sharp curve and gasped in surprise when a figure came into view. Quickly, she steered to the side of the road and pulled to a stop. When the person turned toward her, Bella realized it was a woman. "Ma'am, can I help you?" she called out after pushing the Model T's side curtain out of the way.

Hard shudders racked the thin form, and the reply was unintelligible. Worried, Bella climbed out of the car and went to the lady's side. Her legs were bare beneath her faded, frayed coat and her well-worn shoes were soaked. Blonde hair peaked out from a too-big knit cap, one that surely belonged to a father, husband, or son and not the woman herself. Her face had a waxy, ashen appearance. How long had she been outside and why she was walking in such weather? Was there some emergency at her home? "I'm sorry. I didn't understand you, ma'am."

The woman, still shivering, pointed across the field and mumbled again but her teeth chattered so badly that Bella still wasn't sure what she said. "Does someone at your house need help? A child or your husband? One of your folks?"

"My husband," the woman finally managed to say in a hoarse, weak voice. "He's near our fence line. Down the side road. Just short of our house."

Unsure which house belonged to the woman and her family, Bella merely said, "Get in the car, and we'll go to him."

The woman let Bella assist her into the vehicle. She tried to say more but a series of coughs rattled through her slight form.

"Just rest, ma'am." Bella grabbed a blanket from the rear seat and tucked it around her passenger, who murmured her appreciation. After climbing behind the steering wheel, Bella headed the car in the direction indicated by the woman.

Only moments passed before the lady began gesturing to the left side of the car. "Turn here. He's down this way."

Bella pulled off the main road and stopped. Although the snow was melting, driving any farther was likely to get them stuck in the soft earth. "We need to walk from here." She glanced at the woman again. "You could stay in the car since you're already chilled."

"No. I want to go with you."

Bella didn't argue. Instead, she fell into step beside the woman.

When they had gone about thirty feet, Bella saw a form slumped on the ground. A lantern was next to his right hand. She and the woman both rushed to the man who lay on his side. Only part of his face was visible, but red stained the snow around him. For a moment, shock held her silent. When Bella spoke again, her voice was hoarse. "Do you have any idea what happened to him?"

Although the woman continued to tremble, she managed to speak intelligibly. "I think he was shot."

Bella knelt beside the body. With a shaking hand, she touched the side of his neck. During her time in France, she learned how to check for a heartbeat. But no pulse was evident, so she slowly and carefully levered him to his back. A gasp escaped her when two bloody chest wounds became visible. After staring for several moments, she recognized the man. It was Gus Schwarz.

"I'm sorry. He's gone."

The woman put her hands over her face as another cough racked her slim form. "We need to get you out of the cold. Let's go to your house and call the constable's office."

"We don't have a telephone. That's why I was walking to town for help." Again, coughing assailed her.

Unsure what course to pursue, Bella finally decided having help come to them was better than going into town. "We need to get you somewhere warm as soon as possible. Is there a neighbor who has a telephone?"

"Yes. Jacob Jones is only a half-mile down the main road. He had one put in when his mother was dying."

Bella wondered why Mrs. Schwarz hadn't walked there instead of the miles to town, but she didn't ask. The woman was cold and sick. The croupy cough only emphasized the latter. "We should head there."

"I don't know if he'll let us use his telephone. He and Gus had a falling out last spring. They haven't spoken since."

Yesterday morning's altercation again flashed in her mind, and anxiety gripped her. Bella had only a passing acquaintance with Jones, but nothing in her memory indicated he was anything but a decent man. "I'm sure Mr. Jones will allow me to make a call. You don't even have to go inside."

"All right," the other woman replied.

***

Jones lived alone in a compact cottage settled in a copse of trees. After parking in front of the home, Bella went to the door, knocked, and waited. A look of surprise blanketed the slim man's face when he answered. Once Bella explained the situation, the farmer led her to the telephone. Several moments passed before the operator connected her to the constable's office, and Bella breathed a sigh of relief when Nolen answered. She quickly relayed the issue and returned the earpiece to the candlestick cradle after the call disconnected. "Thank you so much. I need to get Mrs. Schwarz home. She's chilled and sick."

Jones' expression grew grim. "Helene is with you?"

"Yes, in my car. She was walking to town for help, but she's in no shape to be out in the cold, damp air. She said they don't have a telephone. Don't they have a vehicle, either?"

The man's expression went from grim to angry. "Gus didn't want a phone. As for the truck, I heard it broke down a few weeks ago, or so he told folks. He only has a passing acquaintance with the truth, so hard to say. He uses the wagon, but Helene wouldn't be strong enough to hook up the horses." Jones turned away and went to a large wooden trunk in the corner of the room. In a moment, he was back with two faded quilts. "If she's cold, these should help."

"Thank you," Bella replied. Two more covers would be useful. "Now, I really should go. I told the deputy we'd be waiting at her house."

"Of course." Jacob nodded in agreement.

With that, Bella went back to the car, opened the passenger door, and piled the blankets on Mrs. Schwarz. "These will make you a little warmer."

The older woman again murmured her thanks, but her croupy cough continued off and on until they arrived at the house. As she drove down the short drive, Bella couldn't help but notice the poor condition of the property. No paint remained on the house or barn, leaving them both a faded gray-brown. Several moments passed before Bella realized this place had once belonged to the Culpepper family. Was this woman related to them? Jones had called her Helene. Sudden realization hit Bella. Her passenger must be Helene Culpepper.

As she parked, Bella brushed those thoughts aside, got out of the car, and walked toward the house with Mrs. Schwarz. The back porch listed sideways, forcing her to step carefully as she helped the older lady up the uneven stairs and into the kitchen. While spotless, the room showed as much wear as the exterior.

"We should get you settled in the parlor." Hopefully, that room was warmer. When they stepped inside, Bella quickly realized it wasn't. Nor was it in any better condition than the outside. The wood floor, while clean, was scuffed and scratched. The oak planks had long ago lost any finish, and the area rug covering them was faded and frayed. Torn upholstery covered the chairs and divan. Closer inspection revealed the furniture was of excellent quality, but it had been hard used over a long period of time.

Once her hostess settled on the divan, Bella got a fire going in the empty hearth. When a cheerful blaze began to warm the room, she turned back to the other woman, who was watching her.

"Thank you. You're very kind, and I don't even know your name."

"I'm Arabella Stewart. From Ballantyne."

A soft smile curved Mrs. Schwarz's lips. "Of course. I haven't seen you since you were a girl, but you favor your mother. I would sometimes accompany my mother and her friends to Ballantyne for luncheon. You probably don't remember because you were young, and usually on the golf course."

The woman's words brought forth more memories. The Culpeppers had been well-to-do, educated, and genteel. Gus Schwarz did not fit any of those categories. He and Helene Culpepper seemed to be an unlikely couple.

"Could I get you a cup of tea? You must still be chilled."

"That would be lovely."

After a nod, Bella went to the kitchen. She stirred up the coals in the stove and put the kettle on. The sound of a car drew her attention, and Bella peeked out the threadbare curtain to see Jax emerging from his green roadster. A resigned sigh left her. Of course, he—not his deputy—would come. Before going to the back door, she prepared the tea. Any delay was useful since she needed to bolster her emotional reserves before facing him.

When he tapped, she opened the door. "Thank you for coming."

He swept off his cap and wiped his shoes on the ragged rug by the door. "Nolen told me Gus is dead," Jax said without acknowledging her words or offering a greeting of his own.

A sigh left Bella. So much for niceties. Evidently, Jax no longer used them. "I'm afraid so. Mrs. Schwarz was walking to town. When I saw her, she wanted to go back to her husband. Since I thought we might be able to help him, we did—but it was too late."

"Nolen also said Gus was shot."

"Yes, more than once."

Jax ran one hand over his face. "I don't suppose she knows how it happened."

Bella shook her head. "I don't think so, but she hasn't talked a lot. She was trembling with cold, and maybe shock, when I picked her up. She could hardly speak. I got a fire going in the parlor and made some tea for her."

"Doc Smedlay is on his way, mostly because I need him to look at the body but he can check on Mrs. Schwarz first." He unbuttoned his jacket. "Let's go in and see her."

With a nod, she picked up the tea and led the way to where Helene Schwarz was resting against the arm of the divan. After setting the beverage on a table, Bella took one of the chairs flanking the fireplace. The older woman settled the blanket around her thin shoulders before picking up the cup and saucer.

"Constable Hastings is here, ma'am. He wants to speak with you about..." Bella, uneasy about referring to the woman's dead husband, let her voice trail off.

"Of course," the older woman murmured. Her faded blue eyes focused on the constable.

Jax sat down in the other chair, hat in hands, before he spoke. "I'm sorry about your loss. I know this is a very difficult time, but I have a few questions."

"I understand."

"Bella said you were coming to town for help, Mrs. Schwarz. Do you know what happened to your husband?"

Before replying, the older woman took a sip of tea. "I've had a bad cold, so I went back to bed after preparing breakfast for Gus. That was around seven. I fell asleep again right away and didn't wake up until nine o'clock. Gus wasn't back in the house, which was very unusual, so I got dressed and went looking for him." Several coughs briefly interrupted her. "I went to the barn first. Gus wasn't there, but both horses were gone. Only the horses. The wagon was there, which was odd. The horses are a team, so there's no reason for Gus to take them out alone. We don't ride them."

Jax's brow furrowed in confusion. "Were the horses with his body?"

"No," Helene replied. "I think they got out. Or someone let them out. That happened once before, a while back, and Gus went looking for the horses then. I suppose the same thing happened today."

"We never found out who did it," Jax admitted in a rueful tone.

A low sigh left Helene. "We've had problems since April and those crimes haven't been solved, either."

"We've tried, Mrs. Schwarz," Jax replied in a defensive tone.

She gave a slight nod but said nothing.

"So, the horses are still missing," Jax went on.

Mrs. Schwarz nodded. "I didn't see them when I went out looking for Gus, or when I was walking to town."

"We'll hunt for them later, ma'am," Jax assured her. "Was there anything else missing?"

"Only the horses, I think," she replied.

"I'm going to head out and see..." Jax stood up, but knocking interrupted him. "It's probably Doc."

"I'll let him in," Bella said before hurrying to the front door. She greeted the town physician, a robust man in his fifties, and led him to the parlor.

Doc immediately went to Mrs. Schwarz's side. "Helene, I was so sorry to hear about Gus. How are you feeling?" A series of rattling coughs emanated from her. "How long have you had this?"

"A few days," she said in a ragged whisper.

The physician glanced at Jax. "I need to examine her and see if it's only a cold, not bronchitis or pneumonia. I'll be along as soon as I can."

"All right," Jax agreed. "I'll head out now." He turned to Bella. "Exactly where is he?"

"Off the main road a bit. I would never have seen him if Mrs. Schwarz hadn't guided me. I should probably go with you or you may not find him, either."

For a moment, Jax looked like he wanted to object. Then, he nodded in agreement. "Let's go."

Bella turned up her coat collar and preceded him to the kitchen and out of the house. When Jax held the passenger door open for her, she murmured her thanks. Once they were on their way, she provided directions. Within a few moments, she gestured to the side of the road. "He's over that way," Bella said with a wave of her hand. "You better park here because the ground is very soft. I didn't drive back here for fear of getting stuck."

Jax nodded before getting out and falling into step beside Bella. He glanced around. "I guess you and Mrs. Schwarz made these footprints, such as they are. It's pretty slushy. I can't tell if anyone else was around here, although that must have been the case."

The implicit criticism in his words that she'd somehow disturbed the crime scene annoyed Bella. "The temperature went above freezing overnight, so some snow must have melted before Gus came out here. It was a wet mess when I brought Mrs. Schwarz back."

His green gaze met hers. "That's too bad. Some decent footprints might be useful."

The pair continued to the body. "He must have been out here looking for the horses. I've seen his team and they're Belgians, so they couldn't jump the fence."

"I noticed a gate a bit farther up the road was ajar," Bella told him. While she hadn't consciously filed the information in her mind before, it quickly came back to her.

His gaze locked on Bella. "I know the one you mean. I've been out this way more than once to check on vandalism. That gate is never unlocked."

"It is now," she replied.

"I'll look once Doc gets here. For now, I need to take a better look at Schwarz." Jax focused on the dead man.

"He was shot more than once, wasn't he?" Bella asked as she came to a stop next to Jax.

"Yes, he was shot twice." Jax had dropped to his knees and levered the body sideways before pointing to the bloody holes in the back of Schwarz's jacket. "There are exit wounds, so the bullets went through him. He probably bled out quickly since there's a fair amount of blood on the ground and on his clothes."

Only a short time ago, crimson had stained the slush. Now that more melting had taken place, the ground was very wet—with water and blood. "Do you think you can find the bullets?"

A half-shrug lifted one shoulder. "I'll certainly look, but they could have travelled a ways." Jax got to his feet and surveyed the ground. "I don't see any shells, so the killer had sense enough to pick them up. Unfortunately."

Bella chewed on her lower lip. "You don't know what kind of gun was used?"

"No. Without bullets or shells, it's hard to know. Right now, I'd say he was shot with a handgun at close range. It was probably still dark when it happened, so shooting from a distance isn't likely. Stay here while I see if I can find anything," Jax said before walking toward the trees in the distance. As he went, he scanned the ground.

The order made Bella want to object, but she maintained her silence until he returned. "You didn't see any bullets?"

"Afraid not. I didn't really think I would, though. They could go fairly far after passing through him."

Bella nodded before speaking again. "He must have discovered the horses missing right after breakfast, so it probably happened not long after seven o'clock."

Jax turned toward her. "That sounds right, and I'm guessing he came out here looking and was shot shortly after that. The sun doesn't rise until almost eight, so this lantern must belong to Gus, but his killer had to have some sort of light. The moon was just a sliver last night."

"If the same person let the horses out, he must have had some familiarity with the Schwarz place. Of course, as you say, he probably had a flashlight or lantern." As Bella glanced around the area, she reviewed the current details and what she already knew about recent crimes in the area. "Do you think the killer might have drawn him out here by letting the horses go? If Gus had seen the gate open before this morning, don't you think he would have fixed it?"

"Good points," Jax said.

Bella wasn't sure if he was surprised, dismayed, or encouraged by her remarks, but the sound of a vehicle approaching kept her from inquiring. She turned to see George Forrester, a tall man in his early forties, and Doc Smedlay emerging from the mortician's Auto Hearse. Although Forrester also used the contraption to transport seriously ill patients to Doc's or to the nearest hospital, uneasiness sent shivers through her. Bella hadn't been home for her parents' funerals, but she could imagine both riding in that same vehicle to their final resting places. The thought was not a pleasant one.

"Not a good way to begin Christmas Eve," Forrester said as he and Doc joined Bella and Jax.

"No, it isn't," Jax replied before turning to Doc. "How is Mrs. Schwarz?"

"I left some cough medicine with her. I'd like her to come to town and stay in one of our patient rooms so my wife and I can keep watch over her, but she doesn't want to. She asked me to contact Gus' cousins. I'll place a call when I get home."

"That's good," Bella murmured. "I'll check on her when I get my car."

"Thank you, Arabella," Doc said with a slight smile.

The men went to Schwarz's body. When Doc knelt down to do a brief examination, Jax said, "There are two wounds, but the bullets went through him. I searched the immediate area. Couldn't find them or the shells."

"That's too bad," Doc replied. "From the size of the entrance wounds, he was shot at fairly close range. Perhaps a pistol or a revolver. I may know more when I do a thorough exam. Unless you object, we'll take him back to town now. George will drive me to get my car later."

"That's fine," Jax said. "I'll look around here a bit more, but I think I've seen it all. Not much good evidence yet."

The older man nodded. "The autopsy may reveal more."

After Smedlay and Forrester went about their grim task, Jax turned to Bella. "I'll take you back to the house to get your car, but I'd like to take a closer look at the gate first since it's not far."

"Fine," she replied.

***

Jax drove the short distance, stopped, and went to the fence. He wasn't surprised when Bella got out of the automobile and followed him, but his focus was on the gate and its shattered lock.

"It looks like someone hit the lock with a hammer," she observed.

"Or the butt of a handgun," he replied, bending to take a better look. After a moment, Jax extracted a handkerchief from his pocket and picked up the lock.

"Do you think you can get fingerprints from it? I know they've been used in some cases, but how would you examine for them?"

A sigh escaped him. "I wouldn't. I'd need help, probably from a bigger department, but there may not be prints anyhow due to the damage. I'm guessing the killer kept banging on it until it broke completely apart."

The expression of excitement on Bella's face fled. "It's in pretty bad shape."

"I'm afraid so." He walked the fence line until a depression in the snow came into view. Curious, Jax bent down to study it.

"Did you find something?" Bella asked.

He shot her a quick glance before continuing his perusal. "Possibly, but stay where you are."

"What did you find?"

Of course, she wanted details. Jax figured she'd come over and look for herself if he didn't offer any. "There's a tire track. A narrow one."

"Maybe from the killer's vehicle?"

"It's a strong possibility." Jax rose to his feet, but he continued to scan the shoulder and road. No snow or slush on the highway meant determining the motorcycle's direction was impossible. A heavy sigh escaped him.

"What's wrong?"

Jax shrugged. "I'm pretty sure a motorcycle made the impression, but I can't tell which way it came or went since the pavement is clear." Freeze and thaws were common during Ohio winters, but this particular warm spell was especially unwelcome since it had destroyed possible evidence.

"Why do you think it was a motorcycle?"

He pointed at the faint impression. "Because it's very narrow. Too narrow for a motor car."

"That should help you find the killer."

"Maybe." When he glanced back at her, Jax noticed she was shivering and got to his feet. "You're getting cold. Let's go."

***

Once they were on their way back to the house, Bella shifted to look at him. "Do you think the person who has been vandalizing property is the same one who let the horses out and killed Gus?"

"That's possible."

The answer was terse, but she went on. "You don't have any leads on the vandals? You said Gus Schwarz had plenty of enemies. Do you suspect any of them?"

Jax ran a hand over his face. "You already know Gus had words with Curt and Owen yesterday morning, but you and I only heard some of the confrontation. It started inside, and several people heard that part. Gus rarely comes to Moreley, but when he does, it goes about the same as yesterday. He argues with someone. Often, a former soldier. It's like he's always spoiling for a fight."

Fresh anxiety spilled through Bella. "Are you going to talk with all of the soldiers about the murder?" Curt had left Ballantyne very early, but she kept that information to herself. Surely, he had a good reason. An innocent one.

Jax's expression shuttered. "That's police business. I can't share it with just anyone."

Bella recoiled at his cold tone and clipped words. *Just anyone.* Was that how he saw her now? As simply another resident? He'd changed, but so had she. Taking the comment to heart would be foolish, but it stung. "Of course not," she murmured, her voice equally chilly. She glanced out the side of the vehicle until the farmhouse came into view. As soon as the car pulled to a stop, she got out. "I'll check on Mrs. Schwarz before I head for town."

With that, Bella turned and strode away.

***

Jax ground his teeth as he watched her rush off. The urge to call her back and apologize hit him full-force, but he resisted. If Bella was mad at him, she wouldn't be insinuating herself into the case as she'd been trying to do with her questions. The previous morning, he had revealed a lot about local crime and the veterans because Curt lived and worked at Ballantyne, so Bella needed to know. He'd probably been too forthcoming with information on the motorcycle tire tracks because it was easy, far too easy, to fall back into their old pattern of camaraderie.

With a heavy sigh, Jax turned his Chummy toward the roadway and away from Bella. She was nothing if not intrepid. Her haste to join the Army Signal Corps and go to France as an operator still made him feel uneasy. She'd come back safe and sound, but that was pure luck, and Jax wasn't planning to rely on luck to protect her now, and protect her, he would.

Chapter Five

Despite —or perhaps because of—Jax's cutting words, Bella wanted answers, and asking the right people could help. After ensuring Mrs. Schwarz was comfortable, Bella continued to town and made the mercantile her first stop. The Downings, who owned the store, were a lovely couple of middle years. She had always liked them despite their nosiness and gossiping. Now, those traits seemed more appealing. In the past, the idle chatter, even if some was factual, hadn't been of interest. Her life had centered on Ballantyne and golf, not town goings-on and who was stepping out with who.

As a girl, she hadn't fully understood the close connection between town and resort. Now, she did. If lesser crimes kept visitors away, how much damage would an unsolved murder do? Finding the killer quickly was crucial, and Bella planned to do whatever she could to help whether Jax liked it or not.

No other customers were in the shop when she entered, an additional sign of lagging prosperity. However, both proprietors issued warm welcomes. Mrs. Downing, petite and round, came from behind the counter to hug Bella. Mr. Downing, only slightly taller than his wife and nearly as rotund, joined them.

"It's so good to see you, my dear," the older woman exclaimed. "Welcome home." Her husband offered similar sentiments as he took his place back behind the counter. Mrs. Downing continued to clasp Bella's hands in hers.

"Thank you. It's very good to be here."

"I'm sure it is, but we're so sorry about your parents and Matthew." The older woman's voice was soft with sympathy. "They're terribly missed."

"I appreciate that," Bella managed to say over the lump of grief clogging her throat. Many more condolences were likely to come her way and, although she appreciated expressions of kindness and sympathy, each one was a stab to her heart.

"How is Mac?" Mr. Downing put in. "Doc said he has a bad cold. I'm sure seeing you was a tonic."

Grateful for the change of subject, Bella smiled. "He seems to be better today."

Mrs. Downing released Bella's hands and stepped back. "Can we help you with something, dear?"

Bella briefly explained the reason for her visit. She chose gifts for Curt and Carl, a box of fudge for the younger Molitor and one of rock candy for the older as they each had particular tastes in sweets. Since the Downings didn't mention the murder, Bella realized word must not have spread to them so she shared the news. "Such a terrible thing," she said in summary.

The Downings exchanged a stunned look before the older woman replied. "How awful. What a shock for his wife."

"First murder here ever," he said almost as if trying to absorb the information. For a moment, he fell silent. "I suppose you know about the other crimes."

Bella nodded. "I could hardly believe those things have happened. Moreley has always been such a peaceful and safe community."

A frown pulled down the corners of Mrs. Downings' bow-shaped mouth. "When we send men away to war, they come back changed. My grandmother always said that was so for my grandfather and uncles. They were proud to fight for the Union, but it took a toll. Some are more different than others. Heaven knows what they saw and did over there. Shocking things, I'm sure."

Bella frowned. The note of condemnation in the words evoked exasperation. "Our soldiers suffered terribly in the trenches, but that doesn't mean they aren't still the same at heart." If others felt like the shopkeeper, it was little wonder visitors stayed away.

Color surged into Mrs. Downing's cheeks. "I wasn't finding fault with our brave boys," she hurriedly said. "I'm simply saying we cannot expect them to be exactly as they were."

Somewhat mollified, Bella nodded, but the comment still upset her. Did people think war veterans were violent? Moreley had more returned soldiers than many communities, but they were all good people.

Mr. Downing broke into her thoughts. "I believe what my wife means is many went away naïve young boys, but they have come back experienced men. They aren't as likely to accept criticism from folks, including their elders."

The last statement provided another clue about what had precipitated the confrontation with Owen, Curt, and Gus. "Jax and I saw Mr. Schwarz arguing with Owen and

Curt yesterday morning. Evidently, it wasn't the first time they've clashed."

Downing ran his fingers through his coal-gray hair. "I'm afraid not. Curt had words with him long before now. I'm sure you remember Gus tormenting Carl. Curt always took up for his brother, which is as it should be. Carl got teased too much. It was bad enough from other youngsters, but a grown man like Gus should know better."

"It seemed like Gus started yesterday's argument," Bella observed.

"Probably so," Mr. Downing replied. "He's always quick to find fault and pick on others. Once we entered the war, he blamed everyone for the anti-German actions in other areas. Nothing happened here, but Gus still went on and on. He got worse once our boys started coming home. Now, he's convinced all of the crimes are due to him and Meyers being German. No one here spoke against them. None of the soldiers have, either. But the trouble started after they came home."

Bella let the man's mischaracterization of Schwarz and Meyers go although both had been born in Ohio, not Germany. She was accustomed to some townsfolk referring to second and even third generation Americans by the country of their ancestors. "Curt was among the very last to get back."

"Yes, he was. He and Owen Carlson were both hospitalized for a while and didn't get home until March. The first vandalism happened in early April. That's what made people suspicious—the timing of it. Nick Nicholson was still constable then. He investigated but didn't find enough clues to arrest anyone."

"He thought it might be kids making mischief," Mr. Downing added.

Bella frowned. "It doesn't seem like kids would be so persistent, and they'd probably talk about it, so word would get out sooner or later."

"That's what most of us thought," the man agreed. "I don't know that Nick spent a lot of time on the case. He'd already decided to take a job with the Toledo police, and he only worked a few weeks after the first trouble."

"Did Jax become constable in May?"

"Yes, he did," Mrs. Downing replied. "He worked with Nick for a couple of weeks. Then, he was on his own. The town council refused to hire a deputy until October. Even now, Nolen only gets part-time work."

Although Jax had said as much, Bella still found the decision surprising. "I know there aren't as many people now, but there used to a constable, two full-time deputies, and a clerk. A constable and a part-time assistant don't seem to be enough."

"I agree with you," Downing said. "Especially with so many crimes lately, Nolen should be working full-time. Jax doesn't let him put in extra hours without pay because he won't take advantage of the boy. Instead, he works almost constantly himself."

The observation didn't surprise Bella. Jax had always been a hard worker, and it was reassuring to know something about him hadn't changed. Since the conversation had wandered away from Bella's initial focus, she moved it back.

"Gus seemed very adamant about veterans wearing their uniforms."

"It's been one of his excuses to harass them, and it's what he tells them and anyone else who will listen," Mrs. Downing replied with a frown. "Gus finds seeing any part of army uniforms very offensive, and he's said so more than once. Of course, he often goes on to say they need to put the past behind them, get jobs, and make contributions to the community."

Bella frowned. "That's mean."

"Yes, it is," Mr. Downing concurred, "but petty and mean describe Gus quite well."

"They do and always have," his wife put in. "Fred Snyder and Warren Ritter were still boys when they left for France, and they've both grown inches since then. I'm sure their old pants would be above their ankles. As for Owen, he hasn't found a job so I doubt if he can afford to buy anything new, and he's so thin now. Curt has been fortunate because Mac hired him last summer, and he has a place to live. He may wear parts of the uniform since some of the others must."

"I'm sure that's the case," her husband added.

Mrs. Downing nodded. "Owen's wife left him a few months ago. Since then, he's been very withdrawn. As far as jobs, there are few here and, with the theater closed, he can't go back to his old job as projectionist. Movie houses are more common now, so he could get a job elsewhere but he doesn't want to move away from home, I s'pose."

The Picture Palace had been a source of community pride since few small towns had such facilities when it opened. Owen had been equally proud to be the projectionist. Remembering how he'd looked the previous day—forlorn and frustrated—filled Bella with anger and sadness. How dare Gus attack Owen or any of the veterans for their attire? "Yesterday's conflict started inside the café, so we didn't see that part. Do you know what else was said?" With luck, the town gossip mill was still going.

Mr. Downing ran one hand over his face before exchanging a look with his wife. When he turned back to Bella, his face was lined with concern. "I heard Curt called Gus a Hun and said he ought to go back to Germany if he doesn't respect those who served this country. I imagine that lit a fire under Gus."

"Oh, no," Bella murmured. "Has Curt said such things in the past?"

"Not that I've heard," Downing told her. "I guess they came close to blows yesterday, but you and Jax may have arrived in time to put a stop to it. Abner Smith had stopped for breakfast at the café, and he saw how it started. He told us it was very heated. Curt got Owen outside, but Gus followed them. Abner was worried, so he went out, too."

"Did he plan to intercede?" Bella asked, recalling the postmaster's presence the previous morning.

Downing shook his head. "I don't know. Abner wouldn't be much of a match for Gus. Never was. Not in size or in personality. Gus picked on him when we were all in school together. They were a couple of years ahead of me, but I recall Gus singling out poor Abner often."

Bella nodded. "I see," she murmured before returning to the veterans. "Curt seems quiet and withdrawn, so I'm surprised he reacted so strongly. Except for the fact that, as you say, he probably still feels responsible for men in his platoon." Her brother, she knew, would have been the same way. But what about Jax? As constable, he couldn't take sides, which had to be difficult, especially when it involved men he'd been with in France.

"Yes, and it's hard for all involved," Mr. Downing said.

Bella could only agree. After exchanging holiday greetings with the couple, she left the store feeling troubled. While she had gotten more information, it disturbed her because Curt could be a suspect—a strong suspect.

Chapter Six

After depositing her packages in the car, Bella went to the post office. Purchasing stamps wasn't a priority, but speaking to Abner Smith was since he had observed yesterday's conflict both inside and outside the café. On top of that, the man not only knew everyone in and around town, he was in the perfect position to hear and spread "town news" as he had always termed the latest gossip.

"Arabella," the postmaster called out from behind the counter as she stepped inside. A smile curved his fish-like mouth. Not for the first time, Bella was reminded of a guppy. A friendly guppy. "How good it is to see you again. Welcome home, my dear. I didn't get a chance to give you a real greeting yesterday." Smith had changed little in Bella's time away. His wire-rimmed spectacles perched precariously on his narrow nose and his bald head shone brightly in the glaring light from the ceiling.

"Thank you, Mr. Smith, it's nice to be home," Bella replied as she crossed the cramped lobby. Her gaze flickered around the place. It hadn't changed much in her absence, either. Narrow and long, the front area boasted the same number of postal boxes and mail slots as it had all of her life. The dark floor and equally dark woodwork were still polished to a high shine. Some things in Moreley remained the same, which was reassuring.

Smith's voice broke into her thoughts. "I was so sorry to hear about Matthew. Such a terrible loss, as were your parents' passings." His expression had gone from pleased to somber.

Bella nodded and thanked him before hurrying on to another topic. "I need to buy stamps."

"Of course, my dear." Mr. Smith opened a drawer and pulled some out.

As she completed her purchase, Bella went on to briefly describe her side trip on the way to town. Smith looked as shocked as the Downings had at the news of Gus Schwarz's death. When he didn't reply, she continued. "You went to school together, didn't you?"

"Yes, we did. I can't say I liked the man, but I'm sorry to hear about his death. You say he was shot?"

"I'm afraid so."

Smith shook his head as if in continued disbelief. "Terrible."

His responses were terse, which was unusual for the chatty postmaster. If she wanted more information, Bella realized she needed to be blunt. "You said you didn't like Mr. Schwarz, so you weren't friends when you were young?" The Downings had said as much, but it was a starting point.

"No, not at all. We were in the same class until Gus quit school in the ninth grade. He only stayed that long because of Mrs. Hastings. She was a one-woman committee keeping us kids in school. She wasn't Mrs. Hastings then, of course. She was Miss Oliver. New to town and new to teaching, but kind and caring. Of course, Mrs. Culpepper supported her efforts. Gus wasn't much of a student, and his father, who worked for the Culpeppers, wanted him to help more. Old Schwarz drank a lot and didn't always do his job. Mr. Culpepper was patient about it, but he needed a real worker. A small cottage went with the position, so old Schwarz couldn't afford to be fired. To help more on the farm, Gus quit school. Mrs. Culpepper tutored him for a while from what I heard." Smith pushed his spectacles back in place. "I can't say I missed seeing Gus on a daily basis. He picked on some of us quite badly."

The postmaster was once again voluble, and his last statement confirmed what Mr. Downing had said. Bella searched her mind for a response that might garner even more information. "You were at the café yesterday when the confrontation started. Jax and I only saw the end of it, but I heard Gus had been criticizing some of our veterans for still wearing their uniforms."

A low snort left Smith. "Fred Snyder and Warren Ritter wear parts of their uniforms because they can't afford new clothes, and they both went from boys to men in France, so I'm sure their old things don't fit. The others have been wearing their uniform coats since the cold weather hit us. Owen Carlson is forced to wear almost all of his uniform. He dropped weight and hasn't worked since he got back. Then, his wife left. In any case, it was none of Gus Schwarz's business, but he could never keep his mouth shut." His gaze narrowed on her. "He even scolded you for wearing your uniform."

"Yes, that surprised me," Bella commented.

"I wasn't surprised. He's—was—a nasty person."

The postmaster's tart tone stunned Bella. She had always found Mr. Smith to be soft-spoken and pleasant, even when he was sharing the latest tidbits of "town talk." Obviously,

Gus Schwarz evoked strong feelings in many people. All bad. "So, Mr. Schwarz started by talking about Owen and Curt wearing their uniforms?"

Smith nodded. "I imagine Gus only went in because he saw Curt and Owen. The man doesn't frequent the café. Too stingy. Curt bought breakfast for Owen, and they were on their way outside when Gus stopped them. Gus was at his worst, picking on Owen for wearing his uniform and saying it was no wonder his wife left him since he's living in the past."

Bella gasped at this additional piece of information. "Poor Owen."

Again, the postmaster nodded. "His wife was never happy here. Before the influenza and such, there was more to do, and she flitted around, getting involved in everything. After Owen went to war, all she talked about was moving to Toledo or Cleveland. Said Moreley was becoming a ghost town, and she didn't want to stay and die with it." He paused for a moment. "I'm guessing she couldn't convince Owen to leave, so she went herself."

"That's likely," Bella said as she absorbed the speculation. "Did Owen say anything yesterday morning?"

"Not that I heard. He looked badly upset. Curt stepped in like he usually does."

"Curt and Owen were in my brother's platoon, and Curt was the sergeant. I'm sure he feels like he still needs to defend his men." But how far would Curt go? Bella wondered.

"I suppose you're right," Smith said. "Curt has always been loyal. Yesterday, he not only defended Owen, he defended his brother."

"Carl? Why? Did Gus say something about him?"

A humorless laugh left the postmaster. "Once Gus gets going, he doesn't have sense to shut up. When Curt spoke, Gus turned on him and said he had gotten as mindless and as useless as Carl."

Anxiety gripped Bella. The confrontation had been much worse than the Downings had known, and much worse than she and Jax had heard. Had it been bad enough for someone—Curt even—to seek revenge this morning? "How horrible."

"That it was," he agreed. "Took a few moments for any of us to react. Sam Push saw what was happening from behind the counter, hurried to the door, and told them all to stop or they wouldn't be welcome there again. Curt grabbed Owen's arm and pulled him outside, but he said something under his breath to Gus. I don't know what although we could all hear the reaction clearly."

"What did Gus say back?"

A long sigh escaped Smith. "He told Curt to be careful or he'd be the one who was sorry."

Uneasiness crept through Bella. What had Curt said to evoke that reply? The possibilities were troubling. "That must have been shortly before Jax and I saw them."

"It was. I was relieved when you two arrived because I still worried about them coming to blows, and someone could have gotten hurt." Smith paused for a moment. "I was a little concerned when you got out of the car because I don't think Schwarz would hesitate to hit a woman. In fact, it's more likely than not that he'd go after whoever he saw as the weakest person...not that I'm saying you're weak. You never were." A rueful smile touched his lips. "And you still aren't, I'm sure. After all, you served in France."

Bella smiled in return, but she now understood Jax's displeasure with her. He knew Gus Schwarz better than she did and had been trying to protect her, not command her.

When the front door bell jingled, Bella turned to see a balding man of medium build enter the post office. She immediately recognized him. "Mr. Windsor, how nice to see you."

The man blinked at her for a moment. Then, recognition flashed in his dark eyes. "Arabella Stewart. It's good to see you safely home," he observed before offering condolences about her parents and brother.

As she did with everyone, Bella thanked him.

"When did you return?" he asked.

"Yesterday morning."

"You stayed longer than most of the operators," he said. "We all owe you a great debt."

"Thank you, but I didn't do anything more than others, or nearly as much as many." Bella had left with the last of the operators, but primarily because she'd had no family or sweetheart waiting for her.

The doorbell jingled again, and a slight young man with dark hair and dark eyes entered. Mr. Windsor laid one hand on the boy's slim shoulder before turning back to Bella. "Arabella, may I present my nephew, Garlan Dubois. Garlan, this is one of my former pupils, Miss Arabella Stewart. She just returned from Europe after serving in the Army Signal Corps." Garlan gave a slight bow, but it was his pale face and wide eyes that were most noticeable. A shiver rippled through him, and a long moment passed before he spoke.

"Hello. How do you do?" His dark gaze briefly met hers before skittering away.

He had an accent that Bella couldn't quite identify. Mr. Windsor's parents had emigrated from England, but the boy didn't sound British. "It's very nice to meet you, Garlan. Are you visiting your uncle?"

Garlan's gaze went to Windsor who answered for him. "My nephew has come to live with me since he lost his family." He briefly squeezed the boy's shoulder before turning to Mr. Smith. "I want to collect our mail. We are on our way to Cincinnati to spend Christmas with some relations, so I won't stop back until we return this weekend."

Smith retrieved the mail and handed it to Windsor. "Here you go. Enjoy your holiday, both of you."

"Thank you," Windsor replied. "Merry Christmas, sir, and to you, as well, Arabella." Then, he and his nephew—his dark head bowed—quickly exited the post office.

Once they were gone, curiosity overcame Bella. "Mr. Windsor's nephew has an accent that I couldn't quite identify. It sounded a bit French, but also a little Dutch."

Smith inclined his head. "The boy is from Louvain, Belgium."

Bella's hand flew to her mouth. "He must have seen terrible things."

"I'm afraid so," the postmaster agreed. "Before he arrived last winter, Anthony told me about Garlan. He was only twelve when the Germans invaded Belgium and sacked Louvain. His father was a Belgian Army officer, killed shortly after the war started. The boy and his mother, Anthony's younger sister, were fleeing to the countryside where the father had family. She was killed. Garlan somehow got to England where he stayed with some British cousins for a time. Since he is Anthony's only nephew, he was able to come here."

"The poor boy," Bella said with real sadness. "I met some Belgians when I was in France, and they had terrible stories about what happened after the German invasion. Many tales in the papers were exaggerated, but it was an awful time, especially for the children."

"Garlan doesn't say much. Keeps to himself, but he does some odd jobs for folks."

"He looks to be school age. Doesn't he attend classes?" Bella asked in surprise. He appeared to be quite young but, if he was twelve when the Germans invaded, he must be about seventeen.

"Nearly eighteen. Not many boys that age are still in school here and, if they are, they're about to finish. His schooling in Belgium was interrupted. I don't know the details, but I heard the boy got in some pretty bad fights. Now, Anthony tutors him at home."

"He seems so shy. It's hard to believe he'd brawl with other boys."

Smith shrugged. "You can never tell what's inside a person. Anthony is generally a quiet man, but I've heard him argue with Schwarz about the war."

"Really?"

"They were both in here one day to pick up mail. That was before the nephew got to town. Anthony lost his sister and brother-in-law, as I said, but he lost some British cousins, too. He can get on his soapbox about things. Always been that way."

"I recall him having strong opinions when I was in his class," Bella said before turning her thoughts back to the matter at hand. "I've heard Mr. Schwarz suspected veterans of crimes at his farm. Curt especially."

"That seemed to be the case, although I think Gus was wrong." Smith brow furrowed as if in concentration. "He singled out Curt, but he also had a couple of run-ins with Harold Horton."

"I'm surprised. Harold has always been such a calm person. Did Mr. Schwarz confront him when he got home after being wounded?"

"I believe so," the postmaster replied. "We bought a motorized delivery vehicle a while back. Nice, but we can't give it hay." A low chuckle left him. "Anyhow, I took it for a fill-up as Gus was pulling out one day. Harold was plenty upset. When I asked about it, Harold only said Gus was a typical Hun. He didn't want to say more, so I let it go."

Use of the epithet "Hun" surprised Bella. Did all of the soldiers now use the pejorative with their German-American neighbors? Maybe some had changed more than she cared to believe. Since she now had a lot to consider, Bella drew the talk to a close. "I should get on my way. I suppose you'll be leaving soon."

A big smile wreathed the postmaster's face. "That I will. I'm heading to my son's house for Christmas."

After exchanging holiday wishes with the man, Bella took her stamps and made her way back to the car. She looked up and down the street, but saw no other townspeople out and about. With a sad sigh, she climbed into the Ford and headed to Ballantyne. On the way, she planned to see Harold Horton. Perhaps he could tell her more.

Chapter Seven

Harold welcomed Bella and extended his sympathies before asking, "Need a fill-up?"

Although the Model T's tank wasn't close to empty, Bella nodded in agreement. While the man checked under the hood for oil and water levels, she got out of the car and stood beside him. She wanted to ask about his confrontation with Gus, but wasn't sure how to begin.

When he turned to smile at her, a shock of light brown hair fell across his forehead. With one hand, Harold brushed it back. "Mac done a good job keeping her in shape."

She offered an answering smile. "That's good." Bella scanned his face. Like the other veterans, Harold looked older than his thirty-four years. "How are you feeling now?"

A half-shrug lifted one of his muscular shoulders. "The wound don't give me much trouble anymore, and I have work so I'm luckier than some."

Bella nodded. "How is business?"

After closing the hood, he turned to her with a grimace on his face. "Not as good nowadays. Most of the folks left here are loyal customers. We're lucky for that. We're also lucky so many around here bought motor cars. A few still rely on horses, but not many."

"Most, but not all of the locals come here?"

"Only a couple don't these days. Werner Meyers and Gus Schwarz don't." He paused to study her face. "I heard you saw Gus get after Curt and Owen yesterday morning, so you won't be surprised that Schwarz and Meyers go to Boxwood for repairs. Neither gets to Moreley often which suits me fine."

Bella carefully studied Harold. His tone and expression indicated a dislike of Schwarz, but neither revealed any knowledge of the man's death. "You probably haven't heard the news about Gus Schwarz."

Harold looked at her in confusion. When he finished filling the Model T's tank, he asked, "Got into another quarrel?"

She chewed on her lower lip while considering how to reveal the news. "He might have because his wife found him shot to death a couple of hours ago."

Harold's hazel eyes rounded in what appeared to be shock. "What?"

"When I was driving into town, I saw Mrs. Schwarz walking along the road. She was coming for help, but I took her back to her husband's body. He was dead."

Anger tightened the man's sharp features. "Is Helene all right? She shouldn't be out walking in the cold, and she wouldn't have been if that...if her husband kept the truck in running order. She's too frail to hook up horses."

"She couldn't have done that in any case because the barn door was open when she went looking for Gus, and the horses were gone."

"What?" Again, he seemed to be taken aback.

Bella hesitated. Why was she revealing so much? What she wanted and needed was more information. "I don't really know any details."

"But Helene is safe." Anxiety replaced anger in his gaze.

"Yes, she has a bad cold but Doc examined her and said she should be fine." Bella paused briefly. "You thought Mr. Schwarz got into another argument. I've heard he had disputes with a number of soldiers. Were you one of them, Harold?"

His gaze moved to a distant point. "We never got along. I don't like bullies. When he used to bring his truck here, I had my brother work on it and deal with him."

Bella absorbed the words. "Did you dislike him because he was a bully, or did you two have a confrontation?" She knew they had, but would he admit it?

Harold shrugged his broad shoulders. "He never liked me, and I never liked him." Harold stopped for a moment. "He's not only a bully, he is...was a brute."

She tried another tack. "Do you know anything about yesterday's run-in?"

"Not much. One of many, and they're usually the same. Schwarz looks for trouble and finds it at times."

"And Curt always comes to the defense of his men from what I've gathered."

Harold bobbed his head. "Curt's a good man. I do the same if I see Schwarz causing trouble for the boys, but I'm mostly here or home."

Bella started to ask another question, but two cars pulled into the station. "I'll let you go," she said before exchanging Christmas wishes with him and heading to Ballantyne.

As she got on the road again, Bella mulled over what she had learned. What had Curt said to rile up Gus Schwarz? None of the probabilities gave Bella any peace. Neither did Curt's absence. The previous day, after her nap, Bella had seen Carl. The greenskeeper had said not to expect him or Curt for dinner because they planned a late meal of sandwiches in their suite. After that, Bella decided to take a tray to Mac and eat in his room with him. She'd seen no sign of either brother all evening, and only Carl had come to breakfast this morning. At that time, her query about Curt met with a brief reply from his brother—he was visiting a friend for the day. None of that seemed important earlier. After all, Curt didn't have to report his comings and goings to her or Mac. But why had he left so early?

Harold's replies hadn't added much, but his dislike—more than dislike really—of Gus Schwarz was obvious. Bella wished she could talk to Jax about the case, but his dismissal of her as *just anyone* still rang in her ears.

***

When she got home, Bella found Carl and Mac in the kitchen drinking coffee and eating cookies. "I see you found the baked goods."

"I hope ye dinna mind, lass, but I thought a bit of a snack was in order," Mac told her with a smile.

"No, of course not, but don't fill up on sweets. I have a special dinner planned for tonight." Bella laid her purchases on the counter. Uneasiness continued to plague her. Curt was nowhere in sight, and his motorcycle had not been outside.

"Looks like you were busy in town," Carl observed with a shy grin.

"I picked up a few items," she replied, not wanting to reveal that two of them were presents for the Molitor brothers. Bella focused on Carl. In what she hoped was a casual tone, she asked, "Where is Curt? He'll be here for dinner, won't he?"

"Yep," Carl replied.

"You said he was visiting a friend. Someone in Moreley?" She tried to make the query sound off-hand.

Carl shook his head. "He went over to Boxwood very early to see Wyatt Berringer."

"I know Wyatt," Bella said. "He was in my brother's platoon, too. Does Curt visit him often?"

"Every week or so. Sometimes, more often," Carl replied.

Maybe Curt had an alibi, but did he usually spend an entire day with Wyatt Berringer? Before she had a chance to ask, Mac spoke.

"Were there many folks in town?"

Bella busied herself with pouring a cup of tea before replying. "Not really. I only saw the Downings at the mercantile, Mr. Smith at the post office, and Harold Horton at the filling station. I ran into Mr. Windsor and his nephew, too. Not many people were shopping on Christmas Eve afternoon. In fact, I think the Downings locked up behind me."

Mac frowned. "I hope business will be better for all of us next year."

A harsh sigh left Bella. She hated to put more of a damper on Christmas, but withholding Schwarz's murder wasn't a good idea. "I'm afraid there's more bad news."

Mac's gray brows pulled into a frown while Carl looked both surprised and dismayed. "What now?" Mac asked, his tone wary.

Bella leaned back against the kitchen counter. "Gus Schwarz was found shot to death early this morning." She provided details about seeing Mrs. Schwarz and the events that followed. "There isn't a suspect yet."

Neither man replied. As Bella watched, she saw that Mac was clearly taken aback while Carl seemed completely shocked. Did he know about Curt's confrontation with Gus the previous day? Curt had only mentioned seeing Bella in passing when he'd brought up Matt's death. He hadn't indicated where or why their meeting had occurred.

"Sorry to hear it," Mac said when he finally spoke. "Poor Mrs. Schwarz. Losing loved ones is nay easy, but at Christmas..." His voice trailed off.

Carl clasped his hands on the table and focused on the plate in front of him. "Jax called about a half-hour ago," he said. His attention went to Mac. "You were sleeping."

"What did he want?" Bella asked.

The greenskeeper turned his ashen face to her. "He wanted to talk to Curt. I said he wasn't here because he left very early this morning. I hope I didn't cause no trouble for my brother."

"Telling the truth can nay cause trouble, lad," Mac assured him.

Carl looked skeptical, so Bella added her reassurance although she was uneasy herself. "Mac is right. Besides, Jax will talk to a lot of people. That's his job as constable. Interviewing Curt won't mean he's a suspect."

The greenskeeper nodded. "I know Curt didn't do it."

"So, do we," Mac put in. His tone was firm and reassuring.

"Of course, we know that," Bella said, but doubt remained. The ringing of the phone interrupted, and she headed to the lobby's front desk to answer.

The call took no more than a minute. When she went back to the kitchen, the men were drinking coffee in silence but they both looked at her. "That was Jax again. He wondered if Curt was here." Bella was annoyed that Jax had telephoned twice. Curt shouldn't have to answer questions tonight. After all, it was Christmas Eve. Jax's tone hadn't helped, either. Of course, his earlier characterization of her as *just anyone* continued to bother her. Consequently, she had sidestepped saying she would let him know when Curt got back.

Even after Mac and Carl cleared out and Bella started supper, her irritation with Jax lingered. Why should she help him when he'd been so dismissive?

When Curt appeared an hour later, Bella didn't call the constable's office. Instead, she decided any interviews could wait until after Christmas. A niggling finger of guilt prodded her conscience, but Bella ignored it. If Jax called, she'd tell him Curt was back but, if he didn't, that was his problem.

***

At the constable's office, Jax waited to hear from Bella. As time passed, he grew increasingly anxious. He and Nolen had spoken with all of the other veterans still in town except

Harold and Curt. He'd planned to stop at the Hortons' filling station on his way to Ballantyne. Now, with darkness falling and Harold likely to close early due to the holiday, Jax slipped on his cap and coat and headed out.

When Jax got to the filling station, he went inside where Harold working on a car. His former sergeant immediately addressed the murder. "I was sorry to hear about Gus. It had to be terrible for Helene to find him."

Jax wasn't surprised that word of the death had spread. News traveled fast in a small town. For several moments, he studied the other man.

Horton, although muscular, was shorter than Jax. Even so, he exuded strength and stability and maturity which had made him a valuable platoon leader. When he'd been wounded early in the Meuse-Argonne offensive and sent home, Jax had missed his second-in-command. Nolen, more than a decade younger than Harold, had done an admirable job in the older man's shoes, but losing his original sergeant had been a blow for the entire platoon.

"She was distraught," Jax told him.

Concern darkened the other man's gaze. "At least she wasn't hurt, was she?"

"No, she has a bad cold and went back to bed after she fixed breakfast, so she was in the house when it happened."

"And she didn't see or hear nothing?" He still sounded anxious.

"No, she didn't." Jax paused before continuing. "Did you see any unusual activity this morning, or did your brother open the station?"

"I always open at seven o'clock, and he usually closes, but he has young children so I said I'd stay late today. He was going out to cut down a tree. Then, they'll decorate it. I'll go over on my way home." He rubbed his stubbled jaw with one hand. "I can't say I saw anyone or anything unusual this morning. The farm is down the road a few miles, but so are a lot of other farms. Don't pay much attention to traffic. Early morning is our busiest time, although not Christmas Eve. Didn't have no customers 'til around nine."

Jax nodded before posing another question. "Did Schwarz ever bring his truck to you for work on?"

Harold hesitated briefly as if considering his response. "Before the war. Since then, he goes over to Boxwood. You already know he don't like soldiers much. I heard the truck broke down and it's been sitting useless in his yard. If he'd fixed it, Helene wouldn't have been walking this morning."

The town gossips had been busy, Jax decided. "How well do you know Helene? You and she are about the same age, aren't you?"

Harold glanced at a point past Jax's right shoulder. "We were in school together."

The terse reply revealed very little, but Harold's genuine worry about her was evident to Jax. "I never knew either of them well, but I don't recall seeing her in town often."

Harold's gaze moved back to Jax. "She's stayed mostly on the farm for years."

The statement bothered Jax, but he wasn't sure why. "Do you know if she felt the same as Gus about being targeted as German-Americans?"

"Helene's people weren't German. Her father's great-grandparents came from England, and her mother was French Canadian."

Jax offered a rueful smile. "I'd forgotten that, but my mind used to be more on golf than anything else. I don't remember much about her parents." All of his spare time, and most of his attention, had been on the game.

Harold shrugged. "Her parents were good, kind people like Helene. They wouldn't have held no grudge against anyone, and they wouldn't have found fault with us soldiers, either. Don't know how she lived with that man for years. They got nothing in common. Nothing at all." The words rolled out of Harold like a floodtide, a roiling floodtide.

The bitterness in the other man's voice caught Jax off-guard. His former sergeant could be passionate in the face of injustice. Otherwise, he was a calm, steady person. Keeping both sides of the man in mind, Jax proceeded with care. "The Culpeppers were well off, so I'm surprised the house has no telephone."

A guttural sound escaped Harold. "Phones weren't common out in the country when they were alive, and Gus didn't want Helene having any niceties." Again, his voice was harsh.

"Why?" Jax asked.

His jaw tightened. "Lieutenant, we both know Gus was ornery. He wasn't nearly good enough for Helene, and keeping her isolated out there was one way to control her. At least he didn't infect her with his hatred." He grimaced. "You know he's picked on all of us who fought the Huns. Gus had a run-in with Curt and Owen yesterday."

Jax massaged his right temple where a headache was beginning to bloom. "I witnessed part of it. Curt was furious, and Owen was upset." Jax released a pent-up breath. "I need to talk to Curt, but I haven't been able to locate him."

"He was here an hour or so ago. Said he went to Boxwood early to see Wyatt Berringer. The two of them get together often. They're fighting some of the same troubles." A frown pulled down the corners of his wide mouth.

The disclosure about Curt being at the station was disturbing. Where had he gone from here? If he was at Ballantyne, Bella would have let Jax know. Wouldn't she? As he thought about their earlier exchange, Jax realized he'd ask her to call him but she hadn't actually said she would. Doubt flared within him as he remembered his harsh response to her earlier query. She would never be *just anyone* to him, but if she knew the truth about his role in her brother's death, he wouldn't be anyone at all to her. Despite his troubled thoughts, he pushed on. "How did Curt seem?"

"About the same."

"Did he say where he was headed from here?"

"To Ballantyne."

The confirmation rankled. "I'll go out there now. If you hear something or think of anything that might be helpful, let me know."

Harold nodded his dark head. "I can't believe any of the men are responsible for the crimes around here."

"I don't think so, either," Jax said before pausing for a moment. "Thanks for the information." He was about to take his leave when the former sergeant spoke again.

"It was good to see Bella this afternoon. She seemed happy to be home, but troubled over the murder."

Jax froze in place. Now, the source of Harold's information became clear. "She mentioned the murder?"

"She more than mentioned it. She told me about picking up Helene and also asked questions about the past incidents and how Schwarz had reacted. She asked what I knew about the confrontation that Owen, Curt, and Gus had yesterday, too."

"What did you tell her?" Bella had seen part of it. Why was she asking for more details? Was she inserting herself into a murder investigation? He wouldn't be surprised, but he was uneasy. She'd put herself in danger by going to France, but she shouldn't be taking risks now that she was home.

The other man shook his head. "Not much. She knew more about it than I did."

Jax's brow furrowed in consternation. "How would Bella know anything about it other than it happened and what the two of us saw?"

Horton shrugged. "She'd been at the mercantile and the post office. You know the Downings and Smith. Good folks, but gossipy. Smith told her some details about how the argument began."

His consternation turned quickly to irritation. "Did she share them with you?"

"Nope. Didn't have a chance to talk too long since people came in for gas. I'm guessing it's a matter of time before Smith tells all to anyone who will listen. You know how he is."

"I suppose so," Jax replied, although Smith had not revealed everything to him. The man had been busy when Jax stopped at the post office on his way back from the Schwarz farm, so Jax had asked only a few questions. Then, he'd called the mayor to let him know about the murder while Nolen interviewed the other veterans. With so much to do, and so little help, Jax hadn't been free until well after Smith left for the holiday. He definitely had to talk with the man on the twenty-sixth.

After exchanging Christmas greetings with Harold, Jax made his way to the resort. He wanted to find out what Smith had told Bella, and he planned to tell her to stay out of his investigation.

Chapter Eight

Ten minutes later, Jax pulled the Chummy to a stop in front of Ballantyne Inn and leaned back in his seat. His gaze went to the front door festooned with the large wreath. Yesterday morning, Bella had been touched by the decorations, but so had he. They brought back happy memories. The warm light spilling from the windows was familiar, too, but everything else was different. Mostly, he was different. He wasn't here as a welcome guest, or a good friend, but as the constable. The constable who had to question two of Bella's employees, one of whom had been her brother's sergeant, the man who had held Matt as his life slipped away.

A now-familiar ache formed in Jax's gut. If Bella was protecting Curt, that was hardly surprising. He not only lived and worked at Ballantyne; he'd been with Matt at the end. Despite those facts, her failure to call bothered Jax although not as much as her snooping in town. He'd told her the case was police business which meant it was none of hers, yet she had questioned the Downings, Smith, and Harold. None of them was apt to hurt her, but what about the unknown killer? The possibility of her getting hurt, or worse, made Jax sick at heart.

With reluctance, Jax emerged from the vehicle. Although he wasn't anxious to face Bella, he mounted the stairs and knocked on the door.

Mac's deep voice called out, "Come in."

Jax entered to find the old pro seated by the fireplace. A faded plaid wool blanket was wrapped around the man, but

Mac looked better than he had the previous morning. Much better. Maybe having Bella back had put him on the mend. "I'm sorry to bother you," Jax said as he swept off his cap and wiped his feet on the door mat before crossing the wide foyer to stand by the roaring fire.

"Ye are never a bother, lad, and ye nay need to knock," Mac observed. "We will always welcome ye here."

The older man was sincere, but Jax doubted if Bella felt the same way. Why would she? Even so, he forced a smile. "Thank you."

"Bella dinna say she'd invited ye for supper, but I'm very glad the lass did."

Jax glanced away from Mac's steady gaze. "She didn't invite me. I'm here on business, I'm afraid."

The old pro's good humor faltered. "Ye want to speak with Curt and Carl about Gus Schwarz's murder."

"I don't want to spoil the holiday, but I wasn't able to find Curt earlier. Just a bit ago, I was at the filling station, and Harold said Curt stopped on his way back to Ballantyne." Jax shifted uneasily from one foot to the other. Although he needed to talk to the former sergeant, he harbored a faint wish that Curt wasn't around. Then, there would be a viable reason for Bella not calling him. "I'd like to speak with him and Carl."

"Just speak with them?"

"For now, yes." He paused before continuing. "I'd like to talk with Bella briefly, too."

Mac didn't speak for several moments. "She told us what happened to Schwarz. Tis a terrible thing, but the lass dinna believe Curt did it, and nay do I."

The urge to say he agreed hit Jax hard, but entertaining personal feelings was a luxury no constable could afford. His job was following facts no matter where they led. "I can understand that, but I don't like her questioning people. Civilians shouldn't be involved."

"Civilians?" Bella's voice preceded her entry into the lobby.

Jax pivoted to see her cross the distance between the kitchen door and where he stood. Fire flashed in her dark gaze. Before he had a chance to respond, she spoke again.

"By civilians, I suppose you mean me."

He gritted his teeth until a muscle jumped in his jaw. Jax wasn't sure of her motivation, but he could easily see her resolve—something he'd witnessed more than once in the past. "You aren't a law officer," he said in a flat tone that hid both his anxiety and aggravation.

"That means I can't ask people questions?" Her voice was sharp, almost piercing.

Jax took a long breath to rein in his emotions. In the muted light of the kerosene lamps, her dark hair—cut in a stylish bob—shone like polished mahogany. The silky locks framed her lovely features. She didn't look as tired, he noted, but she still seemed vulnerable. Very vulnerable. Her brother's words echoed in Jax's mind. *If I don't make it back, look after my parents and Bella.* Jax had readily agreed. Sadly, he'd gotten home too late to help the elder Stewarts. Standing in Matt's stead for Bella was crucial, not that Jax wouldn't have protected Bella in any case. Still, revealing his promise wouldn't ease the breach between them. Nothing would. He'd made a terrible mistake, a mistake that had led to Matt's death.

A wrenching sigh escaped Jax. "It would be best if you didn't get involved. An amateur digging around could get into a bad situation, and I don't need another murder to solve." When she started to speak, he hurried on. "I asked you to call when Curt got back, but you never did. Instead, I found out from Harold that Curt was on his way here more than an hour ago. And you talked to the Downings and Postmaster Smith." A moment's pause preceded his next statement, but it didn't mollify his frustration or his fear. "Impeding an investigation is a crime."

Bella recoiled as if struck, and Jax had to glance away from the hurt and shock in her eyes. He knew—once again— his words sounded harsh, and her reply confirmed that she saw them as such. But she needed to stay out of the case. She needed to stay out of danger.

"I certainly wouldn't want my death to be an added complication for you," she shot back. "But you forget that I studied all of my grandfather's old murder cases with him the spring I had scarlet fever. We went over his scrapbooks and discussed them in detail, and we even read a lot of mysteries and solved the cases in them. We compiled a memoir of his work, and Grandfather said I was as good as any of his men at figuring out whodunits."

Abruptly, Jax remembered her maternal grandfather's tales about police work and her fascination with it, neither of which qualified her to poke around in a homicide investigation. "Bella, helping your Grandfather Moore write his reminiscences doesn't make you an expert investigator.

Neither does reading all of the Sherlock Holmes tales," Jax pointed out, his exasperation clear in his clipped tone. "You're being stubborn and childish, and it's long past time you got over both."

While she hadn't expected Jax to welcome her help, Bella was stunned by his criticism. Stunned and wounded. The words *just anyone* again flashed in her mind. War had changed him, but he seemed like a stranger. A complete and utter stranger. With effort, she kept the sorrow from her voice and only let her anger show. "I am not a child, and I never suggested I was an expert investigator. However, I daresay I have more familiarity with murder cases than you do as Grandfather was instrumental in solving more than a dozen, and he shared all of the details with me when we worked on his memoir." When dark color rose in Jax's face, Bella knew her barb had found its mark. Normally, she would have never said such a hurtful thing to anyone, but part of her actually enjoyed his discomfort. Although she wasn't proud of the reaction, she couldn't deny it. "I dug out the old notebooks and scrapbooks when I got home today, and I went over some of them."

His nostrils flared with a sharp intake of breath. "Bella, you need to stay out of this. I don't care what you learned from your grandfather or what you found in the old notebooks or gathered in scrapbooks. There is a killer on the loose, and I don't need you, or any other amateur detectives, getting in my way."

His reaction further agitated Bella, and her chin went up. "You're still pretty much an amateur yourself." Again, her harsh words were out of character. If Jax wanted the chasm between them to grow, he had achieved his goal. On her way home from France, she had thought—even, hoped—they might return to some sort of friendship. She had wanted to hear an excuse and an apology for his behavior after Matt died. Now, that seemed highly unlikely.

An audible breath escaped him. "The town council hired me, not you, as their constable. I'll say this one last time. Stay out of this case."

"Or what?" she asked in a voice as cold as his.

Several seconds of silence ticked away before he responded. "Or I'll arrest you for interfering with a police investigation."

Heat rose in her cheeks. "You wouldn't."

When Jax spoke again, his voice was soft but firm. "I will if it comes to that."

For a moment, she simply looked at him. Not a trace of the boy he'd been was visible. Nor was there a vestige of the young man who had marched off to war. Going back was impossible. Going forward was the only choice. Abruptly, Bella turned her attention to Mac. "I have supper in the oven. It will be done in an hour. In the meantime, I'm going to change clothes. I'll be back in time to get the food on the table." With that, she spun on her heel and disappeared up the wide staircase without another glance at Jax.

***

For long moments, he stared after her. His emotions in turmoil, Jax massaged his taut neck muscles. He was still gazing at the staircase when Mac's voice intruded.

"Sit down, lad."

Jax stiffened. Caught up in the heated exchange with Bella, he'd forgotten about the old pro's presence. With weariness dragging at him, Jax nearly collapsed in the chair across from Mac. He'd gotten little sleep last night which wasn't unusual, but he had barely stopped all day. As a result, he was exhausted. That was no excuse for his poor handling of the situation with Bella, he supposed. And he had handled it poorly. Very poorly. In fact, he had handled every moment since Matt's death like a complete fool. He continued to grapple with the aftermath, and he had the sleepless nights and bad dreams to show for it. Finally, Jax glanced at Mac. "I'm sorry for the scene."

A low laugh rumbled out of the older man. "It was entertaining."

Warmth rose in Jax's face. "I could have gotten my point across in a more professional manner," he admitted.

"It's hard to be professional when ye are emotionally involved."

The observation startled Jax, but he immediately objected. "There's no involvement on either side, Mac."

"There used to be a friendship that could have become more."

The statement hung in the air for what seemed like an eternity. Jax wanted to deny Mac's observation, but it held a note of truth. Maybe more than a note. "It could have, although there's no guarantee that it would have."

"It still could if ye two weren't so prickly with one another. I dinna ken why that is."

Relief sapped some of Jax's tension. Bella hadn't told Mac about their encounter after Matt died. "War changes a lot of things, Mac. It changed me, and not for the better."

The older man held Jax's gaze. "Ye've kept to yerself since coming home. I was surprised when ye took the constable's job and even more surprised when ye never played last season. Golf was the center of ye life. I dinna want to pry, but are ye wounds the reason for both?"

If anyone else had asked, Jax would have brushed off the queries, but he'd known Mac since he was six. The older man was like a grandfather to him, a beloved grandfather. In addition, Mac had been role model, friend, and teacher. Even so, Jax's hands tightened into twin fists, and he stared into the crackling fire as he formed an answer. "My right shoulder and arm give me enough trouble that tournament golf is out of the question. I couldn't play thirty-six holes in a day. In fact, I doubt if I could make eighteen at this point." After leaving France, he'd kept his debility to himself. Not even his men knew the extent of damage from his last wounds, so this was more than Jax had admitted to anyone other than Doc Smedlay. More than he wanted to admit. He didn't allow himself to think about the death of his dreams, let alone talk about it.

"So, tournament golf is out but ye could still be a club pro," Mac suggested. "I'll be retiring at some point, and we would welcome ye here."

Jax started in surprise. Long-held hopes, the ones he'd thought were dead, rose within him. So, did the yearning to go back in time. Back to before Matt had died in his place. Back to when he and Bella might have had a future together.

Going back wasn't possible. "You saw how Bella reacted to my advice, Mac. She wouldn't welcome me here."

A half-shrug lifted one of Mac's shoulders. "As ye said, ye could have handled the situation better. Even so, she'll get over her annoyance."

Jax wasn't sure that was true, and allowing too much familiarity would be foolish. What could have been between them was no longer possible. He'd seen to that with one terrible decision. "I should talk with Curt and Carl and get on my way."

Mac nodded. "They're in their suite off the kitchen. The one Julia used."

"Thank you," Jax said before turning away.

Chapter Nine

Jax quickly walked through the familiar kitchen. Memories were everywhere at Ballantyne, but he couldn't afford to get caught up in them. He had a job to do, and it needed to be his only focus. When he reached the door to the suite, he tapped lightly and called out, "It's Jax Hastings."

The door opened almost immediately to reveal Curt Molitor. His gaunt face and hollow eyes didn't surprise Jax. The man had looked much the same for months, long before they'd left France. Now, though, he seemed almost haunted. But who among them wasn't?

"Lieutenant," he murmured, "What can I do for you?"

"I hope you can help me with some information," Jax assured him in an even tone he'd often used with his men when they were under duress. Unfortunately, Curt seemed to be under more duress now than he had been in the trenches. Undoubtedly, Carl had shared the news about Gus Schwarz...if it was news to Curt.

Curt nodded and stepped back. Carl, who was sitting by the pot-belly stove that dominated one corner of the large room, got to his feet. His expression was grim, but he put his hand out as Jax crossed the room. "Sit down. Curt, get another chair."

Once all three of them were seated, Jax spoke again. "You already know why I'm here."

Curt nodded. "I didn't kill him, lieutenant, and I didn't do none of the things that he and Meyers have accused me of." He braced his elbows on his knees and clasped his hands in front of him. "I'm not the same as I was," he said in an almost inaudible voice, "and may never be. I wouldn't kill anyone or anything, and I wouldn't mess up no property, either. I saw more than enough killing and damage in France, enough to last me a lifetime."

"Believe me, I understand." Jax blinked away the ugly images suddenly floating in his mind's eye. Trench warfare was horrific. So was the devastation in France and Belgium. Many towns had been wiped off the map, and graveyards had been everywhere. "Even so, I need to ask you both a few questions." He looked from one brother to the other. Curt, although three years younger than Carl, had once been the more outgoing and sociable one. Now, both were quiet and withdrawn. Not for the first time, Jax wondered if he'd done the right thing by taking the position of town constable. He hated questioning them, but that was his job, and he had to fulfill his duties.

Jax reached into his jacket pocket and pulled out a pencil and notepad. "Were you both here at Ballantyne early this morning?"

"I left around seven to go to Boxwood," Curt replied.

"I couldn't find you this afternoon. Did you spend the day there?" Although Harold had suggested as much, Jax needed to hear Curt's response.

"I go over to talk with Wyatt Berringer. Sometimes, I stay a few hours. Maybe more," Curt said.

Jax looked up. "How is Wyatt?"

"Worse than I am, if you can believe that." Curt shook his head. "He's tried working in his folks' store, but he has trouble dealing with people, so he feels useless. Most nights, he don't sleep at all. Neither do I, though. He called yesterday wanting me to come over."

A harsh breath left Jax as he saw Curt's tightly clasped hands begin to tremble. Talking with fellow veterans could be helpful although it could also create additional turmoil, particularly if they weren't adjusting well, as seemed to be the case with both Wyatt and Curt. Concern for the veterans of Moreley, his men and Matt's, would always be with him. "How often do you see Wyatt?"

Curt's dark gaze flickered away. "About every week, and whenever he calls me in-between."

"Even when you're feeling uneasy yourself?" Jax asked.

A slight smile tugged at one corner of Curt's mouth. "Lieutenant, there's hardly a time when I'm not uneasy."

"You were a big help to me working on the course last summer." Worry darkened Carl's gaze as he studied his brother.

Curt turned to Carl. "I don't have your gift, but I enjoyed it. The golf course is peaceful, especially first thing in the morning when we head out," Curt observed. "And being busy gave me less time to think." He looked back at Jax. "I like the early morning now, the calm and quiet. Even at this time of year, I spend some time alone as the sun rises. That's what I did yesterday. Left here around seven and didn't get there until almost eight-thirty because I stopped for a while."

"I see," Jax said as he made more notes. Dismay filled him. He'd wanted Curt to have an ironclad alibi. Instead, there was a significant gap of time when he'd been alone—time when Schwarz had died. "Did you take your motorcycle?"

"Yep, we don't have no motor car and don't need one. Mac lets us take the Model T. Mostly, I use the bike," Curt told him.

"Did you see anyone on your way to Boxwood?" Jax asked. What he really wanted to know was had someone seen Curt.

"Not until I was almost to town. Like I said, that was around eight-thirty. Wyatt and I planned to meet at the diner, but he wasn't there. The owner will know I was, but I spent more than an hour watching the sunrise," Curt admitted. "I know that's not good, lieutenant."

"Did anyone see you there?" The temperature had gone above freezing overnight, but sitting in the damp air couldn't have been pleasant. Not that they hadn't dealt with worse conditions in France.

"Afraid not. I pulled off the road. There's an old, abandoned barn about halfway between Moreley and Boxwood."

Jax nodded. "I know the place." And he knew it was remote, too remote for anyone to see Curt watch the day begin.

"Like I said, I didn't kill Schwarz or bother his livestock or nothing like that." Curt's voice was a rough whisper.

"Did Wyatt say why he was late?" Jax asked.

Curt shrugged. "He's late a lot. Sometimes, he leaves his house before dawn and heads to his grandparents' old place." He ran one hand over his face. "Being in the trenches was bad enough. When he was wounded and left for dead in No Man's Land..."

Jax's nostrils flared with a sharp intake of breath. "I heard he was out there almost two days."

After a sigh, Curt nodded. "His wounds got infected. He was out of his mind with fever and pain when we were finally able to get our dead. We thought Wyatt was one of them—that's how still and stiff he was. Even worse, when he recovered, he got put back on the line. Lieutenant Stewart tried to get him sent home, but the commander wouldn't hear no excuses. Wyatt was never the same. Second time he got wounded, he wasn't himself at all." Curt's hazel eyes clouded with sadness. "He still isn't."

"It's good of you to talk with him, Curt," Jax said.

A rueful smile tugged at the other man's mouth. "Mostly listen and sit with him. It's about all I can do."

Again, Jax hesitated before asking another question weighing on his mind. "Do you know if Wyatt owns a handgun?"

Some emotion flashed in Curt's gaze before he looked away. "Yes, he does. He sometimes uses it for target practice out at his grandparents' place." When Curt returned his attention to Jax, his expression was solemn. "We both do at times. Mine is in a box under the bed in the other room, if you want to see it."

Jax wished he could say *no,* but he had to check. The tire track and bullet holes in Schwarz were the only evidence. "Yes, please."

Curt quickly returned with the weapon—a service revolver—and handed it to Jax. "Wyatt and I did some target shooting after we ate. I always clean my guns afterward."

The truth of the statement was immediately obvious to Jax who gave the gun back to the other man. "It's a good habit," he replied. Jax had few questions for Carl and, once he asked them, he got to his feet and put the pad and pencil back in his pocket. "Thanks to both of you for speaking with me."

Curt stood up, an expression of surprise on his face. "That's it? You're not going to arrest me?"

"Of course not," Jax said. "I have no reason to do that, Curt. Right now, we're gathering information from anyone who might have seen something this morning. I may need to speak with you again, and with some others, as well. That doesn't mean you'll ever be arrested." He certainly hoped that wouldn't be the case but, at the moment, both Curt and Wyatt were suspects.

"Thanks, lieutenant."

More than once, Jax had thought about correcting Curt. After all, neither of them was still in the army, but Curt probably used the title because he felt more comfortable doing so. Since Jax didn't want to add to the former sergeant's distress, he gave a nod before saying, "I'll see myself out."

Crossing paths with Bella again seemed like a bad idea, so Jax took the short hall from the suite to the back door. As he did, the enticing aroma of ham and cloves reached him. Suddenly, his insides knotted with longing—not so much for food as for the past. Christmas Eve dinner. He'd shared many with the Stewarts and Mac. He quickened his steps but, before he got to the door, Bella entered the hallway from the kitchen. Without making eye contact, she thrust a large picnic basket at him. "Mac wanted to send supper home with you."

Jax ground his teeth. Of course, the generosity was the old pro's idea. Not that he didn't appreciate the gesture. "Thank you, and Merry Christmas." With that, he took the hamper and walked into the night.

**

A blast of cold air hit Bella when Jax opened the door, but the real chill was inside her. Although she had followed Mac's suggestion and prepared a basket for Jax, she hadn't given it to him with genuine generosity. Quite the contrary. Her gesture had been grudging, at best. Bella had resolved to forget about Jax's cold dismissal of her after Matt's death. Not everyone grieved in the same way, after all. On her way home from France, she wondered if they could return to being friends. Then, she'd seen him in the train station, and bittersweet memories had gripped her. Along with the recollections had come disappointment. Jax had seemed almost as cool and distant as he had that day in France. Now, he clearly wanted to keep her out of the murder case which was galling. She knew a few things about investigations, so he hadn't needed to be so haughty and high-handed. With that thought souring her mind, Bella went back to the kitchen determined to forget about Jackson Hastings and the murder case for now.

**

Jax returned to an empty office. He'd told Nolen to leave early, so his absence came as no surprise, but Mayor Cawlings' arrival, moments after Jax had removed his coat and cap, did.

"Good evening, mayor. Is there something I can do for you?"

"I came to drop off the wife's plum pudding since you're working this evening." The tall man, elegantly clad in a black coat of the finest wool, laid the covered dish on the counter where Jax had just deposited the basket from Ballantyne. "I see someone else had the same idea."

"Thank you, and yes. It's dinner from Ballantyne."

Cawlings swept off his hat, patted his close-clipped ebony hair, and leaned against the counter. "Did you talk to the Molitor brothers?" As he spoke, the mayor wiped his wire-rimmed spectacles.

As soon as he'd returned from the Schwarz farm, Jax had alerted Cawlings about the murder. Now, he recounted the latest information. "I plan to send Nolen to Boxwood day after tomorrow to see if anyone saw Curt."

The mayor fingered his dark moustache which hid his upper lip. However, tension was clear in the set of his trim form. "So, you have several suspects and none can present an alibi."

Jax shifted from one foot to the other. "I don't know that I'd call any of the veterans a suspect. We're following every lead, but speaking with some people wasn't possible today. It is Christmas Eve."

The mayor nodded. "I understand. I know you don't want to believe any of your men have been involved in the crimes, especially a murder, but it's important that you show no partiality, Jax."

The undercurrent of warning in the man's voice rankled. So did his intense scrutiny. "They weren't all my men, mayor."

"A turn of phrase," the older man observed with a wave of the hand. "Most of you went to training and on to France together since you were in the same National Guard unit."

Because he couldn't disagree with that statement, Jax nodded. "Yes, of course. But if I had evidence that one or more of them committed a crime, I wouldn't ignore it." With effort, he controlled the resentment rising inside him. Did the mayor really have so little regard for him?

Cawlings clasped his long, lean fingers in front of him. "I hope you'll seek evidence without bias, and I hope you'll do so quickly."

The accusation underlying those words made Jax feel even more defensive. "It's been less than twelve hours since I got the call about Schwarz's death. I searched the scene and found little evidence. Nolen and I are talking with all of the veterans, and we'll speak with others who may have information. Doc is performing an autopsy as soon as possible."

The older man nodded. "I understand it's Christmas, so there's bound to be a bit of delay, but some in town are concerned you won't aggressively pursue suspects who were with you in France." The man took a long, slow breath before speaking again. "I haven't told you before, but there are also those on the town council who didn't support hiring you as constable. In fact, you got the job by a narrow majority—a single vote."

Surprise hit Jax full-force. He wasn't the most qualified person, but he was surprised that four out of the nine councilmen had voted against him. He knew all of those men, and he had for most of his life. Which four had voted *no*? "I see," he murmured, because no other response came to mind.

"I'm sorry but, at this point, I think you need to know. You still have a lot of support. Even so, people are getting uneasy due to the rise in crime. We were all counting on more summer visitors last season and some over Christmas. Now, with Schwarz being murdered, it's certainly added to the discontent."

Cawlings' dark eyes held a note of sympathy, but Jax didn't like that any better than the doubt the mayor had already expressed. Some townsfolk had gossiped about needing a better qualified constable long before now, but knowing he'd been chosen by such a small margin hit Jax hard. Nick Nicholson, the previous constable, hadn't given the town much notice about his resignation, which had been a factor in Jax's favor. So had his father's reputation. Although he'd died more than eight years earlier, Hannibal Hastings still had friends on the council and in town. "Do you want me to resign?"

Surprise blanketed the mayor's chiseled features. "No, of course not. I know you need more time," he hurried to add, "but you may need more help, too. This is the first murder in our area, so all of us are shocked and worried."

Jax frowned. "What do you mean by more help? Can Nolen work more hours while we're solving the case?"

The mayor looked away. "That's a possibility," he replied. "But it might be helpful to ask Richard Jenkins to consult with you. I believe you know him. He's retired now, but he's been a senior constable in Karston, as well as a chief detective in Toledo. In his capacity as a detective, he investigated a number of murders. He occasionally consulted on cases during the war when many small departments were short-handed. He still does."

"He was a friend of my father's," Jax said, but he was still absorbing the suggestion. "He's a good man."

Cawlings smiled. "Yes, he is, so I hope you won't object to him helping out."

Whether he objected or not probably wouldn't make much difference, Jax thought with disgust. Even though he liked and respected Jenkins, an outsider taking over seemed like repudiation. Briefly, pride and necessity warred within Jax. He could quit, but what would that accomplish? Without a job, he'd be even more rootless and restless than he was now. "No, of course not."

"Good. I spoke with him late today, and he'll be able to come day after tomorrow. You probably won't interview anyone else until then. I'll bring up Nolen working more hours at the next council meeting. That will be day after tomorrow at nine o'clock. Stop by my office around eleven o'clock in the morning. I should have an answer then."

"Fine," was all Jax managed to say.

Cawlings clapped his hat back on his head. "Merry Christmas," he said before exiting the office.

Merry didn't describe how Jax viewed the holiday, or anything else, for that matter.

Chapter Ten

Quiet descended on the office for the rest of Christmas Eve and Christmas Day. Between making rounds, Jax spent his time going over information gleaned from the few interviews he and Nolen had already done. When dusk fell on the twenty-fifth, he was frustrated and exhausted, so his deputy's arrival was a welcome respite.

"Since you gave me last night and today off, my mother wanted to make sure you had Christmas dinner," Nolen said, setting a big basket on Jax's desk. The younger man glanced at the papers strewn across the battered surface. "Any leads in this mess?"

The note of amusement in Nolen's voice made Jax smile. "Not really. We need to talk with more people, but the mayor agreed doing so on Christmas wasn't necessary. Of course, some potential suspects and possible witnesses are out of town."

Nolen's hazel eyes widened. "When did you talk with the mayor?"

"He stopped last evening." Jax pushed back his chair and stood up. "I think I'll eat at the table," he said before picking up the basket and heading to the corner of his cluttered office. "This is very kind of you and your mother."

"It was kind of you to work both days and let me off," Nolen observed. "Most bosses would have done it the other way around." He crossed the room and took a chair across from Jax.

"Your mother has been alone the past two Christmases. She deserves to have you with her."

"You could have joined us for dinner." He paused before going on. "Mother thought you might stay at Ballantyne last evening or go today. You used to spend all the holidays there." His attention went to the other basket, now empty, sitting on the table. "Did someone else bring you a meal?"

"They sent food home with me last night when I left Ballantyne," Jax commented. Before Nolen could say more about past celebrations at the resort, Jax hurried on. "I spoke with Curt and Carl." Briefly, he summarized the exchange.

Nolen's freckled face lost any hint of humor. "It's not good Curt was alone when someone killed Gus Schwarz."

"No, it isn't." Jax pulled the plate of turkey, dressing, mashed potatoes, and gravy out of the basket.

"You should eat while it's warm," Nolen observed before glancing at the old stove in the corner. "It's chilly in here. I'll put some coal in."

"Thanks," Jax replied. "I got busy and hadn't noticed." After eating several spoonfuls, he spoke again. "As far as the case, Mayor Cawlings told me he doesn't want me overlooking any veterans, not that I would have."

Nolen scowled. "None of them threatened Mr. Schwarz or even brought up his German roots. They just said he needed to stop blaming us for his troubles. Most asked to be left alone, but he refused to do that."

Jax grimaced. "Some added he had no idea of what it was like in the trenches, and he ought to be grateful to the soldiers. Not that I disagree with those sentiments," he said before taking another bite of dinner.

Nolen slumped back in his chair. "Neither do I. No one understands how it was over there. At least folks in Belgium and France know it was bad. Here, people don't know, and a lot of them don't care."

With a sigh, Jax studied his young deputy. He couldn't deny what Nolen said since he'd experienced the same attitudes himself. "Not every family had someone in the trenches and, even those who did don't always understand," he observed, "but that's what we fought for. We didn't want war coming to our backyard or to our families and friends. We succeeded, and I try to remember that." His words and tone masked his own pain and guilt, but Jax had kept up a firm façade for his men in France, and he always would. His inner demons were his own to battle.

"You're right," Nolen replied. "I just wish people were nicer to guys like Curt. He looked after Carl and their mother when Mr. Molitor left. Then, he watched out for Carl once she passed. That wasn't easy because kids made fun of his big brother all the time. Even though I'm a lot younger, I remember."

"I know. Carl had trouble learning. My mom said he was smart, but letters and words confused him, so school was hard. He's really talented with plants, though. I've never known anyone who took better care of a golf course."

Nolen nodded. "I hope Ballantyne will stay open. Maybe now that Bella is home, they'll get back to normal."

"That's what they want."

A smile curved his deputy's mouth. "Good. If Ballantyne does well, maybe Moreley will, too." For a moment, the younger man looked optimistic. Then, his face fell. "This murder won't encourage people to come here."

"Solving the case quickly will help."

Nolen nodded, but his expression remained solemn. "I hope the killer isn't anyone from Moreley."

The younger man didn't need to say he hoped a veteran wasn't guilty. They both hoped that, Jax was sure. "So do I, but we need to follow the evidence, even if we don't like where it takes us. Right now, we have to talk with others who had run-ins with Gus. Tomorrow morning, I'm going to have you head out to Boxwood. Stop at all of the houses right on the highway. With luck, you'll find at least one person who noticed Curt's motorcycle passing by. Farmers are up early, so someone might have seen him."

Nolen frowned. "Mother and I still don't have a motor car. Do you think the town council will buy a department vehicle soon?"

"I wouldn't count on it, but you can take my Chummy."

Nolen immediately brightened at the suggestion. "Thanks, Jax."

"You have to have transportation," he replied with a smile. Slowly, his good humor faded. "Curt and Wyatt Berringer met at the Boxwood diner, so go there and see what you can find out."

"I've heard they meet about every week, usually after the busy time."

"You need to speak with Wyatt, too. I want to make sure he and Curt have the same story."

A worried expression shadowed the deputy's face. "You don't think either of them was involved in the murder, do you?"

"I don't want to think so, but Curt said the two of them went target shooting at Wyatt's grandparents' old house after breakfast." He slumped back in the chair as fatigue and uneasiness overtook him. "Curt showed me his pistol, and it had been cleaned very recently. He always does that after using it, but still..."

"Do you want me to ask Wyatt about his pistol and see if it's been used or cleaned?"

"Yes. It won't be a big help since we don't have bullets or shells. Plus, we know he used it yesterday." Jax studied his deputy's troubled expression as he spoke. "Is something wrong?"

"Wyatt is still struggling."

Trepidation was in the boy's face and tone, and it echoed inside Jax. "That's what Curt said." Jax grew pensive. "Have you seen Wyatt lately?"

Nolen shook his head. "I went over to see him when we got home. I knew he had trouble after the first time he was wounded, but he was a lot worse than I expected."

"I've only seen him once, and he was very withdrawn." Jax frowned at the memory. "He barely spoke at all."

"I've seen him a few times. Sometimes, he is quiet, but a couple of times..." Nolen's brow furrowed. "He got angry talking about the war, the Germans, and our losses. Then, he suddenly started to cry, sob really. I didn't know what to say or do...I just put an arm around his shoulders until he finally calmed down."

The revelation caught Jax off-guard. Wyatt was more fragile than he had imagined. "That was the best thing. Do you know if Wyatt breaks down often?"

"Twice with me," Nolen said. "I haven't seen him since the last time."

The young deputy looked as troubled as Jax felt. "Do you know if he's been like that with any of the other men?"

"I haven't mentioned it to anyone else because Wyatt asked me not to. Maybe I should have told you already."

"You made a promise, so you did the right thing," Jax assured him. His heart went out to Wyatt, and all of the former soldiers still struggling, but he didn't have time to deal with the situation now. At present, his concern had to be the Schwarz case. "We'll see how we can help Wyatt once the murder is solved. Curt may know more, so I'll talk with him when I have time."

"Maybe we can help all of them."

"We'll do what we can," Jax promised before going back to Nolen's assignment for the next day. "Just ask Wyatt what he and Curt did, other than eat breakfast. If he mentions target shooting, ask where he keeps the pistol and say you'd like to see it. Try to make it as casual as you can."

Nolen nodded. "Yes, sir."

With that, Jax went back to their immediate duty. "I need to meet with the mayor in the morning and give him an update on the case." He gestured toward his paper-strewn desk. "That's why I have such a mess. I'm trying to get the basic facts in order."

"I can stay and go over the information with you. Mother was taking food to Mrs. Groves, and she'll be there for a while."

Some of the tension left Jax. "Another head would be helpful. I've reviewed everything more than once, and I'm getting stale. Let me eat your mother's excellent meal. Then, we'll get to work."

Within a short time, Jax finished dinner and laid his notes out. "You did a good job getting details about Fred and Warren yesterday," Jax observed. "They're completely cleared since their families can vouch for them, and so can some neighbors. Curt says Wyatt gets up early when he can't sleep. Most often, he goes to his grandparents' homestead. I want to know where he was early Christmas Eve morning since he didn't meet Curt until nine o'clock."

A frown knit Nolen's brow. "We have a lot to do, and I'm only supposed to work twenty hours each week."

"I asked Mayor Cawlings about having you work more until we solve the case, and he thinks it's a good idea."

Nolen grinned. "That would be great."

The younger man's enthusiasm made Jax smile, too, but that was tempered by the mayor's other decision. "Cawlings also told me he's spoken with Richard Jenkins from Karston. He's a retired senior constable, but he worked as a chief detective in Toledo earlier in his career. He'll be coming tomorrow to assist us."

"Is he taking over?" Nolen asked in clear consternation.

"No, my understanding is he'll just be helping. He was friends with my father, so I knew him years ago. He's a fine man. Having him here should be a good thing."

***

After another hour, Jax leaned back in his chair with a sigh. "We've put the information together which will be really helpful when Jenkins gets here tomorrow. By then, Doc should have done the autopsy, and he can probably confirm that the murder weapon was a handgun. I can go over everything with the mayor, as well. Before then, I should be able to talk with Postmaster Smith again. He was busy when I stopped on Christmas Eve, and he headed out of town as soon as he closed."

"You saw him at the café when Owen, Curt, and Gus had words, right?"

"Yes, and Smith was inside the café when the exchange began. I'm hoping he heard something useful. Now, I'm guessing your mother is back home, so you need to be there, too. Thanks for taking part of your holiday to work and thank her for the meal. It was great."

Nolen got to his feet and shrugged into his jacket. He hesitated before speaking. "I wouldn't be here to celebrate the holiday if it wasn't for you, Jax. Most of us from your platoon wouldn't be. You and Matt were the best kind of officers. You worried about us more than yourselves. And I know you risked your life more than once to save one of the men. Harold wouldn't have made it back if you hadn't gone out and gotten him."

His voice, a low murmur, was filled with banked emotion that echoed inside Jax. Nolen was obviously sincere, and much of what he said was valid. Jax's primary worry had been his men, and the same had been true with Matt. But

Nolen didn't know everything about Jax's shortcomings. No one except Matt did, and he was lying in a French grave.

Jax tightened his hands into fists as he fought for control. Part of him wanted to admit his guilt, but why should the younger man have to share his burden? What would be gained by revealing that just once, he had put himself first, and doing so had led to his best friend's death? "Matt was a fine officer and a good man. I wouldn't compare myself to him, but I appreciate the sentiment."

Nolen shook his head. "I visited Harold in the field hospital. I'd been promoted to sergeant, and I wanted to know how I could serve the men and you like he'd done. He said I'd be fine as long as I followed your lead in most things." The deputy bowed his head for a moment. When he lifted his gaze to meet Jax's, his eyes were dark with emotion. "Harold said your only weakness was taking on too much and putting yourself in danger too often. Of course, those were good things for your men," he hastened to add.

Jax stood up and grasped the back of his chair. Once again, conflicting feelings buffeted him. "Thanks, but I didn't do anything different from most officers."

Nolen released a humorless laugh. "We both know that's not true. See you in the morning."

"I'll be here," Jax replied.

The younger man paused at the door. "Don't stay too late."

After Nolen left, Jax considered going over their notes again. But he was tired. So very tired. Maybe a good night's sleep would help...if he could sleep, because—like Curt and Wyatt—Jax found real rest elusive.

Chapter Eleven

Jax didn't get a good night's sleep. As usual, nightmares plagued him so he rose before dawn and went to the office. His meeting with the mayor was scheduled for late morning which gave him time to go over the notes again.

When Nolen arrived at seven-thirty, Jax briefly reviewed the plan for the day. "I'm going to head to the post office and interview Smith before he actually opens up. After that, I'm talking with Mayor Cawlings. I should be back around noon. Then, you can go to Boxwood."

After their discussion, Jax headed out. The café was closed until the New Year and no other businesses had opened yet, which meant the streets were quiet as he walked the short distance to the post office, situated just off Main Street. Since it didn't open until eight-thirty, he wasn't surprised to see the *CLOSED* sign in the window. Smith often arrived early, though, so Jax knocked once, which caused the door to immediately open. "Mr. Smith, it's Jax Hastings," he called out. The greeting got no response, which put him on alert. The postmaster never unlocked until the official opening time.

Jax stepped inside, scanned the narrow lobby, and pulled his service revolver out of its holster. Slowly and cautiously, he headed toward the counter. Nothing seemed out of order, except Smith wasn't in sight. As Jax paused at the customer window, he looked around. Where was the postmaster? Again, he called out, "Mr. Smith. It's Jax Hastings." When no reply came, he leaned over the counter and froze. Smith was sprawled on the floor.

Immediately, Jax tried the door separating the lobby from the back room. When it opened easily, he moved to the postmaster's side, dropped to his knees, put his fingers to Smith's neck, and breathed a sigh of relief. The pulse was weak, but steady. A quick review showed no obvious injury, so Jax hurried to the nearby telephone. When the operator came on the line, he outlined the situation and asked her to alert Doc Smedlay.

Smith eyes fluttered open, and he glanced around. "What happened?"

The weakness in the older man's voice disturbed Jax, who hurried to reassure him. "Help is on the way. Just rest quietly."

The postmaster's response was to close his eyes and give a slight nod of his head.

Within minutes, the physician arrived on the scene. "Annabelle caught me just as I about to make house calls before doing Schwarz's autopsy. I got called out to deliver a baby on Christmas Eve and didn't get home until yesterday afternoon." He knelt at Smith's side. "She said you found no sign of an injury, and that seems to be right," he said after a cursory examination. "It's very likely his heart."

"A heart attack?" Jax asked with concern.

"Not necessarily. Abner has a weak heart. He's been taking digitalis for a couple of years. He really needs to retire, but I've had trouble convincing him." A long sigh left the doctor. "I called Forrester in case we need to transport Abner to the hospital. I can't provide proper care at our house if it was an attack."

Doc had barely gotten the statements out when George Forrester arrived dragging a stretcher behind him. "I thought you might want him to go to the hospital, since you did the last time."

"You're right," Doc replied before turning back to Smith. "Are you in any pain, Abner?"

"Not now...but I was..." Smith's voice was weak.

"Chest pain? Just nod your head. No need to talk," the physician said.

The postmaster gave an affirmative nod and pointed to his chest. Smedlay looked back at Forrester. "Let's get him on the stretcher, but carefully."

"I'll help carry him out," Jax offered.

After the men moved Smith to the Auto Hearse, Doc spoke again. "I'm going with them. The mailmen should both be here shortly. They'll know what to do since they had to pitch in when he last had a spell."

"I'll wait for them to get here," Jax assured the doctor. Then, he stood on the curb as the vehicle pulled away, taking one of his witnesses with it.

***

By the time Jax met with the mayor and got back to the office, his frustration had increased. Not only had his planned talk with Smith been foiled, two of the councilmen had joined his meeting with Cawlings. Within moments, their displeasure with Jax became obvious, and it was no longer a mystery as to who two of the four *no* votes had been. Jax knew his anxiety must be written on his face when Nolen frowned and said, "Did the mayor say I can't work more hours?"

Jax removed his cap and coat before joining his deputy at the scarred counter. "You can, but Lyle Fike and Martin Hopkins were in the mayor's office. Both of them think Senior Constable Jenkins should be put in charge of the case."

"What did the mayor say?"

"A lot of nothing," Jax bit out. "You know how he is. Never wants to offend or upset anyone. His final word was *we'll see how things go.*"

Nolen grimaced. "I've heard him say that before."

"So have I. Too often." Jax paused before continuing. "At least you can work as many hours as necessary until the case is solved."

A grin brightened the younger man's freckled face. "That's good news," he replied before becoming serious again. "Did Mr. Smith know anything helpful?"

A half-shrug lifted one of Jax's shoulders. "I don't know. I found him on the floor. Doc came. He and Forrester took Smith to the hospital. It's probably his heart."

Worry wrinkled Nolen's forehead. "I hope he's all right."

"So, do I. I would have come back to tell you, but I waited for the mailmen to arrive. They had to make arrangements to deliver the mail and man the office. By the time I got away, I had that meeting with Cawlings." A harsh sigh left him. "The bottom line is that, if Smith has information, I won't be getting it any time soon." Or perhaps, not at all. Heart ailments were serious, as he knew all too well. Shortly after Jax's eighteenth birthday, his father had died of heart failure.

"Do you think Mr. Smith knows anything important?"

"He was the only one who might have heard what Gus, Owen, and Curt said inside the café, according to the other witnesses at least. Of course, when they were shouting at each other, everyone in the place could hear." Again, Jax silently berated himself for not going back to speak with the postmaster on the day of the murder. Now, he might never know what the man had heard...unless he talked to Bella. But would she talk to him? After their exchange on Christmas Eve, Jax doubted it.

Nolen looked as glum as Jax felt. "Maybe Mr. Smith will be able to talk later today."

"I hope so. In the meantime, we'll go ahead with other interviews."

"Yes, sir," Nolen said before making his way to the door to don his jacket and cap. "I'll be back when I can."

Jax nodded and once again looked over his notes. Surely, some clue would arise. Hopefully, sooner rather than later.

***

After parking the Model T across from the constable's office, Bella hesitated to get out. Picking up the basket should be a benign task, but she didn't want to face Jax after their harsh words on Christmas Eve. If it was up to her, she would have left the basket there indefinitely. Unfortunately, Mac hadn't agreed with that idea. Instead, he hinted she and Jax needed to call a truce. A big part of Bella realized he was right, but she wasn't going to make the first move. After all, she wasn't the one who had created the initial breach between them—or worsened it on Christmas Eve. She hadn't referred to him as *just anyone* or used the word *civilian* as an epithet. Even so, Bella had agreed with Mac's suggestion while secretly hoping Jax would be out when she arrived. Determined to simply retrieve the basket and get away quickly, she left the vehicle and crossed the street. As soon as she opened the door, Bella realized her wish had not been granted because Jax was stoking the fire in the stove.

"Hello, Bella." Both his tone and expression were guarded as he rose to face her.

She cleared her throat. "Good day. I thought I'd pick up the basket while I was in town." No sense in making matters worse by saying the suggestion had been Mac's.

"Sure. Of course." Jax's gaze met hers before moving away. "It's in my office. Let me get it for you."

He hurried off before she could say more, so Bella went to the counter and waited for him to return. While he was gone, she scanned the room. The office looked as forlorn as most of Moreley did. The paint, she knew, had once been blue but now it appeared to be faded gray. A row of four wooden chairs still lined the wall across from the counter. Only a few years ago, the furniture had shone with varnish. Now, the finish was completely gone in places. As a dripping sound interfered with her assessment, Bella peeked over the counter to see a bucket.

"We need a new roof," Jax said as he returned with the basket. "The snow has been melting steadily since Christmas

Eve morning, and water is leaking through the roof and ceiling. It takes a while for all of it run through." He frowned as he studied the almost full bucket. "That's the worst place, but I need to get a couple more buckets because some leakage is starting in my office."

"Is the town really in such desperate straits?" The sadness squeezing her heart made Bella forget about her anger with Jax. She loved her hometown and hated seeing it so downtrodden.

He shrugged. "It's not in a good situation. Everyone hoped last summer would bring a return to normal, but it didn't. Now, the town council doesn't want to pay for any extras."

"A roof to keep water out is an extra?" she asked in surprise.

A half-smile tugged at one corner of his mouth. "Supplying the constable's office isn't a top priority."

"Is that why Nick left?"

His humor faded. "I think it's a big part of the reason, and it's probably why the town gave the job to someone who is completely unqualified."

The stark comment startled Bella. When was the last time Jax had been so open with her? She could barely remember, and that fact—along with Mac's entreaty—softened her defenses. "You aren't completely unqualified."

His blonde eyebrows rose a fraction. "That's not what you said on Christmas Eve."

Heat bloomed in her cheeks. "I didn't say you were totally ill-equipped for the position." Regret over her callous, cutting words assailed her. He shouldn't have been dismissive with her, but she shouldn't have been rude, either. All the same, Bella struggled to ease the breach between them. Offering a real apology seemed like a major challenge, which didn't speak well for her, and she knew it. Maybe the war had changed her more than she had thought. Or maybe her losses had.

"You didn't say anything that wasn't true. I am pretty much of an amateur when it comes to police work, but I'm trying to do a good job." He took a long, low breath before continuing. "I didn't act professionally on Christmas Eve when I berated you. I was already upset when I got to Ballantyne because I thought you'd let me know when Curt returned, and you didn't. On top of that, you questioned the Downings, Mr. Smith, and Harold. The worst part was I tried to talk with Smith earlier in the day. Since he was busy, I let it go. I should have gone back earlier since he was the only who heard the entire confrontation among Owen, Curt, and Gus. Knowing I'd made a mistake put me more on edge. I shouldn't have taken it out on you."

His detailed explanation and sincere regret combined to make apologizing easier on Bella. "I shouldn't have said what I did. I didn't even try to see things from your viewpoint. We both could have acted more courteously."

Jax nodded. "I won't argue but, at the risk of making you angry again, please be careful talking to people. We have suspects, but no clear candidate yet, and the killer must be someone from this area. If you ask a lot of questions, it will get out. Then, whoever it is may go after you. I don't want that, Bella, and not because another murder would complicate my job." He cleared his throat and glanced away. "I was your brother's best friend, and I don't want to see you hurt."

His last words confused Bella because she remembered their last meeting in France all too well. His curt dismissal had hurt her, but that had been emotional distress. Jax was referring to physical harm now. "I only spoke with the Downings, Mr. Smith, and Harold. Surely, you don't suspect any of them."

Jax hesitated a moment. "No, I don't, but gossip spreads fast. By now, the killer may know you've been asking questions. Evidently, you told Harold that Smith revealed details to you."

"Mr. Smith will tell others. He's such a gossip."

A harsh sigh left Jax. "He won't be telling them any time soon. I went to talk with him this morning, and he was unconscious on the floor of the post office."

Alarm made Bella gasp. Only two days ago, the man had been fine. "Is he all right?"

Jax pinched the bridge of his nose. "I don't know. Doc came, and he thought it was Smith's heart. Evidently, he's had problems for a couple of years. When Forrester arrived, they all went to the hospital. Since yesterday was Christmas, Smith didn't have a chance to tell anyone else around here, although I'm sure he regaled his son's family with the tale."

"You didn't get much information from him?" Bella asked.

Dismay flickered across his face. "I didn't get any. Like I said, he was too busy to talk when I first went on Christmas Eve, and I didn't get back before he closed."

For a moment, Bella was silent. She should reveal what she knew. After all, Jax was in charge of the case. "If you want, I could tell you what he told me."

"I'd appreciate it since Senior Constable Jenkins from Karston will be here soon."

"Why is he coming?"

"The mayor and part of the town council think we need outside help."

Bella nodded because the idea seemed sensible. "You are short-staffed with Nolen only working part-time and not having a clerk."

"Nolen can work more for now, but Constable Jenkins is experienced with murder cases, and he's a good man. He and my father were friends, so I already know him." Jax hesitated a moment before continuing. "If you have time, we could talk right now."

"That's fine."

"Let's use my office. Nolen is gone, so I'll have to keep an eye on the counter and an ear for the telephone."

"Where is Nolen?" Bella's curiosity remained in place, but she wondered how Jax would reply. She was willing to share information. Was he?

Jax hesitated only briefly. "I sent him to Boxwood to talk with Wyatt and some others. He's going to stop at the houses along the way and see if anyone saw Curt early the other morning. I'm hoping it will give Curt an alibi."

"I hope so." Curt's possible involvement troubled Bella.

"Come on. We can use the table," Jax said before heading to his cramped office.

Bella had never been in this part of the building, but she wasn't surprised to see it looking as shabby as the front office. The ping-ping-ping of water hitting metal cups didn't surprise her, either. As Jax had said, there were more drips in his bailiwick. She absently wondered how often he had to empty the small vessels. That would be an annoying chore, especially when he had a murder to solve. No wonder he needed more buckets. At least they wouldn't need to emptied as often as small cups.

When he pulled out a chair for her, she murmured her thanks and sat down. Jax joined her. Bella started to rest one elbow on it, but the table tilted precariously, which had him hurrying to rebalance the piece of furniture. "Sorry, I need to put something under a couple of the legs."

"You need a new table," she said with asperity.

He shook his head. "We're not likely to get one any time soon." Jax pulled a notepad off the stack of papers and grabbed a pencil stub. Briefly, his features contorted, as if in pain. With his left hand, Jax massaged his right shoulder.

The gesture reminded Bella that he'd been wounded late in the Meuse-Argonne offensive. From what she knew, he'd gone back to his platoon in only a few days. At the time, she had figured his injury wasn't serious. Now, she wondered. "I heard you were wounded shortly before the armistice. Was it bad?"

Abruptly, he stopped the massage. "It still gives me a bit of trouble at times."

The tense set of his features belied his assertion. "More than a bit, I think. How bad was it? I heard you went back soon afterward."

For a moment, Jax said nothing. When he spoke, his voice held no trace of emotion. "The doctors patched me up pretty well, so I felt okay. Besides, we knew the end was near, and I didn't want someone else with my men when the armistice went into effect." His gaze returned to the notepad.

Again, Bella knew he wasn't revealing everything. "Was it a shoulder wound?"

Seconds of silence preceded his response. "Shoulder and upper arm. There's a little shrapnel left. That's what proves troublesome at times. I've been driving and writing a lot these last couple of days. Both can cause a little discomfort."

Bella was sure *a little discomfort* was an understatement, but she didn't press him further. His reluctance to talk about it was clear. Instead, she said, "I know shorthand. I haven't used it a lot lately, but I can figure out my notes and transcribe them for you."

Jax hesitated only a minute before handing her the pencil and paper.

Chapter Twelve

After Bella revealed what Smith had told her, Jax felt even more unsettled. "Gus saying Curt better watch himself, too, is disturbing." He clasped his hands together and laid them carefully on the table top. "Second-hand conversation wouldn't be admissible in court, but it could turn a lot of people against Curt if it gets out that he may have threatened Gus."

"I haven't told anyone except you, and I won't. I'm sure it was an idle warning. People often say they hope someone gets what's coming to him, but they don't plan on making it happen."

"True, but I appreciate you not mentioning it to anyone. I need to keep an open mind, and I hope others will, too."

"I don't want to hurt Curt," she told him in a solemn tone. Bella glanced away before she continued. "I suppose that's why I didn't call you when he got back to Ballantyne. I hoped you'd wait until after Christmas to question him."

Jax lightly massaged his forehead. A headache was starting again. "I didn't want to question anyone on Christmas Eve, but that's my job. The mayor approved of not conducting interviews on Christmas, but mostly because many people went to see relatives."

"I know," she replied. "It's the first Christmas we've all been home since before the war, and I wanted it to be like it used to be for everyone which was impossible, of course."

Her very clear disenchantment echoed inside him. "I wanted that, too," he admitted. "I wanted the men to enjoy the holiday with their families, not worry about being suspects in a murder case. They deserve better."

"What about you?"

The question caught him off-guard. Obviously, he hadn't been successful in covering his slip-up. Jax didn't want Bella, or anyone else, feeling sorry for him. "I didn't want to have a murder at all." The last statement was intended to distract her. Revealing his emotional turmoil was something Jax planned to avoid. Civility was fine. Familiarity was something else entirely.

Before either of them had a chance to say more, the bell on the outside door chimed. Jax got to his feet and hurried to the main office. "Let me see who it is." Relief filled Jax when he saw Senior Constable Richard Jenkins. Now, he wouldn't be subjected to additional scrutiny from Bella. "Thank you for coming, sir." He crossed the room and offered his hand which the older man immediately accepted.

"Good to see you again, son." Jenkins, a strongly-built man of medium height and late middle years, shook Jax's hand with enthusiasm. "I should have gotten over here to congratulate you sooner. I'm pleased you've taken your father's old job, and I know he would be, as well."

"I suppose he would," Jax replied. "He's certainly a big reason that I got the position."

The older man's steel-gray eyebrows flattened as his smile turned into a frown. "I'm sure you were hired on your own merits."

Jax shook his head. He'd known Jenkins most of his life and saw no reason to hide the facts from him. "The mayor told me on Christmas Eve that four of the nine council members voted against hiring me. I met with him and two of them this morning. It was more than clear that I need to solve Gus Schwarz's murder quickly."

The older man didn't respond for a moment. "I'm here to assist, Jax, and I've told Mayor Cawlings as much. I've helped other departments, especially during the war when most were short-handed. The investigation is yours to direct, and I know you'll do it well."

"Thanks," Jax murmured.

Jenkins looked past him and said, "Welcome home, Arabella. It's good to see you again. I heard you just arrived."

Jax turned to follow the senior constable's gaze. How long had Bella been standing in the door? Long enough to hear his admission? Fresh uneasiness filled him as she moved to join them. Was she glad to know others found him as lacking as she did?

"It's wonderful to be home again," she said, "and to see you, too."

"I didn't know you two were acquainted," Jax commented.

"Only in passing. I was still working full-time in the years before Arabella left for France, so I played most of my golf at Ottawa Park in Toledo. My wife and I spent a few weekends at the resort, and I saw Arabella when I did. You've grown up since then." Jenkins took both of her slim hands in his broad ones and expressed his sympathy over her losses.

Jax was immediately aware of the difference between the older man's heartfelt compassion and his own weak acknowledgments of her grief. His guilt had kept empathy in check in France. Even at the train station, he'd been afraid to let his guard down with her. He still was.

"What brings you to the constable's office? Not trouble at Ballantyne, I hope," Jenkins asked as he looked from Jax to Bella.

"I came to get a basket," she replied.

Jax explained about the Christmas Eve meal from Ballantyne, and Richard smiled.

Before either man could say anything, Bella spoke again. "Since I picked up the murder victim's wife the other morning, we also discussed the case a bit."

"Really?" The senior constable looked back at Jax.

Although he would have preferred that Bella take the basket and leave, Jax briefly summarized their discussion. "I wish we knew what Curt said. I'll ask him when we speak again, probably later today. I need to talk with some of the other veterans again. Nolen may get some information to put Curt in the clear. Overall, we need to do a lot more digging."

"It takes a lot of legwork and interviews to find and unravel clues. Murder cases are particularly tough. In addition, citizens want them solved quickly. That creates more pressure on a police department," Jenkins observed. "What have you learned so far?"

Jax summarized the issues that had plagued Moreley since spring and reviewed the problems between Schwarz and the veterans.

"I heard about the animals and vandalism," Jenkins said. "As far as I know, there was no anti-German sentiment in this part of the state."

"I don't know of any, either," Jax put in, "but Gus Schwarz was quick to take offense. Sometimes, he was just as quick to cause offense."

Jenkins shook his gray head. "Did he have feuds with others in the area?"

"Over the years, he argued with various people," Jax replied. "We're in the process of running those to ground. Nolen already checked on two of the veterans and eliminated them, but we have a lot more to do. I plan to speak with others who had confrontations with Schwarz, and I also want to talk to Mrs. Schwarz again. Needless to say, she was very upset and able to offer only the most basic facts the morning of the murder."

"You've got your work cut out for you," Jenkins observed.

"I'm afraid so," Jax agreed. "I suppose we better start going over what we know now. Nolen and I reviewed our notes last evening, and I compiled them into some semblance of order. I need to finish transferring the raw notes into a better form and type it all up."

"That sounds like a strong plan. While we're talking, you might go ahead and put our discussion into a main notebook," Jenkins said. "That can be a useful tool."

Jax nodded while he rubbed his aching shoulder and wished his deputy was on hand to take notes. Although Bella had been helpful, Jax didn't want to prolong her visit. "Would you mind taking notes, sir?"

"Normally, I wouldn't mind at all. Not that I'm either speedy or neat." Jenkins raised his right hand to reveal a splint on his middle fingers. "I'm afraid I broke a bone earlier in the week. I should have brought my wife. Jenny often helped with notetaking in the past."

"I'd be happy to help again," Bella offered. "I took a few notes while Jax and I talked about Mr. Smith. I had a shorthand course in high school," she told the senior constable. "Not only that, I am the one who saw Mrs. Schwarz walking to town for help and took her back to the body."

While Bella filled in additional details for Jenkins, Jax saw the chances of getting her to leave diminishing.

The older man frowned. "I'm sorry you had to see that. You were able to examine the scene as well as the victim, son?" he asked after turning to Jax.

"Yes, sir," Jax replied. "Unfortunately, some snow melted overnight. I could tell people had been walking around the area, but distinguishing particular footprints was impossible."

When Jax cast a glance at her, Bella frowned. "Mrs. Schwarz found her husband's body before I went back with her so her prints were already there. Besides, mostly slushy snow was left which wouldn't hold a shoe print in any case."

"That's too bad," Jenkins observed.

"Yes, it is and unfortunately, the bullets passed through him," Jax went on. "And I didn't find any shells or slugs around the body. From the wounds themselves, it looks like he was shot at close range, probably with a handgun, since it would have just been getting light. I also found a tire track, most likely from a motorcycle, near the gate on the main road. The lock had been smashed. With the butt of a gun, or maybe a rock or hammer."

Jenkins shrugged. "A little to go on. I'm sure many men in the area have pistols or revolvers, but what about motorcycles?"

"Handguns are more common, but some have both. Wyatt and Curt do. Others, as well," Jax said. "More of the soldiers have motorcycles than cars since they're cheaper."

"You've gathered good information, son," Jenkins said before looking back at Bella. "It would be wonderful if you took notes and typed them later, Arabella."

The older man's obvious enthusiasm and response kept Jax quiet. He greatly feared Bella would want to continue being involved, but he had no good reason to reject her assistance at the moment. Besides, he wasn't going to verbally wrangle with her in front of Jenkins. As she had observed earlier, he was short-handed at the best of times, and this time was far from good. "Sounds fine. Let's go into my office and get to work."

***

Because Bella saw that Jax, unlike Senior Constable Jenkins, showed no enthusiasm for her continuing help, she dutifully took notes and offered no opinions. She didn't want to give Jax cause to cut her out completely.

After the men had discussed the interviews, Jenkins leaned back in his chair with a sigh. "You asked the right questions. I wish all of the men had the right answers."

"As do I," Jax said. He ran one hand over his face. "Maybe we'll turn up better suspects when we talk to other folks at odds with Gus."

"Once your town doctor confirms that a handgun was used, we'll only need to look at men who own one and who have access to a motorcycle," Richard said. "And who had run-ins with the victim."

"That will limit the number of suspects," Jax replied.

"I'm guessing whoever killed Schwarz was influenced by a relatively recent event. There could have been a long-held grudge, though. Maybe it has something to do with the war, but it may not be related at all," Richard said, "so there's no need to look only at soldiers."

"I don't want to think any of the veterans are to blame for the animals, the vandalism, or the murder," Jax admitted. "I may be partial, but if I thought one or more of them were guilty, I would say so."

"I know you would, son, and I don't think you're biased. You know those men better than anyone else. The average person doesn't understand that we coppers get gut feelings. Over the years, mine have served me well. I'm not saying we don't follow procedure and do the work, but I am saying we can't ignore what our insides tell us, either." Jenkins offered a reassuring smile.

"My Grandfather Moore said the same thing," Bella put in.

"Yes, I bet he did," Jenkins agreed. "I only knew him in passing, but he had a fine reputation as a law officer. I would wager he had some great stories about his cases."

Bella forgot Jax's prior reaction to this topic and answered with genuine enthusiasm. "Yes, he did. I was lucky enough to have him share many with me." She revealed her months of recuperation from scarlet fever, and how she and her grandfather had spent time that would have otherwise hung heavily for a young girl.

"How wonderful," Jenkins told her. "I'd love to read through his memoirs some time, if you wouldn't mind sharing them."

"Of course not," Bella readily agreed.

"Reading about his cases and putting the memoir together must have given you insight into investigations," the senior constable went on.

Again, Bella thought about Jax's reaction. His expression seemed more resigned than upset or angry which was a relief. Despite that, she wasn't sure how far to go along these lines. "Maybe a little," she said at last.

"Actually, Bella wanted to be a detective herself for a while," Jax said.

Since his tone held no trace of sarcasm or rejection, Bella relaxed. "That didn't last very long. Once I was able to be up and about, I returned to the golf course and school."

Jenkins smiled again. "You have a number of talents, much like my Jenny. She was a teacher before we married. Growing up, she helped in her family's restaurant. She didn't serve overseas as you have, but she worked with the Red Cross here at home. If she had been younger, I know she would have been in France."

"She sounds like a remarkable woman," Bella observed. "I hope I can meet her."

"If I'm working with Jax for long, Jenny will want to be here, too. As I said, she's often taken notes for me and typed them, as well." A rueful smile touched his hard mouth. "I probably shouldn't admit it, but she's also provided great insight over the years. She certainly has better instincts than many lawmen I've worked with."

"You let your wife get involved in your cases?" Jax asked with obvious surprise.

A low laugh left the senior constable. "I don't know that I'd use the word *let*. My first case as a new detective was a tough one. I worked long hours on it, but to little avail. We were newlyweds then, and I was seldom home and exhausted when I was. Jenny finally convinced me to share my frustrations with her. Once I did, her perceptiveness amazed me. Without her help, I don't know that I ever would have solved the crime. As the years went on, and I left the Toledo police to become a town constable, she often went with me on interviews."

"Weren't you worried she might come to harm?" Jax asked.

"She was always with me, son, and I was careful to not let her get into any dangerous situations. Besides, once she knew about a case, my Jenny was all too likely to start asking questions on her own. I felt like it was better to know what she was doing than to have her poke around alone. Of course, as she would say if she was here, women have as much right to live their lives and follow their passions as men do. I have no doubt she would have been as good at the job as I am, and probably a lot better." Jenkins glanced at Bella. "Times have changed since Jenny and I were young. You ladies have more opportunities now. You could go into police work yourself. You'd be among the very few women, but the world is different since the war, and it's apt to change more."

The vote of confidence made Bella smile. The senior constable had a refreshing, albeit unusual, viewpoint. Not many men were so open to women going into new fields. Or working at all. Once, Jax had thought she should be able to do anything. Now, he resisted her help. Exactly why wasn't clear. "I have an important job, and that's helping Mac bring Ballantyne back to her former glory."

"I'm glad to hear it," Jenkins told her. "And you're right. It is an important job."

"Very much so," Jax added. "Ballantyne is legendary. Having it regain its rightful status as one of the best resorts and finest golf courses in the state will be important to Moreley, too."

Bella wasn't sure about the source of Jax's enthusiasm, but she was relieved to hear it. "What concerns me now is the murder. I feel sorry about Gus being killed, but do you think having a murder here will keep people away?" She looked from Jenkins to Jax. "I know it sounds terrible to be thinking about business..." Her voice trailed off. Maybe she shouldn't have voiced the concern dwelling in the back of her mind since Christmas Eve day.

A pent-up sigh escaped Jax. "Some businesses planned to reopen last spring, but when the crimes started, word spread quickly. Cancellations at the hotel and the resort put an end to a revival. The same with Christmas visitors. We had none."

"My gut feeling is that the other crimes are related to the murder," the senior constable observed. "Once this case is solved, it shouldn't be an issue. Both Ballantyne and Moreley can move forward."

"I am sorry for Mrs. Schwarz...I just wondered," Bella said.

"I've wondered the same thing," Jax admitted. "It's natural enough, I think."

"Very natural," Jenkins agreed. "Now, our task is to solve the case quickly. That will be the best thing for Mrs. Schwarz, the community, and the resort."

"I have something for you to look at," Jax said as he rose from the table and went to his desk. When he had retrieved a handkerchief from the drawer, he came back and laid it on the table. "As I said, the gate near the road was open, which is a rarity. Here's the smashed lock." Jax carefully opened the handkerchief.

Jenkins bowed his head as if to take a careful look. "You were right. Someone beat on it with blunt force."

"The killer may have opened the gate so the horses would go farther, and Gus Schwarz would follow." Jax studied the lock before glancing back at the senior constable.

"Probably so," the older man said. "I wish it was in better condition. There aren't apt to be fingerprints at all since, as cold as it was, the killer might have worn gloves. Even if some were on it, they've been destroyed by the pounding."

Dismay filled Jax. "I was hoping for fingerprints."

"It was wise of you to retrieve it, in any case," Jenkins said with a reassuring smile.

Unfortunately, Jax didn't feel reassured. He felt frustrated and uneasy. Reviewing the clues helped, but not as much as he had hoped.

Chapter Thirteen

Before Bella left, the men discussed how to divide up the next set of interviews. "Do you think you can talk with all of your possible suspects today?" Jenkins asked Jax.

"I should be able to see three of the four who had rows with Gus recently," Jax replied. "Only one of them, Eric Eddington, lives in town. He and his mother run the boardinghouse. He has a motorbike, but I don't know about a gun. Another, Jacob Jones, has the farm just down from Schwarz, and Oscar Wagner lives out that way, as well. Neither has access to a motorcycle, and I don't know if they would have seen anything, but I want to find out."

"Are there folks at the boardinghouse who could vouch for Eddington?" Jenkins asked.

Jax paused for a moment. "Anthony Windsor, who teaches history, lives there. He and his nephew went to Cincinnati to visit family for holidays. They should be back soon."

Jax mentioning their former teacher made Bella think again about her visit to the post office. "I saw Mr. Windsor and his nephew when I spoke with Postmaster Smith. Mr. Windsor seemed much the same as I remember, but after they left, Mr. Smith said Mr. Windsor and Gus Schwarz had a bad argument once right in the post office. I remember him being opinionated as a teacher, though."

"I do, too," Jax said, "and I'd heard he and Gus were hostile with each other dating way back although I hadn't heard about a heated exchange in the post office."

"The boy may take after him," Bella observed. "He seemed very timid, but Mr. Smith said Garlan had been in fights with other boys."

"I've heard a little about it. Garlan hasn't gotten into trouble since I've been home, though." Jax turned to Richard and provided a brief explanation about young Dubois.

"How sad," Jenkins said.

"He barely looked at me, let alone spoke much," Bella added, "and he seemed a lot younger than eighteen."

Jenkins frowned. "Have you spoken with him much, Jax?"

He nodded his head in negation. "I've seen him in passing and tried to strike up a conversation, but he only replies to direct questions and those answers are brief."

Jenkins' brow furrowed. "Has he argued with Schwarz?"

"Not that I know of, but I've seen him on Eddington's motorbike a few times. I don't know about a gun," Jax replied. "Why?"

"Just wondered. I wouldn't get sidetracked with the boy or the uncle right now, but we may want to keep them in the back of our minds," the senior constable said. "You've already accomplished a lot, and you have a good plan. Hopefully, we'll get significant information in the next couple of days. I'll call Jenny and see if she wants to come. I left her at a friend's house near Boxwood, but I'd like to have her take notes for me since I'm somewhat incapacitated. As far as interviews, I'll talk with Mr. Push at the café. I know you already spoke with him, but we need to follow-up. Sometimes people recall more after time has passed. Since the café is closed for a week, I'll try to reach him and the waitress through your local operator." His gaze went from Jax to Bella and back. "Perhaps, Arabella would be good enough to assist you. I couldn't help noticing that you're favoring your right arm, son. I heard you were badly wounded right at the end of the war."

Bella saw color rise in Jax's cheeks. *Badly wounded.* The phrase echoed in Bella's mind. How did the senior constable know the extent of Jax's injuries? Jax had dismissed the wounds as insignificant earlier, and Bella had believed him. But he'd admitted wanting to be with his men when the armistice went into effect. Had he gone back too soon? Was that why he was still having issues? Before he had a chance to answer, she said, "I'd be happy to help. There's nothing for me to do at Ballantyne right now."

Jax's green gaze narrowed on her. "You've only been home two days, Bella. You ought to take some time to rest and relax."

She smiled. "I did that at Ida's house. "I'll call the inn and let them know where I'll be this afternoon."

"Wonderful," Jenkins said. "Some additional help could be crucial in getting this case off your desk and on to the courts, Jax."

When Jax agreed, Bella slumped with relief.

***

After Jenkins left to pick up his wife, Jax turned to Bella. "I can't go any place until Nolen gets back. I don't know when that will be, and I'm sure you have other things to do. You really don't need to go with me." Although having someone take notes would be useful, he felt uncomfortable around her. More than uncomfortable. He felt guilty because he was guilty. Not for the first time, Jax thought about Matt lying in a French grave, a grave that should have been his. If Bella knew the truth, she wouldn't want to be near him for any reason.

For a moment, Bella simply looked at him. "I said I was sorry for being rude the other evening, and I thought we'd reached a truce. If you'd rather not have me around…"

He quickly interrupted her. "It isn't that, Bella." Jax shoved his hands into the front pockets of his pants. Her steady gaze forced him to look away. In France, he'd been able to make an excuse and walk off, but here and now, he didn't have the option. Guilt again filled him, and Jax struggled to organize his scattered thoughts.

"Constable Jenkins is the one who suggested I take notes," Bella pointed out.

Jax looked back at her. Since he had no good reason to disagree with Richard's suggestion, he said, "I appreciate your willingness to help. I don't want you to feel like you have to do it, though." Nor did he want her in danger. Should he reveal the promise he'd made to her brother? Jax shied away from the idea. Mentioning Matt might lead to her asking about that day in France, and Jax wasn't ready to answer any questions.

"I want Gus' murder solved as much as you do. Mac and I are dedicated to bringing Ballantyne back, and an unsolved murder would certainly stand in the way, especially since the rash of crimes earlier in the year did. Besides, I know Curt isn't involved, but having him as a suspect isn't good for him or us."

Her reasons made sense as did accepting her help. "All right. We'll head out as soon as Nolen returns." Briefly, Jax paused before pursuing her comment about the resort. "You said you and Mac have a lot to do. Are you planning to stay in Moreley indefinitely?"

Surprise flickered in her dark eyes. "Of course. Why wouldn't I?"

He shrugged. "You planned to finish college and teach."

A soft sigh escaped her. "When I thought my brother and parents would still be here, I planned to teach. Now, there's only me to help Mac." She bit her lower lip. "Besides, after the Signal Corps, I can't see being a co-ed again."

"What about teaching?"

"I could teach without a degree, but saving the resort is far more important. Mac isn't young any more, and he can't manage everything alone, especially if business increases, as I hope it will. I don't want to lose Ballantyne."

She didn't need to say *along with my whole family*. The sadness in her dark eyes revealed that. Jax nodded. "I'm sure you and Mac will get the resort back to where it was."

"I hope so," she murmured. "I really do."

***

Nolen arrived a short time later.

"Any news?" Jax asked once the younger man had divested himself of his jacket and greeted Bella.

"I couldn't find anyone who saw Curt on his way to Boxwood. A couple families were gone, though. Several folks saw him as he rode through town but, as he told you, that was after eight-thirty," Nolen replied.

Jax absently rubbed his right shoulder. "What did Wyatt say?"

The younger man shrugged. "Pretty much the same as Curt. Wyatt's been having a bad time with the holidays. His family can't understand why he isn't happy to be home for Christmas, or why he doesn't want to be around them. Wyatt called Curt on the twenty-third and asked him to go over to talk."

"So, they spent Christmas Eve day together?" Jax inquired.

"Yes, and Wyatt said Curt didn't leave until after three o'clock. It didn't sound like they did a lot of talking, though," Nolen explained. "They spent most of the day at his grandparents' house. No one has lived there for a while, but they used the fireplace to get warm." He paused briefly. "I asked about his pistol. Wyatt only has it when he wants to go out there and have target practice. His father keeps it the rest of the time."

"Were you able to see it?" Jax asked.

Nolen nodded. "I talked with Wyatt at his folks' place, and his dad got it out. It's been cleaned very recently, too."

"Which doesn't eliminate either Curt or Wyatt," Bella put in.

Jax heard and saw her dismay. She hadn't been happy when he'd told Jenkins about checking Curt's gun, which wasn't surprising. Bella didn't want to think of her brother's sergeant as a murderer, but neither did he. "No, but it doesn't mean either of them was the killer. We have to check everything out."

"I understand," Bella murmured.

Jax gave a slight nod before turning back to Nolen. "Did Wyatt say why he was late meeting Curt?"

"He lost track of time." The deputy paused for a moment as he studied his notes. "Wyatt had trouble sleeping and left home before dawn. He went out to his grandparents' house and didn't see anyone else."

"How did he act when he told you?" Jax asked.

A soft sigh left Nolen. "Like I said, he seemed anxious and upset. No one told me anything to clear Curt or Wyatt."

Jax drove his fingers through his hair. "That's not good," he murmured.

"No, it isn't. Maybe I should have asked Wyatt more questions..." His voice trailed off in uncertainty.

"Not now. Wyatt's reaction doesn't mean he's guilty, but we'll have to follow-up and see if his story changes. We have other suspects to interview, so I'll go ahead with that today and we can get together later to see how we want to proceed," Jax replied.

His deputy's troubled expression intensified. "Do you think Wyatt might have killed Gus?"

A frown creased Jax's forehead. "I don't know, but we can't overlook it as a possibility. Other suspects are more likely at this point." Jax outlined what he and Jenkins had discussed before explaining why Bella was in the office.

Nolen turned to her with a smile. "We could sure use the extra help. You taking notes will be great because the lieutenant's handwriting is practically indecipherable. I don't know how he reads it himself."

The deputy's candor made Jax flinch, especially when he saw a look of something like distress cross Bella's face. Before he came up with a retort, she spoke.

"He used to have beautiful handwriting," she observed. "All of the girls in school admired him for it."

A low laugh escaped Nolen. "Really? I know a lot of mademoiselles in France admired him, but I wasn't aware it was due to his handwriting."

"Nolen, that's not appropriate, especially in front of a lady." Jax's voice was hard and unyielding.

Bright red blotted out the boy's freckles, and his humor deflated. "I'm sorry, Bella. I wasn't thinking."

"You said nothing wrong, and no offense is taken. I'm still a lady, but I was also a Signal Corps operator so I'm hardly the sheltered girl who went to France almost two years ago," she quickly put in.

Jax turned his attention to Bella. Although her expression and tone were lighthearted, something in her eyes gave him pause. They'd crossed paths a handful of times in France, and they'd once spent several days in Paris along with Matt. During those brief encounters, she had never complained about deprivations or expressed any discomfort. Yet, he knew the operators had experienced both, and much more. War changed people. Had it changed her? Jax had never considered that possibility. Now, he felt foolish. How could she not have been affected?

"You operators did a great job," Nolen said to Bella. "Everyone from Moreley was very proud about you being one of them. We bragged to other soldiers whenever we got a chance, didn't we, lieutenant?"

Jax felt Bella turn to him. He forced a smile and spoke before Nolen could say more. "Yes, the men were pleased and proud to have a neighbor who was an operator since you all played a key role in communications." The words sounded impersonal, but they weren't. He had been far more than proud of her, not that he could admit it now. Eager to end the exchange, Jax strode to the hall tree by the front door and grabbed Bella's coat. "We better get going. I'd like to do the interviews and be back in time so you can head home before dark."

"I'm allowed to stay out until after sunset now, constable."

Bella's comment made Jax feel foolish. So, did the grin on his deputy's face. "Of course," he murmured before helping her with the garment, putting on his own outerwear, and heading to the door.

***

When they got outside, Jax went to the passenger side of the Chummy and opened the door for Bella, but she remained on the curb. "I could drive. My car is right here, and you said driving bothers your arm and shoulder." She kept her expression and voice calm and composed. Jax didn't seem aware of her reaction to Nolen's comment about *mademoiselles,* and Bella planned to keep it that way. Of course, she only wondered about one mademoiselle. The French nurse. Since that was none of her business, Bella pushed the troubled thoughts away. "Besides, the Model T has side curtains, and they keep some of the cold, damp air out."

Jax didn't immediately reply to her offer. After a moment, he nodded, went to the Ford, and opened the driver's door for her.

Bella slipped inside, but said nothing until he was in the passenger's seat. "You said Wyatt may not be a strong suspect, but you seemed very troubled about him being out at dawn."

Jax released a pent-up breath. "I wish he and Curt both had alibis. Because they don't, they'll have to be questioned again if none of today's interviews pans out. I don't know that Wyatt had any dealings with Schwarz, but he spends a lot of time with Curt, who has."

"And you don't want to question them again?" she asked.

"It doesn't matter what I want. I have to do my job."

The tight set of his jaw telegraphed the depth of his frustration. "Yes, you do," she murmured before continuing, "Are we going to the boardinghouse first?"

"That's a good idea," he replied. "Eric is likely to be there."

Bella pulled away from the curb and headed to the Eddington home. "I hadn't heard about any feud between Eric and Gus Schwarz." She hadn't kept up with town goings-on as a young girl or as a co-ed. Then, she'd been in France.

"It's not really a feud, but they had an argument earlier this year from what I've heard. It happened before I got home. Eric did some carpentry work for the Schwarzes, and

Gus wasn't happy with it, so he refused to pay the whole amount. Needless to say, Eric was furious."

"I should think so," Bella put in. "My mother had him make bookcases, and they were extraordinary. Eric does a beautiful job."

"Yes, he does, but you know Gus' reputation. Nick had to intervene, and Gus finally paid. However, every time he sees Eric, he makes some nasty comment about him not only doing a poor job, but also being a coward for not handling the problem himself."

"What did Gus want? A fistfight?"

"I don't know exactly what he wanted other than to annoy Eric."

Bella pulled her car to a stop in front of the boardinghouse. "I hope Eric has an alibi," she said as they got out of the car and approached the sprawling gray clapboard home. Bella was relieved to see it looked much the same as it had when she'd left for France. Twin trellises, now bare but covered with fresh white paint, made privacy screens for the wide porch. In the summer, Bella knew, boarders would enjoy sitting in the wicker chairs. That thought made her ask, "Are there many boarders now?"

"Only two," Jax replied. "That's why Eric has been doing more carpentry work. They need the extra money. Like a lot of people in town, times have been tough for them. More than a few folks have moved away which hasn't helped business at all."

Chapter Fourteen

Once again, Bella realized how much renewed success at Ballantyne could mean for everyone in the area, and that success depended on solving Schwarz's murder and the other crimes.

She mounted the steps ahead of Jax and knocked on the front door. Within moments, Mrs. Eddington, a slender woman in her sixties, answered.

"Arabella, how wonderful to see you. Welcome home," the older woman said with a soft smile. As she offered the usual condolences, Mrs. Eddington patted Bella's arm.

"Thank you," Bella murmured in reply.

The lady looked beyond Bella to Jax. "Please come in, both of you." She escorted them to the large front parlor where a fire crackled cheerfully in the grate. "May I bring tea or coffee?"

"No, thank you, ma'am," Jax replied. "We're here to talk with Eric. Is he home?"

"Why, yes, he is." She bit her lower lip. "Is this about Gus Schwarz?" Her gaze went from Jax to Bella and back.

"Yes, I just want to ask him a few questions, and Bella is here to take notes for me."

Her forehead furrowed. "I see. He's in his shop in back working on a project. I can fetch him."

"That's not necessary. If you don't mind, Bella and I will head out there."

"Of course. You know the way."

"Yes, ma'am," Jax replied.

He and Bella went out the French doors at the back of the parlor and down the stone path to a small gray building tucked away in a corner of the large lot.

"I haven't been back here in years," Bella commented as she glanced around the area. "It looks like they still have a big garden in the summer."

"Yes, they do," Jax said. "During the war, Mrs. Eddington put in all vegetables, but last summer, she went back to half vegetables and half flowers. It was a treat for both the eyes and the nose."

His observation surprised her. "Did you come here often?"

Jax turned to look down at Bella. "Mrs. Adams next door sometimes thinks someone is breaking into her shed or the cellar, or she hears something. Whenever she calls, I come over and check."

"She's been thinking such things for years," Bella said with a laugh.

"As far back as when my dad was constable," Jax agreed. "My mother said it started after Mr. Adams died."

"It's nice of you to come and check for her. I'm sure it eases her mind."

He shrugged. "It's no trouble," Jax replied before knocking on the shop door.

After a male voice called for them to come in, Jax opened the door and let Bella precede him into the building. Eric Eddington, a medium-built man in his early forties, looked up from his work bench without a trace of surprise.

"Good afternoon." He stood up and put his broad hand out to Jax who shook it. Then, Eric smiled at Bella. "I heard you were home. Good to see you again."

"And you, as well."

Eric focused on Jax then. "I don't suppose this is a social call."

"I'm afraid not, but I only want to ask some questions," Jax told him.

After Jax explained Bella's part, Eric nodded. "I'm glad you're helping, Bella. The mayor and council expect far too much of Jax and Nolen. Jax has hardly had a day off since he took over as constable."

Bella turned to study Jax whose jaw had tightened. He would never have admitted that himself, she thought with dismay. She didn't voice her observation. Instead, she simply assured Eric, as she had Nolen, that she was happy to help.

"Let's sit down by the stove. I stay plenty warm while I'm working, but when I take a break, it's cozier over there," Eric told them.

A bench and an old wooden rocker were the only seats. When Eric suggested Bella take the chair, she sat down and pulled out the notepad that Jax had given her. He and Eric sat side-by-side.

"What do you need to know, constable?" Eric asked in a calm, composed voice.

"Where were you Christmas Eve morning between six-thirty and nine?" Jax asked without preamble.

"Right here. I woke about six o'clock, as I usually do. I get the fire going in the kitchen stove and one in the dining room, as well. We only have two boarders now, three counting Anthony's nephew, but they share a suite. Bud Ballinger had already gone to be with relatives over the holidays. Anthony and Garlan left after breakfast. Mother got up a half-hour after me. I'd made coffee by then, so we both had a cup before she put porridge on. We had to let our cook and housekeeper go a year back since we lost most boarders. A girl comes to clean twice a week, but Mother does the cooking and I help where I can."

"What time did Mr. Windsor and his nephew come downstairs?"

"Anthony came down about seven-thirty. Garlan came in later. Louis Thomley sprained his ankle last week, so Garlan has been staying with him. Mostly to take care of the livestock, but also to help around the house. Garlan got back around eight-thirty that morning since Thomley's son was coming to pick Louis up. A neighbor tended the animals for a day or two as Garlan and Anthony went to their people in Cincinnati. Garlan and Louis seem to get along well, so the boy may have a long-term job with him."

"That could be a good thing for him and for Mr. Thomley, who must be close to eighty," Jax observed.

Eric nodded. "I know his family would like him to sell the place, but that might be hard right now. No one has bought any property here for more than a year. In the meantime, it could be good for Garlan, as well. He's done odd jobs at other farms. That's why he bought my motorcycle. We have the Willys-Overland. At my age, a motor car is probably a better choice," Eric said with a grin. "At least my mother thinks so."

"I've seen the boy on it, but when did he buy it?" Jax asked.

"Last spring."

Jax tucked the information away, along with the other dates. "I've heard Garlan got into fights at school, but that was before I returned."

Eric braced his elbows on his knees and leaned forward. "That's true. Garlan swore he didn't start any of the fights. Of course, the other boys claimed differently."

"So, you don't know which is right," Bella suggested.

Eric lifted his head. "No, I don't. All I know for sure is when Garlan came home with a black eye, Anthony took him out of school."

"Was the boy very upset?" Jax asked.

"Not that I could tell. He said kids always picked on him, and he was glad to be away from them."

"Mr. Smith said Garlan lived with some of Mr. Windsor's cousins before he came here," Bella put in.

"He did," Eric told her. "Garlan never met them before then. Anthony and his sister have the same father, but different mothers. His stepmother returned to England when the sister was still young, and she met her husband when he was a university student there. They moved to Belgium after they wed."

"I see," Bella murmured. "Garlan was very reserved when I met him, but I can understand why. Mr. Smith said the boy and his mother were living in Louvain, and the devastation there was awful."

"That it was," Jax agreed. "From what I know, which isn't a lot, the boy and his mother escaped to friends in the countryside, but she was killed at some point. The friends managed to save Garlan and get him to England since his father died shortly after the German invasion."

"Did he witness his mother's death?" Bella asked Eric.

"I don't know," Eric said. "We never discuss the war in front of the boy. Anthony tries to avoid that, too, but he has hard feelings toward the Germans. Not only did they kill his sister and brother-in-law, two British cousins died at the Somme. He talked a lot about them before Garlan came. Now, none of us want to upset the boy." Eric shook his head. "He's had enough to handle."

"To be sure," Jax said. "I want to talk with both of them, but I'll be very careful with Garlan."

A half-smile tugged at Eric's mouth. "You haven't finished talking with me, have you?"

Jax smiled in return. "Do you know if Mr. Windsor owns a handgun?"

Eric's gaze narrowed on Jax. "Why? You don't think Anthony or Garlan killed Schwarz, do you?"

Jax shrugged. "I don't know who killed him, so I have to look at everyone who had issues with Gus. Garlan might not have, but we know Windsor did." He didn't want to reveal the other clues in case Eric shared them with his mother who, although sweet, liked to contribute to the town gossip mill.

"You have a lot of folks to look at," Eric commented.

"I'm afraid so," was Jax's reply.

***

Jax and Bella followed the path around the house and out to the street. When they got to the car, she turned to him and asked, "Aren't you going to talk with Mrs. Eddington?"

"Not right now. I never thought Eric was a likely suspect. Now that I know he sold the bike, he isn't a suspect at all. The bike wasn't even here that morning."

"What about Garlan?"

A half-shrug lifted one of Jax's shoulders. "It's interesting that he has a bike, but that just gives us more to investigate."

His use of *us* mollified Bella, and she made no response until they were in the car and on their way again, Bella said, "You told Eric you don't think Mr. Windsor or his nephew killed Gus, but now you think Garlan is a suspect."

"I don't know. It isn't just whether or not I suspect them, they may know something that will help solve the case. For the same reason, we need to add Louis Thomley to the list. I want to know when Garlan left his place. Eric thought they were here until around ten o'clock. Exactly what time did you see them in the post office?"

Bella chewed on her lower lip as she considered the sequence of events on Christmas Eve morning. "Between the time I left the Schwarz farm and went to see Mr. Smith, I only stopped at the mercantile so I probably got to the post office between ten-thirty and eleven o'clock."

"That's in line with Eric's time frame, so talking with Mr. Thomley is important."

"I hope it doesn't involve Garlan," Bella said. "The Belgians suffered terribly after the German invasion. I met several Belgian nurses. One was from Louvain, and she was still there when it was burned to the ground. Even the library. Thousands and thousands of irreplaceable books were destroyed. Homes were burned and many people were killed. I can't imagine how hard that was on a child."

"I also met some Belgians. The Germans seemed to think they could march right through Belgium and on to France because the country was neutral. When the Belgian Army moved to stop the invasion and civilians resisted, the Germans were brutal. I hate thinking about what those people endured."

"So do I." Bella's brow furrowed as she reviewed their talk with Eddington. "Eric said Mr. Windsor has been very outspoken against the Germans."

"You must remember some of that from before America got into the war. By then, his brother-in-law was dead, and the British cousins were, too. I can't say I heard anything directly from him, but I heard about it."

"You lived in town, so you would know more than me. Besides, I was away at college and, when I was home, I mostly stayed at Ballantyne."

"That's true," he replied in a thoughtful tone. "I remember Mr. Windsor was open about his dislike of Germany. Gus overheard him once, and they nearly came to blows. I didn't see it myself, but Nick said he did. He had to break it up."

"Gus is—was—much bigger and stronger than Windsor, but he didn't seem to back down from arguing. At least, not from what Mr. Smith."

"Mr. Windsor is a man of strong opinions. Evidently, he'd had trouble with Gus as a student. That's why there's more than one reason to see Windsor."

"As Eric said, you have a long list."

"Far too long, but maybe it will be shorter by the end of the day."

"I hope so," Bella said before asking, "Where to now?"

Chapter Fifteen

Jax glanced at Bella before replying. "Let's head to the Wagner farm. Oscar and Gus have had an ongoing dispute about Gus borrowing tools without permission and not returning them. Oscar found several in Gus' shed—all rusty and dirty. He was furious. Gus laughed at him and said to prove the tools were his. Of course, Oscar couldn't, which didn't help matters. He doesn't have a motorcycle, though, or access to one. Even so, I feel like we need his perspective. Besides, the distance is walkable."

"But Mr. Wagner killing Gus Schwarz wouldn't explain the tire track. Besides, the Wagners are such nice people. It's hard to picture Oscar getting angry," Bella observed. "I can still hardly believe all of this has happened. Moreley has always been a pleasant place."

"It was, and it is mostly. Neighbors have had minor feuds for years. I knew because of my dad being constable. Usually, things got ironed out once he talked to both parties."

Bella frowned. "My grandfather never mentioned dealing with quarreling neighbors."

"It isn't the most interesting part of the job, so he probably didn't see a need to put any of that in his memoir," Jax pointed out.

"Or bore me. I was definitely more interested in big cases." She sighed. "I suppose he was going over his scrapbooks and reading mysteries with me so I had something to occupy my time." Out of the corner of her eye, Bella saw Jax shift to study her. "He really did say I was good at figuring cases out, though." Even to her own ears, she sounded defensive.

A slight pause preceded his response. "I'm sure you were. You're very intelligent and insightful."

The praise made her glance at him, but all Bella saw was sincerity in his green gaze. Hastily, she looked back at the road. "Thank you."

"It's the truth," Jax said before swiveling in his own seat to look outside. He cleared his throat. "After we visit the Wagners, I'd like to talk with Jacob Jones. He and Gus were in the same class, and he still lives on his family's farm."

Bella frowned. "I called your office from Mr. Jones' house. It was the closest one with a telephone, but Mrs. Schwarz said he might not let us use it since he and Mr. Schwarz were no longer speaking."

"That's probably because Gus and Jacob had a conflict a while back. Gus accused Jacob's dog of killing some of his chickens, and he shot the dog." Revulsion was clear in his voice.

"That's so mean." Bella's hands tightened on the steering wheel.

"Yes, it is. Luckily, the dog survived but Jacob was irate, as you might expect. Nick was still constable, but he told me that, while some of the chickens were dead, it didn't look like an animal had killed them."

"Did he think Gus did it himself?"

"Yes, he did. Evidently, Gus went to Jacob asking for money to replace the chickens. Jacob refused because he said the dog never left his property. Nick wouldn't step in since he suspected Gus. After a week or so, the dog was shot which only increased Nick's suspicions about Gus."

"Gus Schwarz was really a nasty man," Bella observed. "To kill his own chickens and blame his neighbor's dog. It's awful."

"That's why we have so many suspects."

***

During the rest of the short drive, neither of them spoke again. When they got to the Wagner place, Bella pulled to the side of the road, stopped the car, and looked at Jax. "The drive is a mess." Mud, puddles, and a very few patches of snow covered the yard in front of a small weathered house. "Going any farther seems like a sure way to get stuck."

A rough sigh escaped Jax. "We could leave the car here, but it would be tough going for you."

"I'm wearing boots," she pointed out. "They'll get muddy, but I walked through worse in France."

"I know," Jax murmured. And he did. Hadn't both he and Matt worried about her safety and comfort? Since he knew better than to say he was a man and could endure the cold and wet, Jax simply nodded. "Let's go."

When they got to the porch, Jax let her precede him and rap on the door.

A petite woman answered almost immediately. Her gray eyes widened. "Constable Hastings, Miss Stewart. What brings you here?"

Although the woman posed a question, she did not look surprised. Instead, she appeared wary. Jax swept off his cap. "Good afternoon, Mrs. Wagner. Is Oscar home?"

Her bony fingers clasped the edge of the door, but she nodded and said, "Yes. Out in the barn. He should be back in a few minutes." A tiny sigh left her before she continued. "Come in and sit down."

"We need to take our shoes off," Bella said. "Otherwise, we'll get mud all over your clean floor." Actually, the well-worn wood wasn't simply clean; it was spotless as was the rest of the parlor.

After removing their footwear, Bella and Jax followed Mrs. Wagner to the furniture clustered around the fireplace. Flames flickered cheerfully in the grate which drew Bella to take the chair closest to it. Jax took the seat next to her while their hostess settled on the faded settee across from them. "Ma'am, I'd like to you ask you a few questions, as well. Might we do that while we're waiting for your husband?" He strived to keep his voice soft and soothing in order to avoid upsetting the woman, who already seemed edgy.

"Surely," Mrs. Wagner said in a hushed voice that revealed her continuing discomfort.

"Bella is along to take notes for me," Jax explained.

Mrs. Wagner looked at Bella as if seeing her for the first time. After a moment, she offered condolences which Bella quietly accepted before pulling the notepad and pencil out. Before she bowed her head, Jax saw the look of anguish cross her face and his heart turned over. At the same time, guilt speared him. He had caused a good part of her pain, and the knowledge lashed like a whip.

When the farmwoman spoke again, Jax realized he'd gotten lost in his thoughts. "What did you want to ask, constable?"

He cleared his throat. "You already know Gus Schwarz was killed Christmas Eve morning."

She nodded. "Yes, we heard the news."

"Did you see or hear anything unusual that morning?" Jax asked.

For a moment, the woman simply looked at him. Then, she said, "We don't live close enough to hear much, and we don't spend time looking over their way, either."

"Because of the feud between your husband and Gus?"

Mrs. Wagner lifted her chin a fraction. "Not sure I'd call it a feud. Gus and Oscar were friends once. They were two years ahead of me in school, so I've known them both most of my life. Gus was a nice little boy, but he learned quick how to be nasty from his father who was as mean as a man could be. Oscar knew Gus got beat regularly, mostly protecting his mother. When she was still alive, Gus wasn't so mean. After she died, he got as bad as his old man, but we remembered how he'd been so Oscar tried to get along. He gave up after the tool trouble."

"I see," Jax said. Although he had lived in Moreley all of his life, he was still learning some things. "To your knowledge, has your husband been to see Gus recently?"

"No. As I said, he quit being friendly, and I didn't go no more since last spring. Gus was never nice to me but, by then, he was nasty. My man worried about me over there. Neither of us has had nothing to do with them since."

"And your husband was here with you on Christmas Eve morning?" Jax inquired.

Something flashed in her pale gaze before she glanced at the flickering fire. "Yes, there are plenty of chores year-round, and Oscar gets an early start since we have animals."

The sound of the back door opening kept her from continuing. After a few moments, a short but powerfully built man entered the parlor. His hazel gaze went from Jax to Bella to his wife. "I see we have company," he said without a trace of inflection in his deep voice.

Jax got to his feet, crossed the distance between himself and the other man, and put out his hand. After briefly reviewing what he'd told Mrs. Wagner about the visit, Jax returned to his seat while the farmer joined his wife.

"I already asked Mrs. Wagner, but I wondered if you heard or saw anything out of the ordinary the morning Gus Schwarz died," Jax said.

"Nope. I do chores early, but I don't bother myself with goings on over their way." A rueful expression blanketed Wagner's weathered face. "You know he and I had trouble. Now, I stay away."

"Mrs. Wagner said you and Gus were friends as children," Jax commented.

Oscar took a sidelong glance at his wife before looking back at the constable. "Gertrud and I knowed him in school. This place belonged to my parents, and their place was in Helene's family. She's much younger, but I knowed her from the time she was born. Gus' old man worked for the Culpeppers, and Gus worked there when he got big enough.

Old Schwarz liked to drink, and Gus often done his father's work."

"Why do you think the Culpeppers kept Gus' father on?" Jax asked.

Werner grimaced. "Pity mostly. Schwarz had land once. Lost it after the wife died. Mr. Culpepper looked out for Gus all along. Mrs. Culpepper tried, too, but old Schwarz was cagey. Hid his drinking and such. Gus mostly acted good to the Culpeppers. Helene was way behind us in school. Doubt she saw him bully kids." Wagner laid his broad hand on his wife's smaller one. "He's gotten worse and worse since the war started."

"Do you have any idea why?" Jax asked. "Before I left for France, I didn't notice any anti-German sentiment here, and no one has indicated there was any while we were gone, but that seems to be what really provoked Gus."

"There wasn't," Oscar told Jax. "My grandparents came from Germany, and no one acted bad to us. We heard about problems elsewhere. Don't know exactly what set Gus off, but he got riled up when his cousins' town changed its name. It was New Berlin, but now it's North Canton. People voted for it, which is their right."

"I heard about the change, but I didn't know Gus had family there," Jax commented.

"Several cousins. Don't know any of them, though. Anyhow, the change peeved him. He talked to everyone with German blood and tried to get them stirred up, too. Werner Meyers is the only one who listened."

"Do you know why that was?" Jax asked.

Oscar shook his head. "A while back, Mrs. Meyers and the girls went to Cincinnati to visit kin. There was anti-German sentiment there. Lots of posters about getting the Hun and such. Gisela's uncle worked for the German-language paper, and they were visiting when the offices were raided. All of the editors' homes got searched. Pretty upsetting."

"I'm sure it was," Bella put in.

Oscar nodded. "Werner got real mad, so he let Gus fill his ear with a lot of nonsense. Not that Werner picked on any soldiers. More sense than Gus."

"That's a good thing," Jax said. "So, just to sum up, you were doing chores outside early that morning?"

"Yep. Takes about two hours. When I finished, I got back inside. Gertrud had breakfast ready, so we ate and sat here by the fire much of the day. Of course, had to feed the animals again later. Our girls didn't come home for Christmas as both are expecting. We'll be going to see them when the babes come along."

"How nice," Bella said. "Your daughters are a little younger than I am, but I remember them from school. Please wish them well for me."

"We will," Mrs. Wagner said with a pleased smile.

"Mr. Wagner, I need to ask one more question. Do you own a pistol or revolver?"

For several moments, the farmer looked at Jax. "No, constable. I have two shotguns, though."

Jax nodded as he got to his feet. "Thank you for your time, but we better be on our way."

Chapter Sixteen

After Jax and Bella were again on the road, he turned to her and asked, "What did you think about what the Wagners said?"

"They certainly know a lot more about Schwarz than I ever heard."

Jax laid his gloved hands on his knees. "Same with me, but I spent most of my free time at Ballantyne."

His words evoked a host of bittersweet memories and, for a moment, Bella let herself be swept back to happier days. Jax was right about being at the resort. He'd been a fixture every summer day and, after his father died, every holiday, too. Recalling her inhospitable treatment of him on Christmas Eve, Bella experienced a fresh pang of regret. "What did you do on Christmas?" After a long silence ensued, she glanced at him, but he was looking away from her. "Jax?"

He cleared his throat. "I worked."

"Both Christmas Eve and Day?" Remorse hit her full-force. He'd mentioned letting Nolen spend the holiday with his mother, but had Jax worked the entire time?

"The constable's office doesn't close for holidays."

"Couldn't Nolen have worked one of the days?"

A long, low sigh left him. "Nolen's mother has been alone for two Christmases. It was important he be with her."

"What about you?"

"I don't have anyone who expects me for the holiday."

Bella felt her heart constrict. Mac had invited Jax to stay on Christmas Eve, but she hadn't echoed the offer because his dismissive comments had made her mad.

Before Bella could respond, he spoke again. "Even if I had family, I'd need to work at least one of those days. It goes with the job. Besides, Nolen brought dinner on Christmas Day, and we spent time going over the case."

The excuses didn't make Bella feel any better. No matter how much both of them had changed, Jax's first holiday back home shouldn't have been spent alone. "I'm sorry I didn't ask you to stay for Christmas Eve dinner. You spent a lot of holidays with us. You still can, you know."

His hands tightened into twin fists. "I appreciate the thought, but it's better if I don't."

Surprise flickered through her, and Bella once again glanced his way. "Why?"

"As much as we might like to, we can't live in the past. Everything is different now." Jax paused before going on. "I'm different. My life is different. My golf career is behind me. Sometimes, that's hard to accept and spending time at Ballantyne won't make accepting it any easier."

A chill ran through Bella as she absorbed his admissions. Maybe the Jax of her childhood and adolescence was really gone forever. Despite everything, hope lingered. Hope they could once again be friendly at least. But friendship took two people. "Of course, I understand," she murmured. But she didn't. Not really. Being a golf professional had been his passion. How could he abandon it?

Jax listened with the certainty that Bella didn't understand. The end of his golf career wasn't the primary reason for his discomfort, but if she thought it was, they'd both be better off. Not wanting to pursue personal topics, Jax revisited the case. "If you have time, I'd like to speak with Helene Schwarz on our way back to town. We can see Meyers and then stop back at her place before going to the Jones' farm."

"Of course." Within moments, a two-story white frame house came into view. Bella steered the Ford off the road and pulled to a stop in front of the home.

Jax followed Bella to the front stoop. After he knocked, Meyers let them inside.

"I hope this is a good time for us to talk," Jax said to the other man, who made no greeting.

Meyers, a blue-eyed blonde of middling build and height, frowned as he looked at Bella. "What is she doing here?"

"Miss Stewart is taking notes for me," Jax replied in an even tone that matched his calm expression.

The farmer grunted and said, "Come in, but take off your boots. The wife keeps a tidy home, and she don't need to be cleaning up after the two of you." With that, he turned away.

Bella and Jax exchanged a look, but hurriedly removed their footwear before following Meyers down the short hall to an immaculate kitchen. Mrs. Meyers, who stood at the sink, turned to face them. Slightly shorter than her husband and rather rounded, she didn't have his same sour look, but she didn't appear pleased to see them, either.

"Take a place," Meyers said, jerking his thumb at the table in the center of the room.

Jax held a chair for Bella, who sat down, removed her gloves, and unbuttoned her coat. He did the same once he had taken the seat beside hers.

"Have you arrested anyone yet?" Meyers asked in a gruff tone as he settled at the head of the table and stared at Jax with utter contempt.

Clearly, news of Schwarz's death had reached them. "No, sir, we're still investigating," Jax replied.

"It ain't hard to figure who wanted Gus dead. Course, you're looking out for your men instead of finding which one done it." Meyers shot out the words like a machine gun firing bullets. "It's been more than two days. Someone ought to be in jail now."

Bella felt Jax stiffen beside her, but when he spoke, he still sounded calm and collected. What that must have cost him, she couldn't imagine. Meyers was beyond nasty.

"The holiday put us a bit behind," Jax said.

The other man glared at Jax. "You took off when you got a killer loose around here? Bet if the dead man was a soldier, you'd be doing something."

Meyers looked ready to explode while Jax was obviously fighting for control. The situation made Bella furious, but she struggled to remain calm. "The constable worked both Christmas Eve and Christmas Day. There are many people to be interviewed, and he's doing his very best." Although Jax turned toward her, Bella focused on the farmer. Asking questions and making comments weren't part of her tasks. However, letting the man berate Jax was intolerable.

Mrs. Meyers took a seat at the table and laid one plump hand over her husband's broad one before looking at Jax.

"We're both upset about Gus. It was a shock to learn of his death. We thought of the soldiers right off." She glanced at her husband. "We was with my aunt and uncle in Cincinnati for Christmas. They been Americans for years, loyal ones. Made no matter to folks who mistreated them. It ain't right."

"I agree," Jax told her. "I heard about the problems in Cincinnati, and it wasn't fair. But I have to follow the facts and investigate the leads. That's why I'm here." He turned his attention to her husband. "I'd like to ask a few questions that may help us bring the killer to justice."

Meyers' eyes still looked like blue ice, but he gave a slight nod.

"Obviously, you're aware Gus had run-ins with several of the veterans," Jax began, "and I'm aware he and Curt Molitor had words the day before Gus died. Did Gus ever mention any direct threats?"

"You mean did someone say they were gonna kill him? Course not. But Molitor butted into disagreements between Gus and your men more than once. Everyone knows Curt ain't sensible no more, and he's quick to find fault with anyone who don't bow down to you soldiers," Meyers spat out.

A sidelong glance at Jax told Bella he was still fighting an urge to defend Curt. While she admired his restraint, Bella would have enjoyed interceding herself. Instead, she kept her head bowed and continued to take notes. As a law officer, Jax maintained a high level of decorum. She needed to do the same.

"I also understand Mr. Schwarz had an issue with his neighbor, Oscar Wagner. Do you know the nature of it?" Jax knew, but he wanted Meyers' slant.

The farmer snorted derisively. "Wagner claimed Gus had his tools, but he couldn't prove they were his. Gus told me it weren't the first time Wagner accused him of taking things. It all goes back to when they were kids. Both are ten years older than me, so I don't know no details."

"Do you know anyone else who argued with Mr. Schwarz?" Jax asked.

A harrumph left Meyers. "The whole town knows about Eddington doing shoddy work for Gus and then insisting he get paid full price. The trouble between him and the teacher ain't secret, either. That man Windsor likes to brag about his education. Tried to tell Gus how he should think. He don't get how some of us leave school to work our family farms. It don't make us stupid. And the teacher is British, so he ain't got no right to lecture an American."

Mrs. Meyers patted her husband's hand, but her gaze was on Jax. "You said there weren't discrimination here, and you're right. But German-Americans in these parts are mostly farmers, and farm kids often leave school early. Gus did. We did. Our boys will soon. They miss school because of farm work. The other teachers understand, but Windsor don't."

Jax didn't correct Meyers about Windsor, who had been born in Ohio but was of British descent. Instead, he asked another question. "What about Mrs. Schwarz? I understand their farm belonged to her parents."

"It did," Mrs. Meyers told him.

"Culpeppers had money," her husband added, "and they spoilt their girl with it. Helene had to do some work after she married Gus. Didn't hurt her none."

Jax frowned. "Was their marriage a happy one?"

Mrs. Meyers started to speak, but her husband cut her off. "As happy as any." His voice was firm, and his wife gave an affirmative nod.

Despite Mrs. Meyers' seeming agreement, the farmer's reaction and reply bothered Bella. Before returning to her note-taking, she studied them. Nothing could be discerned in either's face, but Bella didn't think they were being completely honest.

"Have you spoken with Mrs. Schwarz since you got home?" Jax asked the pair.

"No," Mrs. Meyers replied, "but I'm taking food over. We'll pay respects then."

"I'm going, too, so I can help out," Meyers reported. "If you don't have no other questions, I need to finish chores here before we go to Helene."

"I don't have any right now, but we're re-interviewing some people so either Nolen or I may be back to speak with you again. It's also possible that Senior Constable Jenkins may be the one to come out. You might know of him. He's retired now, but he was the constable in Karston for a number of years." Jax got to his feet as he spoke.

"I've heard of him. Anyone who can get the killer is welcome." Meyers' words were as much accusation as observation.

Jax nodded. When he put his hand on the back of her chair, Bella stowed her gear in her bag and rose, too. Neither

Mr. or Mrs. Meyers moved, and neither offered to see them out. "Thank you both for your time. We can find our way."

Then, he and Bella did just that.

***

Once they were in the car and back on the main road, Bella couldn't withhold her observations. "They weren't exactly welcoming."

"No, they weren't, but I didn't expect them to be."

Bella shrugged. "I didn't, either, but he was especially sharp-tongued. I don't how you kept from telling him off." She was surprised when a low laugh rumbled out of Jax.

"You did a good job of berating him for me. Although I'd rather you didn't do it again, I can't say I didn't appreciate the effort."

Warmth spread through Bella as she took a sidelong glance at Jax. The amusement softening his tired face was appealing and yet she feared it was also transitory. Any minute he might retreat into the stranger he had become. "He was obnoxious." The comment wasn't personal so, with luck, it wouldn't re-open the chasm between them.

Jax laid his cap on the dashboard. "Mrs. Meyers was somewhat nicer although we didn't learn a lot from her, either. Both made excuses for Schwarz, but they were friends, so I suppose that's natural enough."

"What I found odd was when she started to answer your question about the Schwarzes' marriage, her husband cut her off. Mrs. Meyers nodded like she agreed, but he seemed too eager to interrupt and tense as he did."

"I noticed that, too." He lightly massaged his forehead. "I need to find out more about Mrs. Schwarz. I know she hasn't come to town much for years."

"Mr. and Mrs. Meyers said she was younger than Gus. Do you know by how much?" Bella asked.

"She and Harold Horton were in the same class, so about twelve years younger."

Bella tapped her forefingers on the steering wheel as she mulled over the information. "What else did Harold have to say about her?"

"Not a lot other than saying she was too good for Gus." Jax's brow furrowed as he reviewed the conversation. "He mentioned they had a truck, but it broke down a month or so ago. Harold thought Gus didn't fix it as another way to keep her on the farm. He was pretty upset about that."

"If she seldom went to town, why would it make a difference?"

"That's a good question. Maybe Gus didn't like her using it at all, and she did when he was gone."

The information gave Bella pause. "You may be right." But why keep her at home? Was he jealous? If so, of whom?

Chapter Seventeen

As planned, the pair went to the Schwarz farm next. "There's a car by the house," Bella said, as she pulled off the road.

The freeze and thaw had left the short drive bumpier than on Christmas Eve morning, and Jax felt every jar reverberate through his upper arm and shoulder. He could only be glad he wasn't driving because the vibration through the gearshift and steering wheel would have further complicated matters. Nonetheless, when they pulled to a stop beside the house, he breathed a sigh of relief. He followed Bella to the front door and reached around her to knock.

A tall, broad blonde man, his grim expression totally lacking in welcome, answered. "Yes," was all he said.

Jax introduced himself and Bella, ending with, "May we come in?"

The big man stepped back but said nothing more as he turned to go down a wide hallway. "We should probably take our shoes off," Bella said to his retreating figure.

"No need." The man didn't look back.

Bella and Jax exchanged a glance before he indicated she should go ahead of him as they followed the blonde

"I'm Ernst Schwarz, Gus' cousin," the big man told them once they arrived in the parlor. "Have you arrested someone, constable?"

"Not yet, Mr. Schwarz. We're still investigating. That's why we're here. I'd like to speak with Mrs. Schwarz again. She wasn't up to many questions the other day," Jax replied.

"Of course not. She had a terrible loss." The words rang with disgust.

"I'm aware of that, sir, but she may know something that can help us find the killer. I'd appreciate it if you'd get her." Jax found maintaining his composure challenging, but he relaxed when the Schwarz cousin agreed and left the room.

"He looks a lot like Gus," Bella observed.

"Yes, he seems to be a younger version."

Further conversation was cut off when the cousin returned with Helene. Behind her, another two burly, blue-eyed blonde men entered the room. Ernst jerked a thumb at the pair. "My brothers, Heinz and Gerhard."

Neither of the newcomers spoke or sat down. Instead, they stood at the side of the room with their arms folded across their chests like matching statues.

Clad in a black crepe dress ending just above her ankles, Helene still looked pale and wan. Her gaze went from Bella to Jax. "Ernst said you want to speak with me again. I thought you would have arrested Gus' murderer by now." Her voice, weak and wobbly, lacked assertion.

"As I told Mr. Schwarz, we're doing a thorough investigation. We have leads, and we're pursuing each one," Jax told her. "My deputy and I are speaking with a number of people, as is Senior Constable Jenkins from Karston. He's retired now, but he's helping us with this case."

"That's good." The woman's tone held no trace of emotion, nor did her ashen face. She seemed to be acting by rote.

Jax cleared his throat. "May we sit down and talk?"

Helene Schwarz nodded her head and took a seat by the fireplace. As she did, she pulled her black shawl around her narrow shoulders. Her husband's cousin Ernst sat in the big chair across from her, leaving Bella and Jax to perch on the horsehair divan. The brothers didn't move.

"You already told me about feeling ill and staying in bed on Christmas Eve morning. Are you feeling any better today?" Jax asked.

"Yes, thank you. Doc left medicine for me the other morning and checked on me yesterday when he was out this way to deliver a baby." Helen managed a slight smile.

"I won't take much of your time, but we need to go over a few things," Jax briefly reviewed the main part of their previous exchange. He finished with, "And you didn't hear anything unusual."

"That's right," Mrs. Schwarz said. "As you know, I was getting over a bad cold, so after I fixed breakfast for Gus, I went back to bed."

"Prior to that morning, had you heard or seen anyone unfamiliar around your property?"

"No. No one."

"But you knew your husband had confrontations with various people in the past," Jax said.

Helene Schwarz chewed on her lower lip before replying. "Gus was not a man who took abuse from others." Again, her voice lacked both conviction and volume. She sounded like she was speaking memorized lines. "I suppose you have suspects."

"We don't suspect anyone in particular at this point, Mrs. Schwarz. As I said, we're gathering evidence," Jax replied. "We've spoken with the veterans, and we're interviewing some again. In fact, we're going to see Harold Horton shortly."

A frown formed on Helene Schwarz's wan face. "Harold would never have hurt Gus, so there's no need to persecute him."

The woman's adamant tone surprised Jax since it was the first sign of emotion from her. "You sound very sure, Mrs. Schwarz," he observed, not revealing that Harold had offered an alibi of sorts.

Color swept into her pale cheeks. "I've known Harold since first grade, and he would never hurt anyone. Besides, he opens the filling station every morning, so he certainly couldn't be here and there at the same time."

That statement intensified Jax's surprise. "How do you know Harold opens the station?"

Her blue eyes went to her lap where she was clasping and unclasping her hands. "Gus has been gone a couple of times in the last year or so, and I went to town because I ran out of several things. Last year, I was on my way to town when something seemed to be wrong with the truck. I stopped and Harold was kind enough to look at it for me. He mentioned he was about to leave since he opens the place. Since he was just back home after being badly wounded, we chatted a bit. He still looked pale and thin, and I wondered he was really well enough to work."

"I see," Jax said with what he hoped was a reassuring smile. The woman's obvious discomfort signaled some sort of distress. What that meant, he didn't know. Not yet at least. Asking more penetrating questions didn't seem wise. For one thing, Helene was uneasy. For another, the cousins appeared to be intimidating her. If Jax needed to speak with her again, which might not be necessary, he'd have to contrive a way to get her to his office alone.

"Do you have other questions?" Ernst asked abruptly.

"No, that's all for now," Jax responded. "I appreciate your time, Mrs. Schwarz. Again, I'm very sorry for your loss."

Bella flipped the notepad shut and reiterated her own condolences. Helene merely nodded in response. The cousins said nothing although Ernst rose to lead the way back to the door.

"I expect you'll get the killer soon, constable," he said in his harsh tone. "If you can't, my brothers and I will get at it after the funeral."

Jax's jaw tightened. "Don't take the law into your own hands, Mr. Schwarz."

The big blonde grunted. "You ought to do your job, constable. My brothers and I had to go out looking for the horses. You could have at least seen to that."

Jax had no chance to reply because he and Bella were barely out the door when it slammed behind them. Within moments, they were back in the car.

Once they were partway down the drive, Bella glanced at Jax. "The cousins are a lot like Gus, I guess."

"It seems that way," he said on a sigh. "The last thing I need is for them to start interfering."

"You still have people to interview. One of them will surely provide a good lead," Bella suggested.

"I hope so," Jax replied.

"The entire place is not only run-down, Mrs. Schwarz's dress looks like one that her mother might have worn. Or one she wore long ago."

"I don't know much about ladies' fashions," Jax admitted as he considered the observation, "but I guess it could be. Do you think it's important?"

"Maybe. The other morning, she mentioned not seeing me since I was a girl, but I only had a vague memory of her coming to Ballantyne for lunch. Now, I remember her from when I first started school. She must have been a junior or senior, and when our teacher was out, Helene would take over the class. She was planning to go to normal school. I was impressed by her. She was kind, pretty, and stylish. It's no wonder I didn't recognize her."

"I don't recall her ever taking over my class," Jax said.

"I imagine she only took the first and second grade. Besides, if you remember, your class had a lot more boys than girls. I'm guessing the principal substituted for your teachers, when necessary."

Jax chuckled. "I believe you're right. Of course, I never misbehaved at school because I knew whatever teacher I had would go right to my mother if I did."

"I'm sure that was true since she was always in a nearby classroom," Bella replied, her own voice holding a note of amusement.

After a moment, Jax went on, "You said Mrs. Schwarz planned to go to normal school. That's for teachers, but she never taught as far as I know."

"I don't think she did, either," Bella commented. "She and Gus have been married for many years. Do you know exactly how long?"

"I'm not certain, but they wed shortly after her parents died, I believe. I want to talk to Doc about the autopsy, and he may remember when they married. Of course, Jacob may know about their wedding since he and Gus were in the same class."

"Do you want to go to Doc's after you speak with Jacob? We could go on and talk to Harold after that. Mrs. Schwarz didn't reveal a lot, but I wonder about her reaction to you questioning him. They must have known each other well since they were schoolmates."

"That's a good point. Her strong reaction and Harold's obvious dislike of Gus might be something to pursue."

"Harold said Gus didn't fix the truck because he wanted to keep Helene isolated. If he found out she'd been to town and stopped at Harold's station, Gus might have been jealous. Plus, Harold said she was too good for Gus, right? What if Harold had more than friendly feelings for Helene when they were young?"

A brief silence preceded his reply. "Another interesting idea."

Bella scowled. "You don't sound very convinced."

Jax cast a sidelong glance at her. "You make good points. Intuitive points, and I don't deny that they might be pertinent. Even so, I need hard evidence."

"Of course, but I am interested in hearing what Doc might remember about the two of them."

Her interest wasn't a surprise. Jax ignored it when he responded. "You don't need to come along, Bella. I'm already taking up far too much of your time."

A moment passed before she answered. "I have the entire afternoon free, and I'm happy to help."

Her sincere tone and his own reluctance to give up both her assistance and her company influenced his response. "If you're sure."

"Very sure."

Chapter Eighteen

Once Bella parked the car, Jax got out and held the driver's door for her. "I don't have many questions for him, so this won't take long."

When Jax knocked on the door, Jacob answered almost immediately. He smiled in greeting and the two men shook hands. "Good afternoon, constable." His gaze went to Bella. "Good day to you, too."

Jax again explained why Bella accompanied him.

Jacob offered his sympathy on her losses before saying, "I'm sorry I didn't say so the other morning, but you caught me off-guard." Bella thanked him as he ushered them into a small, cozy parlor. "I've been working outside and just got the fire going again. Sit near it, Miss Stewart. You'll be warmer there. You, as well, constable."

The pair sat on the chairs flanking the fireplace while Jones settled in a nearby rocker. "I figured I'd see you eventually," he said, his smile still in place.

"I only want to ask a few questions, Mr. Jones. We're talking to anyone who might have heard something the other morning."

"I'll help in any way I can."

Before more conversation ensued, a large brown dog ambled into the room. He put his shaggy head on Jacob's knee, got his ears scratched, and went to stand between Bella and Jax.

She put her hand out so the pet could sniff it. After doing so, he laid his head on her knee, much as he had with his owner. "Oh, how sweet," Bella murmured as she stroked his silky fur. "What kind of dog is he?"

"Duffy is a real mixture. He came here when he was just a pup. Since no one claimed him, I kept him. He's a lot of company," Jacob observed with a smile.

"Is he the dog Gus shot?" she asked while continuing to pet Duffy.

Jacob's smile disappeared. "Yep. He was in bad shape for a while, but he made it. Now, I watch him close. Of course, he stays within a few feet of me these days."

"Poor baby," Bella murmured. The dog's tail thumped against the floor as she continued to pet him.

"It was terrible." Jacob looked at Jax. "I haven't spoken to Schwarz since, and I admit I was furious about him shooting Duffy. As you can see, he's a real gentle dog. I have chickens here, and he's never bothered them at all. In good weather, he'll even lie in the yard and let them cluck around him."

Jax nodded. "I spoke with Nick when I took this job, and he suspected Gus of killing the chickens himself."

"I'm guessing that's what happened." Jacob shook his head. "I've known him since before we started school. He was a decent enough kid until his mother died. After that, his old man didn't have anyone except him to beat. Gus got meaner over the years. The last few years, he's been real bad."

"So, I've heard. Do you have any ideas why?" Jax asked, hoping Jones would offer something new.

Jacob shrugged. "He never talked much about his German heritage when we were kids. Started doing it a lot once the country went to war. He was furious when his cousins' hometown, New Berlin, was changed to North

Canton. And there were some bad incidents in the papers, not that Gus read a lot but he heard about them from Werner Meyers."

"So, we were told," Jax said.

"I'm not saying those things were right, but no one here bothered Gus or Meyers or anyone else with German blood. Gus took every incident, everywhere personally. I think he looked for excuses to be angry," Jacob said.

"It sounds that way." Jax paused for a moment. "We were just at his place and talked to his wife and cousins."

"How is Helene doing?" Jacob's voice held a note of real distress.

"Fairly well."

"It had to be a shock, but once she gets over that, she may be relieved," Jacob stated.

"Relieved?" Jax echoed. "Why would she be relieved?"

Jacob leaned forward, braced his elbows on his knees, and clasped his hands in front of him. "I don't know it for a fact, but I think he might have been rough with her at times."

Surprise filled Jax who looked at Bella to see she was equally taken aback. "What makes you think so?"

"Last spring, I went over to try to talk sense to him. That was before he shot Duffy. I didn't want no more trouble. Foolish to try mending fences, but we knowed one another a long time." Jacob studied his dog before going on. "It was a scorcher of a day. Helene was out in the back hanging up wash. I noticed bruises on her arms, like someone had grabbed her hard, and I asked if she was okay. She pulled down her sleeves down right off and mumbled how she'd fallen. Gus saw me and came over. He ordered her to get inside, and she went."

"Did you ever see other marks on her?" Jax asked.

"No. I never went over there again, and Helene rarely went to town, especially in the past few years."

The comment supported what they already knew, so Jax nodded. "Do you know when they married?"

The older man's brow furrowed. "Shortly after she graduated. That would have been about sixteen years ago. Her father passed that winter, but he'd been poorly for a while. Her mother passed the following summer. Gus had been working the farm, and I suppose it was easiest for Helene. He was still a good-looking man and could be nice, if he wanted something. Of course, I'm not sure how nice he was after the wedding. They'd only been married a few years when he accused her of flirting with men in town. That's when she stopped going places by herself. Later, she rarely left the farm."

She had gone to town at some point, though, and she had seen Harold. The knowledge bothered Jax. He brushed the thought aside and made his last statement. "I assume you were here alone Christmas Eve morning."

"Yep. Just me and Duffy," Jones replied. "I got no one to back me up, but I had a couple of calls before Miss Stewart stopped. My aunt lives with her daughter over in Boxwood. They phoned early. About seven. My cousin wanted to make sure I remembered when dinner was. Talked to them about fifteen minutes and called another cousin after that since he was picking me up. I got a phone but still use horse and wagon to get around. His car makes a quicker trip. He's got young ones, and they had to get on the line and tell me about Santa coming." A smile lit his lean face. "Took a while. By the time I rang off, it had to be eight-thirty. You can check with Annabelle. She'll know the times. Pretty sure we held up the line a bit longer than she likes."

"Probably so if you talked longer than ten minutes," Jax replied, recalling the local operator's preference for short calls. He got to his feet. "I appreciate your cooperation."

***

"We discovered a lot more than when the Schwarzes married," Jax said to Bella once they were headed back to Moreley.

"Poor Helene," Bella said. "No wonder she looked so different. Being bullied had to take a toll. She's only ten or eleven years older than I am, but she's aged a lot." A soft sigh escaped her. "Everything looks different in light of Jacob's revelations. Someone has to use a strong grip to create bruises."

"I'm afraid you're right," Jax agreed. "I had no idea, but I'm guessing most people didn't know since Helene stayed home so much."

"With no family left, she was at his mercy," Bella murmured. "I'm not as young as she was when she lost her parents, and I've not only been to college, I served in France. Even so, I realize how lucky I am to have Mac."

Jax turned to look at Bella. For several moments, he said nothing. When he finally spoke, his voice was rough and ragged. "I'm glad you have him, too."

His tone and words made her heart beat faster. Bella wanted to say that talking with Mac about the past was almost as important as planning for the future with him, but she hesitated. Jax had put up barriers in France, and she wasn't sure how—or if—to breach them. With effort, Bella focused on other information provided by Jones. "I wonder if anyone else noticed marks on her. Doc examined her the other morning, so he may have seen some."

"Possibly. I'll definitely ask him." He hesitated before going on. "Do you mind stopping by where Gus was shot? Now that most of the snow is gone, I'd like to see if I can find the bullets even though it's a long-shot."

"Of course," Bella immediately agreed.

It only took moments to reach the spot. As she had on Christmas Eve morning, Bella parked on the edge of the road. "The mud and puddles won't make it easy to find much," she observed.

"Probably not, but I want to look. The trouble is, not knowing the exact type of gun means I don't have much idea of how far the bullets travelled," Jax said as he walked toward the trees.

Bella looked toward the Schwarz house, which was only partially visible beyond the trees. "I still think the killer might have only wanted to cause trouble, not kill Gus. We already talked about both of them having a light since it was so early."

"That's quite possible. None of the other incidents of vandalism ended with violence."

"Duffy got shot," Bella pointed.

"Yes, but that wasn't connected to vandalism." Jax paused before saying, "Let me look around here a little more. I want to check along the road again, too. Maybe we'll see something there."

Buoyed by his use of *we* again, Bella readily agreed. For several minutes, the pair covered the ground between where Schwarz had fallen and the trees bordering the farm. "Nothing," Jax murmured at last. "Let's take a look at the shoulder. With the snow gone, there may be some other clue." With long strides, he reached the roadside ahead of her.

"See anything worthwhile?" she asked when, out of breath, she joined him.

A half-shrug lifted one of his shoulders. "The narrow tire mark is even less distinct, but that's not surprising with the snow melt and puddles forming. Not much else to see."

"So, you're still focusing on people with both motorcycles and handguns."

"For the most part, yes. I want to make certain none of the bikes have come up missing. We know Curt and Wyatt have theirs. Harold's brother has one, so I need to check on it."

"And Garlan bought Eric Eddington's."

"True, but we don't know if the boy has a gun or not."

"Are you still focusing on Curt?"

Jax exhaled sharply. "I have to keep him and Wyatt on the suspect list, Bella."

Since she couldn't argue with Jax's assessment, Bella nodded before turning back to the car. Her heart heavy, she glanced at him. He looked as troubled as she felt. Neither spoke as they made their way to Doc Smedlay's place.

***

Bella and Jax had to spend a few minutes in the waiting room before Doc came out to greet them. "I finally got to the autopsy today. I'm sorry I couldn't do it sooner, but I had a full schedule Christmas Eve, a baby on Christmas Day, and Smith this morning. Come into my office and sit down." Doc settled behind his big oak desk while Bella and Jax took chairs across from him. "It's as we thought. Gus was shot at very close range with a pistol or revolver. I can't tell which or what type since we have no bullets or shells."

Jax sighed. "We stopped at the scene before coming here. I looked around the area hoping the bullets might be under the snow, but no luck."

"It would be darn hard to find small slugs. They could have gone a number of feet before hitting something or falling," Doc pointed out.

"Yes, but I had to try."

The older man nodded. "Other than what I've told you, I would guess Gus died quickly, since one bullet hit a main artery. The amount of blood on his clothes and the ground would support that."

When neither man spoke again, Bella said, "We saw Helene Schwarz this afternoon. She seems to feel better, and she told us you checked on her yesterday."

Smedlay nodded. "I stopped on my way home from the birthing. I wanted to make sure she hadn't gone into bronchitis or pneumonia. Gus' cousins arrived while I was there, so I didn't stay. They're anxious to proceed with a funeral, so they weren't happy an autopsy was yet to be done. Now, Forrester can come for the body, and the plans can go ahead."

Bella and Jax exchanged a glance before he continued. "Did you notice anything other than a cold with Mrs. Schwarz?"

A puzzled look crossed the man's face. "No. Did you have something in mind?"

Jax revealed what Jacobs had told them. "We wondered if she was bruised."

The physician frowned. "She wasn't, and even if she had been, I doubt if she would have killed him. In case that's what you're thinking."

"We don't think that, either," Bella was quick to put in. She ignored the dark look Jax sent her. "Did you ever notice bruises on her before?"

"Until the other morning, I hadn't treated her for a number of years," the physician replied.

"She wasn't a regular patient?" Jax inquired.

"No, not recently. I saw Helene when she was a child. I was new to town back then. Her parents worried whenever she got sick, so they always got me. Since her marriage, I've only seen her a handful of times. Twice after she lost babies."

"She lost babies?" Bella echoed.

"I'm afraid so. She lost one several years after her marriage, and another the next year. I shouldn't reveal details, but I will say her husband waited too long to fetch me both times. When I spoke with her, I discovered she may have been with child other times, but wasn't able to carry the babes as long." He shook his gray head. "Gus thought she should be able to deliver a child without help. I never saw bruises at any time, though. If I had, I would have had a serious talk with Gus. As it was, I told him to get me for another baby. Of course, after the second time she was here, there was very little likelihood of that happening." Disdain and dismay were in the physician's tone and expression.

Bella's insides knotted as Doc spoke. Poor Helene had evidently suffered in more than one way at the hands of her husband. "You must have known her parents."

Doc smiled. "Yes. Lovely people. Unfortunately, she lost both of them within a matter of months. She and Gus married shortly after her mother died." He paused for a moment. "I probably shouldn't say this, but I believe she may have been with child when they wed."

Surprise rippled through Bella as she absorbed the doctor's revelation. "I see," Bella murmured. Her heart hurt to think of a young, beautiful Helene alone and at the mercy of someone like Gus Schwarz. Although she knew Jax didn't like her asking questions, Bella couldn't help but pose the one in the back of her mind. "Do you know if Helene and Harold Horton ever stepped out together?"

The older man's brow furrowed as if in deep concentration. "That would have been many years back. But I recall seeing the two of them in his motor car on a few occasions. I believe they were in the same class." A tap sounded at the office door. "Come in," Doc called out.

Mrs. Smedlay, a slender blonde in her early fifties, stepped inside. She smiled at Bella and Jax before turning her attention to her husband. "I'm sorry to interrupt, but your next appointment is here, dear."

"I just had one more question. How is Mr. Smith doing?" Jax asked.

Doc looked grim. "Not as well as I hoped he would. This morning, I called the hospital to check. He may still come out of this, but he's weak and often asleep."

"I see." Jax frowned.

"I hope you do," Doc said. "He isn't up to any questions, but I'll let you know when he is."

"I'd appreciate it." Jax got to his feet and extended his hand to the doctor. "Thank you for your time, sir, and for the information."

"If I can offer more help, don't hesitate to contact me."

Chapter Nineteen

Once Bella and Jax were outside, she turned to him. "I feel terrible for Helene. It sounds like she's had an unhappy life with Gus."

"It sure does," Jax agreed. The more he learned, the more troubled he became. An idea had formed in his mind when Doc revealed Helene might have lost a baby shortly after her marriage. Jax just wasn't sure how to divulge his thoughts to Bella. He didn't want to offend her sensibilities.

Bella cleared her throat before speaking again. "I wondered..." Her voice trailed off, and she glanced away.

Jax turned to face her. "Wondered what?"

Twin splotches of pink bloomed in her cheeks. "When Doc said Helene might have lost a child shortly after she wed Gus. Well, I wondered...he was so much older, and she was only out of high school."

He studied her expression for a moment. "You're wondering the same thing I am, I think."

The color in her cheeks intensified. "If Helene had gone to college as she planned, she probably would have sold the farm. It doesn't sound like Gus could have afforded to buy it, and the next owner may not have kept him on."

"That could have been on his mind," Jax agreed.

Bella chewed on her lower lip. "I wonder how he talked her into marrying him. I know Jacob said Gus was good-looking back then, but he was a lot older than Helene. Do you think...well, I suppose he could have forced her and when she found out about the baby, she felt like she had to marry him?" The last words came out in a rush.

A long sigh escaped Jax. "I'm afraid it seems all too possible. If she was in a family way, Helene probably saw no choice. Gus certainly doesn't sound like a doting husband, so it's hard to believe he courted her with any finesse."

"It's more like she leaned on him because he was the only one there for her. Then, he either forced her or seduced her. Neither is a good basis for marriage."

"You're right. I've certainly learned a lot more about Mrs. Schwarz today. We'll have a number of details to go over back at the office."

"Do you want to talk with Harold now?"

A short silence preceded Jax's answer. "I thought we had an understanding that you weren't asking questions, just taking notes. You already questioned Doc about Helene and Harold." Although the words could have been construed as criticism, he kept his voice and expression benign. Until he had a solid suspect, Jax wouldn't stop worrying about her. Admitting that wasn't likely to dissuade Bella, though. A series of emotions crossed her face, and he braced for an argument. When none came, he relaxed.

"Yes, well, I've been wondering about her reaction to you interviewing him, and about him disliking Gus so much. I can't help but feel there might have been more between them than being schoolmates. Now, we know there was." Bella grinned.

Jax's lips twitched as he tried to repress a smile. "We know they were in his automobile more than once. That hardly makes them sweethearts. As far as talking with

Harold, I think I should see him by myself, Bella. Considering what we know, and what you imagine, he may not be comfortable if you're there."

A frown blanketed her face. "I took a lot of my notes in shorthand, so I'll have to transcribe them. I can do that before I head home."

He only considered turning her down for a moment. "I'd appreciate it."

"I'm happy to help."

***

Both Nolen and Jenkins were in the constable's office when Jax and Bella arrived. "How did your interviews go?" the older lawman asked once the pair had removed their coats and gloves.

Jax glanced at Bella before replying. "Pretty well. In fact, we learned quite a bit about Helene Schwarz. I'm not sure it will lead us to the killer, but it's worth going over. Bella is going to transcribe her notes. Then, we can get started on putting everything together."

Bella looked around the outer office. "I thought your wife would be with you."

"She's in town and should be here shortly. Since the hotel is closed, we took a room at the boardinghouse for a few days. That will be easier than driving back and forth to Karston, especially if there's more snow," Jenkins replied.

Bella nodded, went into Jax's office, and started working on the notes. She was just wrapping up when Jax tapped on the door. "You don't have to knock in your own space," she said with a smile. Spending the afternoon with him had been more pleasant than she'd imagined. Almost, but not quite, like when they were kids. Jax had been at Ballantyne every summer day and, although he'd come as her brother's friend, he'd quickly become her friend, too. Her friend and her champion. Jax, as much as Matt, had encouraged and supported Bella.

He offered a matching smile. "I wondered if you were almost finished."

"All finished actually." Bella leaned back in the hard chair.

"Mrs. Jenkins is here, and she's going to join us since, as her husband says, she has good insight." He hesitated before continuing. "You have good insight, too, so I wondered if you could stay a little longer."

"I'd be happy to stay."

Within moments, the Jenkinses and Nolen joined Bella and Jax. Mrs. Jenkins was a slim woman in her early fifties. Her blonde hair, cut in a stylish bob similar to Bella's own hairdo, held only a few traces of gray. Her gray-green eyes sparkled as she smiled at the younger woman. "You must be Arabella. I'm so pleased to meet you."

"Thank you, Mrs. Jenkins. It's good to meet you, as well."

"Please call me Jenny." The senior constable's wife took the chair next to Bella while her husband settled on her other side. Her gaze went around the table. "All of you."

Nolen sat across the table which left Jax with the seat next to Bella. "Where do you think we should start, Senior Constable?"

"If everyone is calling my wife by her first name, I think all of you should call me Richard." A grin curved the older man's face, but his attention was on Jenny, not the others.

"Certainly." Jax nodded, pulled a notepad off his desk, and handed it to Bella. "Maybe you could re-copy the list as we go and add any new notes?"

"Of course." Bella couldn't repress a smile. This was going far better than she imagined, and she thanked her lucky stars that Mrs. Jenkins—Jenny—was with them. Otherwise, Bella wasn't sure if Jax would be amenable to her continued participation. Just because the last few hours had been pleasant didn't mean he was willing to prolong the situation.

Richard looked back at him. "Did you learn anything particularly important?"

"We got some interesting details, and a little hard evidence." Jax briefly reviewed their meetings.

"So, Eddington, Meyers, and Jones are out," Richard said.

"Unless they're hiding weapons or could borrow a motorcycle easily, yes," was Jax's response. "I'll have Nolen talk with Annabelle to double-check Jacob's story, but I think it's solid. Besides, while he could have walked to Schwarz place, it would be a hard slog in the dark, and that wouldn't explain the tire track by the road. On the other hand, Wyatt and Curt have pistols and bikes. Harold has a revolver, and his brother has a motorcycle. Garlan bought Eric's machine, but we don't know about a gun. Owen has a handgun, but no bike."

Jenkins responded. "I spoke with Owen, and he sold his pistol a few months ago."

Bella looked up. "Who bought it?"

"Louis Thomley," Richard replied. "We stopped out there, and he's not back from his son's place yet, but a neighbor was tending his animals. According to the man, Louis may not be back until later today or tomorrow."

"I don't see Mr. Thomley as a suspect," Nolen said. "He wouldn't be playing pranks on Mr. Schwarz, even if he didn't have a sprained ankle."

"I agree," Jax added, "but Garlan was there until early that morning, and knowing Louis bought Owen's pistol makes me uneasy."

The deputy's brow furrowed. "I used to help Mr. Thomley with chores when I was in school," Nolen put in. "He had a shotgun and a revolver back then. He kept both locked up. Said his wife insisted they were put away. A cousin of hers shot himself playing with a gun when they were kids."

"Mrs. Thomley died a few years ago," Bella added. "I wonder if he's still careful."

"We need to find out," Jax said, his expression grim.

The senior constable put his elbows on the table and leaned forward. "Let's review the information about Garlan."

"From what I know," Jax began, "when he first got here a year ago, he tried going to school but it didn't work out. He got in some fights. According to what we've heard, he claims other boys started the brawls. They say differently." He briefly reviewed Garlan's flight from Belgium.

"After what he experienced, it wouldn't be hard to understand why he had problems," Jenny observed.

"You said the uncle was outspoken about Germany. Has the boy ever expressed any anger toward Germans?" Jenkins asked.

"Not that I've heard," Jax said with a frown. "What about you, Nolen? Do you know anything?"

The younger man shook his head. "No, I don't. Garlan seldom talks to anyone. I tried a couple of times, but he barely acknowledged me."

Uneasiness played along Jax's nerve ends. "My mother often used the adage *still water runs deep.*" For a moment, he hesitated. "Right now, I'd say we have to focus on Harold, Curt, Wyatt, and Garlan."

"From what we now know, I concur. Let's review alibis and possible motives," Richard suggested. "How about starting with Harold Horton?"

Bella glanced back over the earlier notes from the group. "Harold always opens the station at seven o'clock, and the murder must have taken place around that time or a bit later. We don't know exactly when, but Mrs. Schwarz found Gus shortly after nine, and I was on the scene by nine-thirty."

Jax drummed his fingers on the table. "Harold said he opened, but we can't be sure if he was there at seven and stayed. Unfortunately, he says his first customer didn't come until after nine o'clock."

"Since it was Christmas Eve morning, that doesn't seem surprising," Richard said.

"No, it doesn't," Jax agreed, "but it means we can't clear Harold."

Richard nodded. "Even though we can't be sure if he had opportunity, it would help if we knew more about his possible motive."

"We know he and Helene went around together a little. I'll talk to Harold again tomorrow. I don't know if he'll admit much, or even if there's anything to admit, but we also found out a lot more about Helene and Gus." Jax briefly summarized what they had heard from Jones and Doc about the Schwarz marriage and about Doc's comments on Helene and Harold.

"That poor girl," Jenny murmured.

Her husband nodded. "If you're going to see Horton, I'll head out to the Thomley place in the morning. With luck, he'll be back."

"Good," Jax replied. "I'm anxious to hear what he says about storing his guns, especially the pistol." He looked at his deputy. "It will be up to you to open the office tomorrow."

"Yes, sir," Nolen quickly agreed.

"What about Curt?" Bella asked. "Are you going to talk with him again?"

"No. He was very cooperative, so there's nothing more to ask yet. Talking to Horton, Thomley, Windsor, and Dubois are my primary concern right now," Jax replied. "We can wait a bit to talk with Wyatt again. As far as I know, he has no motive to bother Schwarz, let alone kill him."

"I can't see any, either," Richard said.

Noise in the outer office stopped the exchange. After a moment, Mayor Cawlings appeared at the door. "What have we here?" he asked, his attention focusing on the two women.

"We're going over all of the evidence, Mayor," Jenkins told him. "Five heads are better than one."

The mayor's dark eyes widened in surprise. "You're discussing the case with the ladies?" The question indicated dismay.

Bella stiffened with annoyance, but she remained silent since no words of hers were likely to mollify Cawlings. Before she'd left for France, the man had told her parents being an Army Signal Corps operator was no job for a young lady, and they should keep her at home. Luckily, her mother and father had been more modern in their thinking than the mayor. Not that Bella had asked for their permission. After all, she had been of age.

Jenkins smiled but replied in a firm tone. "My wife has worked with me on cases in the past, and Arabella was able to take notes for Jax. She knows shorthand, an invaluable skill. Unfortunately, we law officers seldom have it."

Bella noticed the senior constable didn't mention Jax's wounds and why help was advisable. He also made it sound like both she and Jenny were highly qualified to assist. A small smile formed on her lips as the mayor slowly nodded.

"Yes, well, I'm glad you have good help," Cawlings said.

"It's especially important," Jenkins continued, "since your department is so small. I don't know how Jax and Nolen manage on a daily basis, let alone handle a murder."

When a dark flush crept into the mayor's face, Bella had to bite her lip to keep from laughing. Senior Constable Jenkins knew how to handle the politician.

"Are you honing in on the killer?" the mayor asked.

"We've made excellent progress," Jenkins assured him. "Jax has developed some good leads. The rest of us are here to assist him, as needed."

"Wonderful," the mayor said before bidding them farewell and leaving the office.

Jax grinned at Jenkins. "I wish I had your skill in handling the man."

"You will in time, Jax. You will in time."

A round of chuckles ensued as the group acknowledged the humor.

Chapter Twenty

Because it was late when the group finally dispersed and the usual constable's work still needed to be done, further interviews were delayed until the following day. Again that night, Jax slept little. His mind was too filled with the case. Unfortunately, none of his ruminations helped.

Early the next day, Jax went directly to the filling station where he found Harold Horton working on a car. "Good morning," he said after walking into the garage area.

Surprise flashed across the other man's face. "Good morning. Do you need a fill-up?"

"No, I just wanted to talk with you again."

Horton frowned. "I've already said everything I know, lieutenant."

The use of his military rank registered with Jax as a tacit way of keeping their old connection, especially since Harold had not used the title in recent months. "Bella and I learned some new information yesterday afternoon, and I wanted to get your view."

Harold wiped his hands with a rag before tossing it aside and gesturing to the station's office. "We might as well sit down."

Jax followed him to the tiny room tucked away between the garage and front area. Once Horton settled behind a battered desk, Jax took the chair opposite him. "I talked with Jacob Jones and Doc Smedlay yesterday. Jacob said he'd been at the Schwarz place last spring and saw Helene outside doing chores. He noticed bruises on her. I wondered if you ever saw any marks."

"How would I know anything about that? Helene rarely came to town over the past few years, so I seldom saw her, but I already said as much."

The words didn't match his angry expression. Even worse, his former sergeant's lack of candor troubled Jax. "But she was here last year shortly after you came home." He made it a statement, not a question.

Harold's eyes widened, and he cleared his throat. "Yes, about a week later." He focused his attention on the scarred desk as he spoke. "Gus goes out of town to hunt with his cousins in the fall, and Helene came to town for something, not to see me."

"Didn't she also want to know how you were doing?" Jax was casting bait and hoping to catch something big. He still didn't want to think his former sergeant was a murderer, but Harold wasn't being candid, and he needed to know why.

A half-shrug lifted one of Horton's broad shoulders as he glanced back at Jax. "She asked, but everyone did. It's a small town, and most people appreciated our service."

The responses were sparse, which only increased Jax's uneasiness and suspicion. "Has she been to see you since then?"

The other man shifted uneasily in his seat. "She stopped last month when Gus was hunting with his cousins again. They pick him up, so she had the truck."

"You said the vehicle was broken down in their yard."

Harold cleared his throat as a look of dismay crossed his face. "It broke down some time after she was here. She came in due to a noise issue. Vehicles can be loud. When someone seldom drives, noise can bother them. That's why she stopped both times."

Jax nodded, as if in agreement, but anxiety plagued him. Not for one moment did he believe sounds from the Schwarz vehicle had drawn Mrs. Schwarz to the garage on two separate occasions. "You said she was too good for Gus, so I suppose you didn't think much of her marrying him."

The other man's gaze again flitted away from Jax. "I didn't think much about it at all. Her parents were gone, and he worked on the farm. I guess it was the only way she could keep the place."

"Didn't she plan to go to school to become a teacher?"

After a moment, Harold's attention returned to Jax and darted away again. "She thought she wanted to be a teacher, but once her parents passed, Helene had the farm to consider. As I said, marrying Schwarz was a way to keep it."

The answers weren't in line with the comments of others who thought Gus might have forced Helene into marriage. Perhaps his former sergeant didn't share that suspicion. If he didn't, he had less motive to kill Schwarz. "Do you still have that pistol?"

Harold's ruddy face lost its color. "I do."

Jax thought he probably looked pale himself. "Where do you keep it?"

"I bring to the station with me. It's in the bottom desk drawer." Although the gun was an arm's length away, Horton didn't reach for it.

A sigh escaped Jax. "I'd like to see it." The other man's reply was a stiff nod.

For several moments after Harold handed the pistol to him. Jax looked over the weapon. It wasn't in good shape. The butt end was battered, but it was clean and empty of bullets. "When did you last use it?"

"On the twenty-third. My nephew was here, and I showed it to him. Told him to keep any weapon clean and safely stored away." Harold paused. "He's ten now. My sister-in-law said it's okay for him to learn to shoot, and my brother asked me to teach him."

Jax nodded. Most boys that age were interested in firearms, but troublesome thoughts still filled his mind. "Speaking of your brother, I haven't seen him riding his motorcycle lately."

Harold grimaced. "He crashed it a couple of weeks ago when the roads were wet. Ran off into the soft ground. He was okay. So was the bike, but his wife don't want him riding in bad weather, so it's here for the winter."

The response only increased Jax's apprehension. "Can I see it?"

Again, Harold paused before answering. "Sure." In silence, he led the way to the back of the garage.

Seeing the bike only added to Jax's worry and frustration. He'd learned nothing that pinpointed Harold as Gus' killer, but he'd discovered nothing to clear him, either.

When a vehicle pulled into the station, Harold immediately turned away. "I got to get to work." He headed toward the door and then paused to briefly glance back at Jax. "I don't know nothing else. I didn't see Helene much for years. First, she was married and second, I was in France. Like I said, she stopped when Gus was away but only because of the truck." He walked out to the pumps without a backward glance.

With a sigh, Jax went back to his Chummy and headed toward Ballantyne. He planned to use seeing Curt as an excuse for his visit, but what he really wanted was Bella's opinion on his exchange with Harold. He didn't let himself consider how foolish the impulse was. It would be so very easy to fall back into their old, familiar pattern. Too easy. If they were friends again, she would eventually want to talk about Matt and that day in France. Hiding the truth about his role in her brother's death would be impossible then. As impossible as revealing it was now.

***

After parking in front of the inn, Jax mounted the porch steps two at a time and entered the building to find Bella behind the front desk. Surprise flashed in her chocolate gaze when she saw him.

"Good morning. What brings you out so early?"

Jax closed the distance between them. "I wanted to talk with Curt, if he's around."

Her brow furrowed into a worried frown. "He and Carl are out cutting down some trees. A few fell victim to the heavy, wet snow. Since the weather is a bit better, they decided today was a good time to clear them. They'll be back for lunch in about an hour."

"I see," he replied. "I suppose I could wait. In the meantime, if you have a few minutes, I'd like to discuss something with you."

"Of course. Why don't we sit in the kitchen? It's warmer there, and I have a pot of coffee on the stove."

"Sounds good."

Jax followed Bella to the other room, waited for her to bring two cups of coffee, held her chair, and sat down himself. Once they were settled, she turned a speculative look on him. "What did you want to talk about?"

After a long sip of the hot brew, Jax replied. "I went to see Harold this morning."

"What did he have to say?" Bella asked with obvious anticipation.

"I asked him about Helene Schwarz. She's actually stopped at the station at least twice. Evidently, Gus and the cousins go hunting every year. They pick him up, which leaves the truck with Helene. Harold indicated she was worried about some noise from it, but having the same thing happen twice is odd, especially a year apart. More than that, he said she showed the same interest in his wounds as any of the other townspeople. I'm not sure I believed him." Jax wanted to get Bella's impression of this information before mentioning details about the pistol and the motorcycle.

Bella's brow furrowed. "I don't think he was completely honest with you, either. Helene stopping twice when Gus was gone is interesting."

Jax nodded. "It is. But another issue bothers me. The grip of his pistol is badly battered, and it's been cleaned recently. He's been teaching his nephew to shoot, or so he said."

Bella traced the rim of her cup with one forefinger. "Those things don't help eliminate him."

"No, they don't, and his brother's motorcycle is being stored at the station over the winter."

"Did you ask Harold if he'd been riding it?"

"No, because if he isn't being honest about his feelings for Helene, I'm sure he'd lie about that."

"You're right."

Jax cleared his throat before voicing another issue. "Last night, I went over everything in my mind. You know, what Jacob and Doc said about Helene possibly being beaten, and about what you and I discussed."

"That Gus put her in a compromising situation so they had to marry." Bella's voice was soft and subdued.

He nodded. "Doc seemed unsure, and I don't think it was widely suspected in the community, but she and Harold went to school together. Knowing she's gone to see him twice when her husband was out of town and knowing she and Harold were classmates, I thought he might suspect why she married Gus. If he does know, he would have been furious, I'm sure. He looked very angry when I mentioned Jacob seeing bruises on her."

"I can see him being upset, but furious?"

Jax released a pent-up breath. Bella didn't know why he'd considered that to be likely, so Jax went on. "In France, we were driving the Germans back when we came to a farm. Harold was my sergeant then, and he went ahead into the barn to make sure no enemy soldiers were there. He found a young French girl who had been badly abused by German soldiers. He was well ahead of us, so he was with her for a while before the rest of the platoon arrived. We were all shocked and sickened, but Harold was particularly affected.

He was holding her and singing to her like you would a little baby, and she was letting him. I can't explain it, but there was a bond there. She seemed to see him as an angel who came to save her, and he definitely felt like he was her guardian. We got her to a field hospital, but Harold didn't forget the girl. In fact, he was determined to kill as many Germans as possible to avenge her. That's how he got badly wounded. He was trying to take out a sniper's nest."

"How awful." Bella grasped her coffee cup tighter.

While he had spoken, Bella's gaze widened in shock while the color drained from her face. Regret filled him. "I shouldn't have said so much."

She shook her head. "We heard of such incidents with German soldiers and both Belgian and French girls. They did terrible things to some of the women." She paused to take a drink of coffee. "Do you think Harold thought of Helene when he saw the girl in France?"

Jax slumped back in his chair. "That occurred to me last night when I couldn't sleep. The girl was small and blonde like Mrs. Schwarz. She was younger, probably about eighteen."

"Around the same age that Helene was when she lost her parents and married Gus."

A sigh left Jax. "That's right. Everything considered, including your insight, I have to wonder about the two of them." Bella's grin revealed her satisfaction over his admission, but he had to admit that gut feelings mixed with hard facts might yield better results.

"And you were up all night mulling this over?"

Warmth invaded his face. "Not all night." When her lips twitched, Jax nodded. "A lot of the night."

Bella's teeth toyed with her lower lip. "It could be a clue. Do you think Curt will know anything?"

Because Jax didn't want to admit his primary purpose was to talk with her, not Curt, he shrugged. "He might have some insight since he was only a year behind them in school. Of course, we can't eliminate him, either, so he could lie."

"Is there anyone else who would have been in school with them who might be helpful?"

"The classes were small, as you know. Only thirty or forty in a grade, and not everyone finished school. Several died, a couple in France and a couple from influenza, and some moved away, I doubt if there's more than a handful left here. I'll talk to Curt and see what he knows. With luck, I might be able to find something of substance to move the case forward." Jax yawned. "Sorry."

"You must have left for the office very early."

He nodded. "I did. I woke up around five o'clock and couldn't get back to sleep. I drove by the boardinghouse and didn't see Windsor's car. He parks in the driveway, so it would be there if they got home last night. Nolen is covering the office this morning, but I spoke with him briefly and also with Richard. Richard and Jenny went by the Thomley place after our meeting broke up, but they still didn't find anyone at home."

Bella frowned. "Maybe he'll be back today."

Jax shrugged. "I hope so. I really want to know about the pistol he bought from Owen. Jenny and Richard will drive out again this morning. We'll all meet at the office around one o'clock."

Several moments passed before Bella spoke. "When you say *we,* does that include me?"

Jax hesitated before replying. "I can't expect you to use all your time helping us."

"I don't have much to do here right now, and finding the killer is important to the future of Moreley, which means it's also important to Ballantyne."

"If you're sure..."

"I'm very sure."

Chapter Twenty-One

While Bella went about fixing the noon meal, Jax drank more coffee. They engaged in only casual conversation, especially after Mac joined them.

"Good to see you, lad," the older man said as he took a seat at the table. "How is the case going?"

"Not that well," Jax admitted. "I want to talk to Curt. He may have some useful information. At least, I hope so."

"I saw him and Carl coming this way, so they should be here shortly," Mac said as he settled at the table. The brothers appeared only moments later. Curt stopped just inside the back door, a look of concern on his face. "What brings you out, lieutenant?"

"Just to get more information," Jax replied in a reassuring tone. "Maybe we can talk after lunch, if Bella is willing to take notes for me again."

"Of course, I'm willing," she said as she put a tureen of soup on the table. Shortly after that, Bella brought a tray of sandwiches before settling back in the chair she had vacated.

Mac was the first one to finish eating, and he announced his plan to nap. "'Tis nay something I can do during the season."

A short time after that, Carl stated the same idea. "We got all of the damaged trees down, so I think I'll have a rest, too."

That left Bella, Jax, and Curt at the table. The constable pulled a pad and pencil from his pocket and handed both to Bella who took the items with a smile.

Curt watched the exchange before saying, "I spoke with Senior Constable Jenkins and his wife yesterday afternoon. I didn't know nothing more to tell them than I said earlier. I still don't."

"I'm not here about those interviews," Jax assured the other man. "I wanted to ask you a few questions about Helene Schwarz."

"About Helene? Why?" A look of confusion blanketed Curt's face.

"You were just behind her in school, weren't you?" Jax inquired.

"Yes, but what does that have to do with Gus' murder?"

"I don't know that it does, but do you remember her very well?" Jax asked.

A half-shrug lifted one of Curt's shoulders. "She was a pretty, smart girl. In the lower grades, she wore her hair in braids. Some of the boys liked to pull them, just to get her attention." His expression softened. "Never made a fuss about it. She would have made a good teacher. Too bad she married Gus instead." The gloom returned to his face.

"Why do you say it was too bad?" Jax asked.

"The difference in ages, for one." Curt paused for a moment while he glanced at Bella. "I don't exactly know how to say this, don't know if it's true or not, that's why I never have."

"Say what?" Bella asked as she stopped taking notes. "Do you know anything about why Helene married Gus?"

Color suffused Curt's lean face, and he glanced at Jax, who nodded. "Our ma sometimes worked for the Culpeppers. Mostly, when they had company or during threshing season when extra hands came. She worked there pretty regular when Mrs. Culpepper was ill, and Ma got worried about how Gus was acting like the farm was his. He bossed Ma around and, when Helene tried to intercede, he said to take care of her mother. He'd handle the help."

"So, you think she married him because he took over most of the responsibilities?" Bella posed the question with a quizzical expression on her face.

Curt massaged his forehead. "Not really. Something happened I haven't forgot. My ma was talking with a friend. I was coming down the stairs when I heard them, so I stopped and listened. Shouldn't have, but I was young and curious. She told her friend that Gus might have taken advantage of Helene, if you know what I mean." The color in his face intensified.

Jax cleared his throat. "I believe we do."

The other man stared into his coffee cup. "He was a terrible bully, although my ma said he hid it well enough from Mr. and Mrs. Culpepper, and even from Helene until after her mother died. The woman wasn't in her grave a month when the two of them got married." Curt's fingers tightened on his cup. "I never spoke about it, not even to Carl, because Ma said I shouldn't. She didn't want no one gossiping about why Helene married him, especially when...well, when she didn't have a child after all."

"Do you know if Helene had another sweetheart before Gus?" Jax didn't want to present the idea that Harold and Helene might have been stepping out in case it led Curt to echo the possibility instead of offering it on his own.

A slight smile tugged at Curt's lips. "Most of the boys in school admired Helene. Harold drove her around some. Back then, he was one of the few with an automobile. You know his pa was a blacksmith, but he took to motor cars right away. Started fixing them along with wagons. Harold worked with him and got a vehicle as soon as he could. Culpeppers had one of the first automobiles in town, so Helene was used to the convenience. Anyhow, Harold started taking her places shortly before their class graduated. I don't know that Mr. Culpepper would have considered him good enough for his daughter, but I think Harold would have gotten his approval before Gus."

Bella and Jax exchanged a glance while Curt was talking. In her eyes, Jax saw the same interest that he felt. But what did it all mean? At present, he couldn't make a clear connection.

"Did your mother work for Helene and Gus after they were married?" Jax hoped this might elicit additional details.

"For a very short time," Curt replied with a grim expression. "She wanted to stay on, and Helene wanted her to." Again, he looked uncomfortable. "Ma felt sure Helene with was child."

Jax recalled Doc's observation that Helene might have lost several babies. "What about your mother's friend? Do you remember who she told?"

"Mrs. Carruthers."

Hope that this would be a lead disappeared. "She died from influenza, didn't she?" Jax asked.

Curt nodded. "Carl said she was one of the first to get it, but her health was never good."

"And you don't think your mother told anyone else?"

"I'm sure Ma didn't. She only told Mrs. Carruthers because she was the minister's wife. From what I heard, Ma didn't even want Pastor Carruthers to know. She didn't want to hurt Helene," Curt concluded.

"I can understand that," Jax told him. "Thank you for talking with us."

A worried expression settled on Curt's face. "You won't tell no one, will you? I don't want to hurt Helene, either."

"I may have to share it with Jenkins and Nolen, but I won't tell anyone else."

"Neither will I," Bella assured him.

Curt merely nodded in response, but his expression was troubled.

Fresh apprehension filled Jax, but he went ahead with the next question on his mind. "Has your regard for Helene affected how you feel toward Gus?"

A look of confusion crossed the other man's face. "I'm not sure what you mean."

Jax glanced at Bella, but her head was bowed so he couldn't see her expression. "I know you didn't like how Gus talked to the boys, but is that the only reason you've confronted him at times? Or did what you surmised about him and Helene enter into it?"

"Lieutenant, I haven't liked Schwarz since I was a kid. He bullied my brother every chance he got. He, a grown man, picking on a boy. So, I had more than one reason to dislike him. I can't say I thought about Helene or Carl when Gus was ranting about us getting over the war." Curt shook his head. "Like we ever will."

"I can't argue with that," Jax said.

Curt nodded. "Any other questions?"

"Not right now," Jax replied. "Thanks for your time."

***

When Bella and Jax were alone in the kitchen, she laid down the pencil and leaned back in her chair. "Curt has more than one reason to dislike Gus," she observed in a troubled tone.

"Yes, he does. I had no idea that Mrs. Molitor ever worked for the Culpeppers."

"I didn't, either. I barely remember Helene's father, although I recall her mother. Mrs. Culpepper was petite with blonde hair and blue eyes like Helene, and she had a French accent. I found her speech so charming. I think that's how I first got interested in taking French in high school."

Jax studied her for a moment. "It seems like Helene would have taken French, as well. Of course, she probably learned from her mother at home but, not many schools had a French teacher like Moreley did. Unfortunately, Miss Lavigne moved away a couple of years ago."

Bella chewed on her lower lip. "I wonder where she is now. She might know more about Helene and other beaus."

"I can ask the principal, I suppose. He'll be home from school this week. He may know something about Anthony Windsor and Gus and about Garlan's fights at school."

"You're right, and Principal Fike would know where Miss Lavigne went. Also, he was a teacher when Helene and Harold were in high school, so he might know if the two of them were sweet on one another," Bella suggested.

"That's a good point," Jax agreed before hesitating. He briefly looked down at his plate and back at her. "Would you mind going with me to see Mr. Fike?"

A grin lit Bella's face as amusement sparkled in her eyes. "Afraid he'll remember some of your schoolroom antics?"

His lips quirked. "I didn't engage in antics. Remember, my mother was a teacher and everything I said and did, for better or worse, got reported to her immediately. Just as bad, with a father who was the town constable, I knew I'd be punished as soon as he got home."

Bella's good humor fled. "Your father didn't hit you, did he?" The idea had never before occurred to her. Now, she wondered why it hadn't. Jax's father had been a stern man.

"His punishment was much worse than that. He'd bar me from coming to Ballantyne for a week, sometimes longer. No matter what time of year it was, I hated being away from here for more than a day or two."

The admission slipped past her defenses and confusion. "You are still welcome here, Jax. I know you said it's hard to come and not be able to pursue your dreams. It has to be difficult, but you are welcome."

He glanced down at his empty coffee cup. "It has to be hard for you," he murmured, his voice barely audible. "The memories and the losses. I'm sorry about your parents. I should have said so right away. I should have written to you."

A lump of emotion rose in her throat, and Bella swallowed hard to dislodge it. After her brother's death, she hadn't expected to hear from Jax when her mother and then, her father had passed. She'd hoped, though. "Thank you," she murmured, simply because nothing else came to mind. "I should have come home sooner. Part of the reason I stayed in Europe was not being able to face coming back. Ida was kind to stay with me, but I think it was hard for her, too, because she'd lost Alan." Her friend's fiancé had died only days after her own brother, so they had grieved together.

Jax frowned. "Did Ida see Alan when they were both in France?"

Bella blinked at the change in topic. "When we first arrived, we were in Paris for a few weeks. You remember that." When he nodded, she continued. "As soon as all of you got to France, Alan somehow managed to visit the city for a couple of days. Ida was so pleased." A smile curved her lips as she recalled her friend's happy surprise at seeing her intended. "They both had leave at the same time once after that. Then, it became hard for Alan to even write to Ida, and he said getting close to our billet or meeting her on leave was impossible."

"I'm sure he did," Jax muttered.

Confused by his tone and words, Bella asked, "He did try, you mean?"

Jax stared into his coffee cup. "Yes, of course. It's good you and Ida were together."

"Yes, it was," Bella replied. "There was so much loss and devastation in France and Belgium that our own sorrows didn't seem so unusual. Coming home...well, it is different. But I'm glad to be here, and every day gets a little easier."

"I'm happy to hear that."

The rough quality of his voice was at odds with the sentiment, and it set Bella to wondering again. She wanted to ask why he'd turned away from her instead of offering solace after Matt's death, but she feared another withdrawal. While Jax had always been a bit reserved, he'd never been moody. Time in the trenches had changed other men. How could it not have altered him? She and Jax were working well together. Why spoil that by introducing possibly provocative topics? Besides, she had no claim on him and never had. Instead, she focused on matters at hand. "I'll just clean up the lunch dishes. Then, we can visit Mr. Fike."

***

Although Jax offered to help clean up, Bella suggested he relax in the lobby instead. As tired as he felt, agreement came easily. Unfortunately, although his body yearned for rest, his mind continued to whirl. He'd nearly slipped when talking about Alan Brewster and the secret he'd vowed to keep for the man.

Jax slumped back in one of the leather chairs. Growing up, he'd learned that honesty was the only, not simply the best, policy and Jax had lived the adage. Now, he was hiding two truths from Bella, which was basically the same as dishonesty. Only one of the two would hurt her, but the other could hurt her friend Ida. Besides, he'd made a solemn vow to keep quiet. Just because Alan was dead didn't mean Jax should break his promise.

Restless and haunted, he was happy to see Bella emerge from the kitchen with her coat on. "Ready to go?" she asked with a smile.

"Yes," he replied with what he hoped was good humor. "I have the Chummy parked in front." Since they'd be in town where more people would see them, Jax preferred to drive because he didn't want to be seen as weak or needy. Not when several councilmen, including Fike, found him to be lacking as a constable.

After a moment's hesitation, Bella nodded. Then, they were off.

***

A short time later, they pulled to a stop in front of the principal's house. Located across the street from the red brick school, it was a similar, but smaller, building. A white picket fence surrounded the front yard and neat, white trellises climbed the brick on either side of a long porch.

When Bella saw smoke coming out of the chimney, she said, "It looks like they're home." Jax's response was to move slowly toward the house. "Is there really some reason you don't want to talk with the principal?" she asked as they made their way up the front walk.

He stopped at the base of the porch steps, glanced at the door, and back at her. "You already know four of the council members voted against me. Fike was at a recent meeting with the mayor, so I know he's one of them."

"He is?" Dismay flashed through Bella. "It can't be because you were a poor student or a troublemaker. He couldn't have disliked your mother because she was a lovely woman and a fine teacher, and if he had gotten in trouble with the law, the whole town would know, so he has no reason to hold a grudge against your father. It simply doesn't make sense."

A half-smile tugged at one corner of Jax's mouth. "He doesn't think I'm qualified, and neither do the other three who voted against me. They know I always said I'd never become a lawman."

Immediately, Bella felt angry on his behalf. "That doesn't mean you aren't capable." He was doing a good job. Anyone could see that.

His smile became broader. "I know we've agreed to forget about our unpleasant exchange on Christmas Eve, but you seemed to think I wasn't highly competent then. It's hard to believe you completely changed your mind."

"I can admit when I'm wrong," she replied before mounting the steps and knocking on the door.

It soon opened to reveal a middle-aged man clad in navy trousers and a roll-neck sweater. His dark gaze narrowed on Bella before recognition flared. "Arabella Stewart. I had heard you were home." He offered his sympathies on her losses, but his kindly expression soon turned to a frown when he looked over her shoulder. "Hastings, what brings you here?"

Bella responded before Jax had a chance. "The constable wants to ask a few questions, and I'm here to take notes for him. You might remember me taking shorthand. It was wonderful that Mrs. Ingram taught it for a semester every year. Not many schools the size of Moreley had such courses. Or still do." She knew she was babbling, but Bella wanted to thwart a rebuff from the principal. In addition, she hoped to keep the man from openly criticizing Jax. "I hope we can take a few minutes of your time."

Fike looked as if he wanted to refuse but, after a moment, he stepped back and opened the door wider. "Come in."

He waved them into his library. Three walls of the small room were lined with books while the other one boasted a stone fireplace flanked by windows. The overall effect was one of cozy comfort, yet their host's expression remained cold.

"Thank you," Bella said as she took one of the leather arm chairs facing a mahogany desk sitting in front of the back wall. Fike seated himself, and Jax took the seat next to her.

"We won't impose on you for long," Jax said.

Fike scowled at him. "Good. My wife will be home soon, and we plan to visit friends yet this afternoon."

Bella found the principal's reaction to Jax unacceptable, but she pulled a notepad and pencil out of her pocketbook before smiling again. Perhaps, she could wear him down so that he willingly—and hopefully, helpfully—answered Jax's questions.

"As you know, I'm investigating Gus Schwarz's murder," Jax began in a calm, controlled tone that Bella had come to recognize as his constable's voice.

"Have you made any progress at all?" Fike asked, his own tone hostile.

"I believe so."

Jax sounded serene, but Bella saw fire flash in his eyes. "A lot of progress has been made," she added. When his gaze met hers, Bella saw the flames bank and fade. She offered him a smile before turning her attention back to the pad in her hands. Jax might chastise her later, but she didn't care. Someone needed to defend him.

"Yes, we have made progress, and I hope I can get some helpful information from you, sir."

"I don't know how I might help, but what do you want to know?" At last, the principal's voice lost some of its edge.

"Do you remember when Helene Schwarz was in high school?" Jax asked.

Fike's expression softened. "Of course. She was one of our best pupils. I thought she would go to normal school and come back to teach for us."

"Do you know why she decided not to go to college?" Jax asked.

The principal rested his elbows on the edge of the desk and steepled his fingers in front of him. "I know she wasn't sure about leaving her mother after her father passed. We had discussed it, and I spoke with Mrs. Culpepper. She encouraged Helene to continue her education. That was a few weeks before Helene's graduation and before her mother fell ill."

"Then, Mrs. Culpepper thought she could run the farm without Helene's help," Jax suggested.

"Actually, Mrs. Culpepper was about to sell the place," the principal replied.

"Was she planning to move to town?" Jax asked.

"I believe so. When I spoke with her in the spring, Mrs. Culpepper said there were a couple of good offers. Helene seemed fine with that decision. Happy, in fact."

"What about Gus? Do you know how he felt?" Jax asked.

A frown furrowed Fike's forehead. "He wasn't happy. Mrs. Culpepper told me as much, but she hoped the new owners would hire him. Gus had no other place to go, and his reputation made it hard for him to find other work."

"Do you know why the Culpeppers kept him on?" Bella inquired.

Fike lightly tapped his forefingers together as he seemed to consider the query. "Mostly, because they felt sorry for him. Old Mr. Schwarz was a nasty drunk. Even before he worked for the Culpeppers, Helene's mother saw to it that Gus always had food and clothing. They couldn't do much about his father's meanness, but none of us could."

A sad sigh escaped Bella. The laws were such that a man could beat his wife and his children without fear of punishment. Not for the first time, she was grateful that her own father, her grandfathers, and Mac were good men who would never harm anyone, especially not a woman or child. Her glance strayed to Jax. Despite the changes in him, he wouldn't, either.

"So, they hired Gus after his father died?" Jax asked.

"He was already doing more work on the farm than his father ever had. Gus needed a job and a place to live. I don't think he showed his mean ways there. Mr. Culpepper would not have countenanced that."

"What about after Mr. Culpepper's death? Do you think Mrs. Culpepper was able to handle Gus?" Jax asked.

"She didn't indicate he was a problem. I don't know if she understood how badly he behaved elsewhere. For that matter, I don't think Helene did, either. Gus was probably nicer to them than to others." The principal glanced from Jax to Bella. "Why so many questions about how Gus came to be at the Culpepper place?"

Bella looked at Jax. When he nodded, she answered. "It seems like they were an odd match. I remember Helene a little. Although she's ten years or so older than I am, I recall her coming to my first and second grade classes to substitute when our teacher was out."

A bright smile softened the principal's face. "Yes, she was one of the pupils mature enough to take over a class. She was always ahead in her own schoolwork, so missing a day never hurt her." His smile faded. "I agree Gus and Helene did not appear to be ideal spouses. He was much older, and he'd left school in the ninth grade. In many places, farm children leave earlier." Fike looked at Jax. "Your mother was important in keeping youngsters with us. Parents listened to her pleas to let their children get as much education as possible. Because of her efforts, we still have a high graduation rate." He paused for a moment. "In many places, married ladies weren't allowed to teach, but we were happy to have your mother return when you started first grade."

Jax smiled. "My mother was a big believer in schooling, but Mr. Schwarz wasn't a good student, from what we've heard."

Fike scowled. "He wasn't interested in learning, and I can't say any of us were sorry to see him go. He was always in trouble. On the other hand, Helene loved learning. Not only that, she was very popular with the faculty and her schoolmates."

"You say she was popular," Jax commented. "Did she have a sweetheart when she was in school?"

Again, the principal smiled. "Many of the boys would have liked to step out with her, but her parents favored her going on to college. We don't have many pupils who continue their studies." He paused to once again tap his fingers as if in concentration. "I seem to recall Harold Horton driving her around town. I'm sure he was smitten and perhaps she felt the same, but her mother got ill shortly after graduation. Helene didn't come to town much during those weeks, and Mrs. Fike and I didn't want to stop and disturb them." He sighed. "I saw Helene at her mother's funeral, and Gus was beside her every moment. A few weeks later, they got married. I didn't understand it then, and I still don't, in all honesty."

"A lot of people don't," Jax admitted, although he didn't reveal what they had already learned.

The principal's expression grew somber. "I always wondered..."

"Wondered what?" Jax put in when the man stopped speaking.

The man's gaze went to his desk top. "I don't like to speak out of turn but, as I said, Gus was always a troublemaker. He got worse these last few years, and I had to wonder how he treated Helene, especially when she seldom came to town."

"It's hard to say," Jax agreed although he had a good idea of how Schwarz had treated his wife. "We've heard Schwarz and Windsor had a longstanding mutual dislike."

Fike looked steadily at Jax. "You must have a good reason for asking all of these questions, Jackson. I thought the main suspects were soldiers, since Gus had run-ins with all of them."

A shrug twisted Jax's shoulders. "They're among those who have been questioned, but so are a few others who argued with Gus recently. I've had a chance to talk with everyone in that category except Anthony Windsor. The Eddingtons said he might be back sometime today. Do you know if he is?"

"I haven't seen him, but he may be home by now." The principal picked up a pencil from his desk and rolled it between his hands. "I wouldn't think of Anthony as a possible suspect although I know he and Gus had a few confrontations over the years and, as you say, a shared dislike."

"We've heard they argued about the war," Bella observed.

Fike nodded in agreement. "Anthony has relatives in England, and his sister married a Belgian army officer, as you probably know. Their son is living with Anthony now."

"I've seen Garlan a few times. Since he was helping Louis Thomley out near the Schwarz place, I want to talk with him, too, in case he saw something that morning." Jax paused for a moment before making another observation. "We heard Garlan attended school here for a time. Did you get to know him well?"

The principal gazed down at his desk again. "I can't say I did. He's quiet and reserved, different from most boys his age, but I'm sure that's a result of what he experienced after the German invasion." Fike drummed his fingers on his chair arms. "He made no friends at all, and he got into a number of fights. Fighting isn't unusual among boys that age, but Garlan was quick to take offense and lash out."

"I've heard Garlan accused the other boys of starting the fights," Jax said.

The principal nodded. "Yes, but the others said Garlan was the one who began punching and kicking them. It took a really bad brawl for Anthony to start teaching him at home."

"How bad was it?" Jax asked, knowing about Garlan's black eye but wondering about the others involved.

A grimace shadowed the principal's face. "The Landon boy had a broken bone in his eye socket, and young Hughes lost two teeth. Garlan's eye was blackened, so he wasn't as badly injured as the others."

Bella gasped. "Garlan caused those injuries?"

"I'm afraid so," the principal replied. "Following the fight, the others had their bicycles stolen. They accused Garlan, but Nick never found any proof...just the destroyed bikes in the woods behind the school."

"I see," Jax murmured. "Do you think Garlan did those things?"

"I don't know, Jackson. I hope not."

Jax was quiet for a moment. "Do you know how the problems between Schwarz and Windsor began?"

"It went back to when Anthony was a new teacher and not much older than Gus." Fike glanced from Jax to Bella. "You know Mr. Windsor is a small man, so many of the boys towered over him. Some tried to intimidate him, and they succeeded. I wasn't the principal then, and old Mr. Bower rarely left his office, so Anthony was on his own. Gus got some other boys to play pranks on Windsor. Once Gus left school, that didn't happen as often but he never stopped entirely. Eventually, Anthony got better with discipline, but there was always hostility between them. The war and Anthony's involvement with the Americanization Committee only increased Gus' dislike for him."

"I thought the committee was formed to help German immigrants learn English and become citizens," Bella observed. "Why would Gus object to that?"

"That was its first focus," Fike agreed. "Some members got carried away with their prejudices. Anthony is from Cincinnati, and the anti-German sentiment was strong there. He became more and more outspoken as the war went on."

"We heard that from Werner Meyers," Jax said.

Fike sighed. "Then, you must know that Werner's in-laws were affected by events in Cincinnati. Mrs. Meyers and their girls experienced some of it themselves. She claimed Anthony was involved in efforts to stop teaching German there, and to remove all books about Germany from city libraries."

"Was he?" Bella asked.

A frown knitted the principal's brow. "He might have been. Anthony goes home in the summer, and he joined with others who were harassing editors and publishers of German language newspapers. Once Gus found out, he confronted Anthony. That was shortly before our boys started to return."

Jax and Bella exchanged a long look before he spoke again, "We hadn't heard any of this."

The older man shrugged. "Anthony didn't make his involvement widely known, probably because it wouldn't have been well received here. I'm sure Gus found out from Mr. and Mrs. Meyers. I only know about the confrontation because Anthony told me himself. He and Gus ran into one another over in Boxwood. Anthony claimed Gus threatened him, and he might have. Garlan was with Anthony at the time and, according to Anthony, the boy started to cry and tremble. That night, and for weeks afterward, he had nightmares. Evidently, no one else saw their quarrel. At least, no one else mentioned it, so I didn't, either."

"This was last winter?" Jax asked.

"Early March, I think."

"Nick never said anything about it," Jax observed.

"It happened in Boxwood, so Anthony didn't tell anyone other than me. I suggested he keep away from Gus and let things die down." Fike shrugged. "I'm not sure that was the best advice, but I haven't heard about other problems since then. Of course, I was away over the summer. Anthony and Garlan left a week or two after we did. By then, Gus had turned his attention to the veterans. As far as I know, Gus and Anthony haven't had any confrontations since last March."

A troubled silence filled the room before Jax spoke again. "May I ask one more question?"

"Of course."

"Do you know where Miss Lavigne went when she left Moreley?" Jax asked.

A smile brightened the older man's face. "Yes, she's at the Boxmore Hill School for Young Ladies."

Bella started in surprise. "That's where my friend Ida went to school. It's only a half-hour drive from here."

"We hated to lose her, but with the drop in population, we weren't able to keep her on full-time," Mr. Fike observed.

"My wife meets Genevieve for lunch in Boxwood occasionally, so I know she only planned to be away for a few days over Christmas. She should be back at school by now. All of the teachers live there, you know."

"I'll try to reach her this afternoon," Jax said, getting to his feet. He extended his hand. "Thank you for your time."

"Of course, Jackson. And she might know when Mr. Windsor will return. They've stayed in touch since she left us." Fike stood and shook Jax's hand before smiling at Bella. "It was good to see both of you."

Chapter Twenty-Two

"You seem to be winning Mr. Fike over," Bella observed once they were back in the car.

Jax shrugged. "He was a lot more helpful than I figured he would be, but I think he was nice because of you."

"I'm not so sure," Bella replied before going back to the case. "I'm surprised about Mr. Windsor being involved in anti-German activities."

"So am I," Jax agreed. "Losing his sister and brother-in-law along with cousins had to affect him."

"Probably, along with comments from his family and friends in Cincinnati." A moment of silence passed before Bella spoke again. "The information about Garlan was interesting." A benign word, but she wondered what Jax thought.

"I agree. I want Nolen to speak with the boys involved in the fights. He's closer to their age and may be able to get information I couldn't."

"That's a good idea. As far as Mr. Windsor, we may learn more from Mademoiselle Lavigne since she's still in contact with him. Perhaps, she knows Garlan, too."

A momentary silence preceded his response. "I was planning to take you back to Ballantyne, but do you mind stopping by my office first? I'd like to see if Nolen or Richard has any news. I also need to set up a time to visit Miss Lavigne." Jax steered the Chummy away from the curb and toward Main Street.

"That's fine. I could call Mademoiselle Lavigne if you like, and go with you to interview her. I would love to see her again. She was one of my favorite teachers, and a big reason why I planned to become a French instructor myself."

Jax gave a quick sidelong glance at Bella. As he looked back at the road, he nodded. "All right."

***

Nolen, Richard, and Jenny were all in the office when Jax and Bella arrived. "Any news?" he asked, following her inside.

"We had a bit of excitement in town," Nolen told him.

"What happened?" Jax asked.

"Not much," Richard put in. "Mrs. Adams thought someone was in her cellar, so Nolen went over while I stayed here."

"When I got there, she also said her goat was stolen." Nolen continued the story. "First, I looked in the cellar. I don't think anyone has been down there since the turn of the century because Mrs. Adams can't manage those rickety steps any more. I know how she is, so I took plenty of time poking around. Then, I searched around and found the back gate open. I guess the goat walked away instead of being taken."

"Probably so," Jax said with a chuckle. "He's done that in the past."

Nolen nodded. "I had to spend quite a while hunting for him. Over an hour. Getting him home wasn't easy, either." He glanced at the Jenkinses and grinned.

Both Jenny and Richard laughed. "I stayed here, but my wife helped Nolen. She's not only good with investigations; she has a knack with stubborn animals."

"This one was particularly stubborn," Jenny admitted.

"Evidently, that all happened after I called from Ballantyne," Jax said.

"Yes, and it took up a lot of this afternoon. I hope you made more progress on the murder than we did," Richard informed Jax.

"I think we did," Bella put in before briefly summarizing their findings. "I don't have a solid piece of evidence to support my feelings, but my gut says there's something important about the Schwarz marriage that we don't know for sure. We have guesses, but we need facts."

"It certainly sounds like their decision to wed was hasty," Jenny observed.

"I agree," Bella said. "Harold driving her around when they were in school seems important to me, especially in light of an incident in France." Her attention moved to Jax. "Why don't you tell them about it?"

After a moment's hesitation, he revealed the tragedy and Horton's role. "I'm not sure it's related to the Schwarz murder at all. It certainly isn't hard evidence."

As a constable, Jax naturally focused on facts, so Bella added her own, less substantive, approach. "Maybe not," Bella said, "but Helene speaks fluent French, and you said the French girl looked a good deal like her."

"How did Harold act after the incident?" Jenny asked.

When Jax didn't immediately reply, Nolen spoke. "Harold changed after he found the girl. He was bent on killing as many Germans as he could. That's how he got wounded. He tried to take out a sniper's nest. When I went to see him in the field hospital right before he got sent home, he told me to always follow the lieutenant's orders and to keep the safety of the men first and foremost."

"Do you know why he told you that?" Bella asked.

Nolen shrugged. "Maybe because I seemed young to be a sergeant."

"That wasn't the reason," Jax said. "I told Harold he needed to focus on his job as platoon sergeant, not on avenging the French girl. He didn't listen."

After a brief silence, Bella spoke again. "Harold can be much more fervent than I imagined."

"It certainly sounds that way," Jenny agreed.

"I don't disagree," Jax said, "but we need to focus on verifiable facts. One that could be important is Harold's access to his brother's motorcycle. It's being stored at the garage, so it's easily available to Harold."

"Do the tires match the tracks you found?" Richard asked.

"Pretty much. As you know the tread wasn't visible, only the tire outline. But the tires on the Horton bike are about the same width as the tracks. Most motorcycles tires are similar in size, though. With that being said, we definitely can't eliminate him." Jax exhaled sharply. "It also troubles me that Windsor and Schwarz had a heated argument in Boxwood last spring." Although Bella had mentioned the event in her summary, he felt it merited more attention.

Richard nodded thoughtfully. "I agree. You two uncovered details that need more investigation."

"I was hoping we'd narrow the field down," Jax muttered. "If we don't identify a suspect before the funeral, I'm afraid the Schwarz cousins will interfere."

"We still have several suspects, but there's time before the services to weed some out," Richard observed. "As you've said, talking with Thomley, Windsor, and Dubois is crucial."

Jax nodded in agreement. "If I can arrange it, I'd like to speak with Miss Lavigne today. Bella wants to go along since she was in the woman's classes." He looked from Nolen to Richard. "Can one of you see if Windsor is back and talk to him, if he is?"

"Of course. One of us will and the other will stay here in case any more goats escape," Nolen replied.

The group laughed before setting out again.

***

Mademoiselle Lavigne was back at school and agreed to meet with Jax and Bella, so they were on their way in a short time. "I'm looking forward to seeing her again, and I hope she knows something about Harold and Helene—if there is anything to know." Bella leaned back in the passenger seat and watched out the windshield as scenery sped by. Jax wanted to drive, so she hadn't argued.

"It seems like there is something, but maybe Harold and Helene are the only ones who really know what it was," Jax responded. "Although Gus probably knew, too."

"Evidently, Gus saw an opportunity to own land himself after Mr. Culpepper died. Once he married Helene, everything—the house, the farm, any money—must have belonged to him. He probably did all he could to trap her, especially after her mother became ill."

"It would be like him to do that, but it isn't evidence to catch his killer," Jax said.

"I know, but it seems important overall. Gus treating Helene badly gives Harold more motive."

"True."

"You don't sound convinced."

An audible sigh escaped him. "It's not that. Your perceptions are really helpful and, like Richard says, gut feelings can be important. I can't arrest someone based on insight or intuition, but I can use those things to guide the investigation."

Bella chewed on her lower lip as she contemplated possibilities. "Harold could have gone to the farm early and let the horses out. But he would have needed to wait for Gus to miss them, if he was planning a murder. If he only wanted to leave the horses out as a prank, he wouldn't have been gone long. Then, there's Curt, who knew Gus probably took advantage of Helene, and he thought she was with child. Does that seem like enough motive for him to kill Gus?" Her consternation surfaced in her voice.

"Those are all good points. For now, I simply want to gather more information. Maybe Windsor or his nephew will say something that leads us in a completely different direction. Or maybe Miss Lavigne will." He paused briefly. "I think we need to turn off soon. You said Ida went to school at Boxmore Hill. Do you know which road we need to take?"

"Turn at the next main road. That goes to the school."

***

Ten minutes later, Bella pointed to the left side of the road. "The gate should be coming up on your side."

Two square red brick pillars marked the entrance. Next to them was a large sign proclaiming that this was the *Boxmore Hill School for Young Ladies.*

Jax maneuvered the Chummy between the posts and toward a large building composed of the same brick as the pillars.

As he drove down the gravel path, Bella said, "Mademoiselle Lavigne said the school isn't open, but the faculty dormitory is right behind it. She'll be waiting for us. I remember it from when I visited Ida here. It's a smaller building, but there's a sign and a small parking area."

Within moments, they were standing outside another red brick structure. "I guess this is it," Jax remarked as he opened one of the heavy wooden doors and allowed Bella to precede him.

When they stepped inside, a tall, lithe woman in her early forties greeted them with a smile and extended hands. "How good it is to see you, Arabella."

Bella smiled in return and took her former teacher's hands in a mutual greeting. "It's wonderful to see you again, Mademoiselle Lavigne."

The two women exchanged some words in French which Jax could only vaguely follow. However, he heard his name and saw Bella flush. When she shook her head in negation, both curiosity and concern assailed him. What had their former instructor said?

"I am sorry, Jackson," the teacher said. "We should not be speaking a language you do not know."

Despite her soft voice and kind smile, the woman's observation held subtle criticism. Did the woman realize he'd taken French I during his junior year only to be in the same class as Bella, who had been a freshman? Something in the teacher's penetrating gaze said she knew. He was equally sure that, although Jax had sat behind Bella, she hadn't suspected his motivation, which was some solace. "I wasn't your best student, I'm sure," he mumbled.

"Ah, I do not believe you were very interested in learning the language," she observed with a knowing smile. "Perhaps other things were more intriguing to you at the time."

Heat rose in his face when Bella looked at him with curiosity. Eager to change the topic, he restated their purpose in coming. "We don't want to take too much of your time, so perhaps we should sit down and talk."

"Of course." Miss Lavigne led the way to a small sitting room off the main entrance. "I had our custodian start a fire. Not too many of us are back in the building right now, so it is somewhat cold, I'm afraid." She took one of the two chairs on the right side of the grate while leaving the loveseat on the other side for Bella and Jax to share.

After he and Bella sat, Jax turned back to the teacher. "You already know Gus Schwarz was murdered Christmas Eve morning."

"Yes, I wish I could say I'm sorry, but I am not." The older woman said in a taut tone that telegraphed disgust.

"Why is that?" Jax asked.

She shook her head. "Jackson, you must know the man has long been a bully and a brute. He took advantage of Helene when she was alone and grieving. Otherwise, she never would have married him." Her voice was firm, and her eyes flashed with certainty.

"When you say he took advantage of her, exactly what do you mean?" Jax figured Miss Lavigne might confirm what they had already heard. Hopefully with actual knowledge and not guesswork, which was what they had to date.

His query hung heavily in the air for several moments. During that time, Miss Lavigne glanced at Bella, back at Jax, and down at her clasped hands. "Helene was one of my best students." She briefly smiled at Bella. "You two were on the same level in terms of ability, interest, and dedication. You both loved the language and wanted to share it by teaching. I was so pleased."

"I still love the language," Bella put in. "I don't know that I'll ever have a chance to teach it, but being fluent was the main reason I was able to join the Army Signal Corps as an operator."

"I'm glad you put what you learned to good use. I know you operators were very important in the war effort." The woman's smile faded, and she looked into the crackling fire. "Unfortunately, Helene never got a chance to use her skills. After her father passed, she and her mother wanted to sell the farm, but Madame Culpepper became ill. Her health deteriorated quickly, and Helene spent much of the summer after graduation caring for her. I visited often. Madame enjoyed speaking her native language, and I was happy to spend time with her so Helene could get away. Of course,

Mrs. Molitor came to do housework and cooking, but Helene was young and needed to be out and about more often."

"Did she spend time with other young people in town?" Jax hoped the teacher would mention Harold herself. That would provide a way into a broader discussion.

"Yes, sometimes she joined others in group outings. Not so much when her mother was very ill, but before then."

"With her girlfriends?" Jax asked.

"Usually, although I know she occasionally saw Harold Horton." A smile touched her lips as she looked back at Jax. "He had been driving her around all spring. Helene confided that Harold wanted to court her but was willing to wait until she completed her education. Not every young man will delay his own wishes for his sweetheart. It is a very admirable quality, but a man should not wait too long."

When her gaze narrowed on him again, Jax shifted uneasily. "You said Gus took advantage of Helene." He had already asked the question, and she had changed the topic. Now, Jax pressed the issue. "Exactly what do you mean?"

Chapter Twenty-Three

Delicate color crept into Mademoiselle Lavigne's face. As she looked at Jax and Bella, a sigh left her. "I must remember you two are no longer my pupils, or even youngsters. You are adults who have seen war firsthand, and I need not protect you from ugliness, although I wish I could. I wish I could have protected Helene. I suppose I feel a need to guard her secrets even now."

"Whatever you tell us will be held in the strictest confidence," Bella assured her. "Won't it, Jax?"

"Of course," he readily agreed. "I may need to share it with Nolen, my deputy, and Senior Constable Jenkins who has come to help with the case, but they'll also keep it to themselves."

The French teacher nodded. "I did not know why Helene hurried to wed Gus until months later. Despite everything, I would have cautioned her against it, although I can understand her decision." She took a long, deep breath before continuing. "Several months after their marriage, I saw Helene in town. She was a shadow of her former self—so pale and thin—and her distress was obvious. I invited her to come to my boardinghouse. Mrs. Eddington and Eric were gone, so we had the parlor to ourselves. I made tea, and we chatted. Within minutes, Helene was sobbing. I tried to comfort her, but she cried and cried. It was a long time before she regained control. Then, she told me why she married Gus."

Bella's heart pounded hard in her chest as she waited for her former teacher to go on. Were she and Jax right in their suppositions? In many ways, she hoped they weren't, because Bella hated to think of what Helene might have endured, not only prior to her marriage, but for all of the years during it.

For several moments, Mademoiselle Lavigne simply watched the flames leap in the grate. Finally, she spoke again. "She said one evening after Harold brought her home from a ball game, Gus was waiting outside. Evidently, he saw Helene and Harold kiss good-night. After Harold left, Gus asked if Harold was courting her, and she said no because she was going away to school as soon as her mother was well. I know Helene still hoped for that. Anyhow, Gus had been drinking. He forced her into the barn where he took advantage of her." She swallowed convulsively. "Helene went to her room without seeing Mrs. Molitor, who was sitting with Madame Culpepper. She said Mrs. Molitor asked her the next day if something was wrong, but Helene was humiliated and afraid, so she said no. I remember her being very subdued about that time. Her mother took a turn for the worse, and that seemed to be a logical cause for Helene's melancholy. I wish I had known more."

"You couldn't have known what happened," Bella observed. "Who would think such a thing?"

"I was certainly foolish in not realizing Gus would treat Helene with the same cruelty he did others," Miss Lavigne said. "The next day, Helene said he came to her and apologized. He offered to marry her, too. She refused until she knew about the child. I know Harold cared for her, and

I think he would have married her even under those circumstances."

"I think you're right," Jax agreed. "He was my platoon sergeant until he was badly wounded and sent home, so I know him well. He's a good man."

Bella glanced at Jax, whose expression held both supposition and anxiety. Those feelings echoed inside her, but so did uncertainty. Harold couldn't be the killer, could he? "What happened to the child?"

"She lost it several weeks after they wed. When we spoke, I urged her to seek a divorce. Although it would have been scandalous, she certainly had reason. Gus had the property and money in his name by then. With no family or funds, there was little she could do. I would have helped her get away from him, but I did not have enough money." The woman looked sad, defeated, and angry all at the same time. "I suggested she go to Harold because I know he was heartbroken when Helene wed Gus. I thought he would have married her even then, and he might have helped pay for the divorce, as well."

"But she didn't want to do that?" Bella asked.

"No, she was broken in body and spirit. The loss of her babe caused physical problems for her, and she lost several more babies."

"She spoke with you about that?" Surprise filled Bella.

The teacher nodded. "During the first few years after her marriage, Helene came to town about once a month. They didn't have a telephone, but she would stop to see me if I was home. She tried to make the best of her situation. Despite all of the difficulties, Helene had a good deal of pride. I'm sure most townspeople had no idea how truly miserable she was. Of course, we all knew Gus was bad-tempered, but the two of them maintained the pretense that he was good to her. When she stopped coming to town, he said it was because she had the same sort of weakened constitution that her mother had suffered."

"Do you think that was the case?" Jax inquired.

"No, I do not. After she lost the first baby, Helene's health improved somewhat. For a while, she seemed almost like herself and I hoped she was happier. She certainly pretended to be. That went on for a few years. Then, she had two real emergencies with losing babies. I know Gus came to town for Doc at least once. After that, I visited Helene on a few occasions, but Gus was always present. They both acted as if all was well, but I could see it wasn't. When we entered the Great War, he became furious about discrimination against German-Americans. I agree it was wrong, but nothing happened here and no one bothered him or the others of German descent." She shook her head. "At least that took his attention away from Helene, and I believe he left her pretty much alone in recent years. Of course, she was still under his thumb because he owned the farm and controlled the money."

"We spoke with Jacob Jones yesterday," Jax told her, "and he thought Helene had bruises on her arms at one point."

Disgust filled the teacher's dark eyes. "I wouldn't be surprised. She never mentioned beatings, only that Gus insisted on marital relations even when she said no." Mademoiselle Lavigne looked from Jax to Bella. "You said I might be helpful to your investigation, but I do not see how any of this would be of use. When I arrived at the Moreley train station yesterday, Mr. Geneve couldn't wait to tell me about the murder. He said someone released the horses and opened the gate very early and then killed Gus."

Bella nodded. "That may be what happened. As I'm sure you know, Gus made a number of enemies. One of them seems to be Anthony Windsor. He isn't back from his trip, but Mr. Fike mentioned the two of you are still in touch."

The woman smiled and nodded. "We got well acquainted as fellow teachers and boarders. Now, we correspond on a weekly basis. He keeps me up-to-date on my former students and others in Moreley, especially the Eddingtons. They became like family to me. As far I know, he and Garlan plan to be back today or tomorrow. Some of us get together once a month for supper, and we're meeting this Sunday."

"Good," Jax replied.

"You don't consider Anthony as a suspect, do you?" Mademoiselle Lavigne asked.

"We speak with possible witnesses, as well as suspects," Jax replied, neatly sidestepping a direct reply. "Mr. Fike also mentioned a history of mutual dislike between Windsor and Schwarz." Briefly, he summarized the principal's revelations. "Were you aware of that?"

"Anthony started teaching a few years before I did, but he and others who taught Gus Schwarz told tales of his bad behavior. I was certainly glad he was gone before I came." Her expression grew somber. "As far as Anthony being involved in anti-German activities, I didn't know of it. He was upset, of course, about his sister, brother-in-law, and cousins dying. And about all of the atrocities in Belgium. Who wouldn't be?"

"Are you acquainted with Garlan?" Jax asked.

She frowned. "I have met the boy. He's a very introverted, sensitive young man. I do not know all of what he saw in Belgium or heard from his British relatives, and Anthony has only shared that Garlan frequently has nightmares."

"I suppose that isn't surprising," Jax commented.

"No, not at all," the teacher agreed. "I'm sure that contributes to Anthony's dislike of Gus berating the veterans, but I'm surprised he supported closing down German-language newspapers, banning German books, or the like."

Bella posed a question that had been in the back of her mind. "Would Mr. Windsor have any way of knowing about the Schwarz marriage? I mean, why they got married or Gus beating her?"

Mademoiselle Lavigne put her chin in her hand in a gesture of contemplation. "I certainly never revealed what Helene confided in me, and I don't think he overheard any of our conversations, although it's possible. As far their marriage, I think people eventually came to realize it wasn't a good one, especially after Helene stopped going to town."

"Thank you for your time, Miss Lavigne," Jax said as he got to his feet.

"I'm happy to see both of you again," the older woman replied with a smile. "I knew you'd be a good constable, Jackson. Despite not being a top student in French, you've always been honest, hardworking, and respectful."

Bella grinned when a look of embarrassment covered Jax's face. "He is a good constable," she added, enjoying it even more when he seemed to wince.

"Thank you, ladies," Jax replied. "Again, I appreciate you taking time to speak with us, Miss Lavigne."

"I hope you find the killer soon. I cannot say I shed a single tear over that man dying, but I do not like to think we have a murderer in our midst."

"Neither do I," Jax told her.

Silently, Bella concurred.

Chapter Twenty-Four

When they got back to the Chummy, Jax suggested Bella drive. She quickly agreed without mentioning how tired he looked. As they left Boxmore Hill, Jax cast a sidelong gaze her way. "She certainly confirmed the suspicions and filled in a number of details."

"Yes, and it's even worse than I thought." A long sigh left her. "Harold and Helene cared for one another, so he is a viable suspect and I wonder about his alibi. He could have slipped away for a bit. On the other hand, Curt thought Gus took advantage of Helene, and he has no alibi. It's hard for me to think of either one as a killer."

"I'm with you on not wanting to consider Harold or Curt as suspects. But they both have pistols and access to motorcycles." He paused for a moment. "They have motive, too."

"I know," Bella murmured. "Garlan has a motorcycle, and maybe access to a pistol. He's also acted violently. Plus, we don't know for sure where he was early Christmas Eve morning."

A period of silence ensued before Jax responded. "Garlan came to Moreley last winter, just before Christmas from what I know, but the vandalism only started last spring. Why would he wait so long to harass Gus and Werner?"

"That's a good question," Bella said with a sigh. "Of course, Mr. Fike said Gus and Mr. Windsor had a confrontation last spring, and Garlan saw it."

Jax nodded. "That could be a factor, but why kill him now?"

"Another idea occurred to me. Even though the killer had a gun, he might not have gone there to murder Schwarz. There must be something we don't know yet," Bella pointed out.

"I'm afraid that's the case. We have a lot of information. Maybe we just haven't put it all together correctly. Or we don't have a key piece."

Bella frowned. "Did Curt know about the incident in France? He was in Matt's platoon, but would he and Harold have had a chance to talk afterward?"

Jax sat in silent contemplation for several moments as he tried to recall the sequence of events after the girl had been found. The Meuse-Argonne offensive had escalated the next day, and they had been thrown into heavy combat. Within a few days, he'd been wounded, and then Matt had died. As always, he reeled with guilt and regret when he thought of his best friend. Lost in his remorse, Jax briefly forgot about the case at hand. Not until Bella spoke again did he manage to fight his way back to the present.

"Jax, do you know if they spoke about it?"

He cleared his throat. "I don't know if they did, but they would have seen one another when both platoons got a short break, so they could have talked about it. It was very much on Harold's mind."

"I almost wish we hadn't found out so much," Bella said on a sigh.

"In some ways, I do, too," he admitted, "but I certainly don't want to arrest the wrong person." He didn't want to arrest one of his men or one of Matt's, either. "All of the bits and pieces should help. We already knew anti-German sentiment was strong in Cincinnati. Not only were editors and employees of a German-language newspaper investigated, the symphony conductor and his wife were arrested under the Alien Enemies Act. They were interned and, after the war, deported."

"What had they done?" Bella asked.

"As far as I know, he only spoke against the war. Nothing more."

"I supported the war effort, of course, but many people who didn't were treated terribly, especially after the Espionage Act, and then the Sedition Act, went into effect. Both gave authorities a lot of latitude in questioning and even arresting pacifists and dissenters."

"Imprisoning and deporting people who disagreed was wrong, but not everyone thinks so. Windsor didn't."

Bella nodded. "Both Mr. Windsor and Garlan experienced losses." Another issue occurred to her. "Does the boy speak fluent English? He had very little to say when I met him in the post office."

Jax shrugged. "I've only talked with him a few times. He seems to understand English, but he definitely has an accent. From what I know, he speaks French, German, and Flemish, too."

"Perhaps I should have spoken to him in French."

"Maybe. Your French seems flawless. Miss Lavigne certainly seems to think so." He paused for a moment. "What did she say to you?"

Bella stiffened as if in discomfort. "You took French for a year, and you had to use it occasionally when you were overseas, I'm sure."

He released a short laugh. "As you know, since we were in the same French class, I had no skill with the language. What I used in France was quite basic. Even then, I couldn't understand French people since they talk fast."

"You were able to order coffee and croissants in that little café in Paris." As soon as the observation was out of her mouth, Bella regretted it because Jax tensed up. The memory was such a happy one for her that she could not fathom why it upset him, as it clearly did. Just that once, Jax and Matt had managed to get a few days of leave at the same time, and they had come to the city to see her. Being together had meant a lot to all of them, or so she had thought. "Jax..." Bella's voice was barely audible over the car's motor, but she relaxed a bit when he answered.

"Yes, I could manage that much."

The harshness in his voice didn't match the benign words. Bella yearned to know what made him withdraw so completely at times. Ignorance could be bliss, so she didn't ask. "But you didn't understand anything Mademoiselle Lavigne said." Going back to that point seemed best. Besides, Bella wanted to know what he had grasped.

"Not really. I heard my name, but I didn't get the context."

Bella forced a light laugh. "She said you weren't good at French, but you were well-behaved so she liked you."

When he briefly looked at Bella, his brows rose as if in doubt. "Really?"

With effort, she maintained her amused, relaxed demeanor. "Yes, really." It was a lie, but the truth would create complications, something Bella preferred to avoid.

"I wonder why she chose to say it in French instead of English."

Since doubt remained in his voice, Bella hurried to present an adequate excuse. "She probably didn't want to hurt your feelings by saying you were a poor student. After all, you did well in your other courses."

He shrugged. "Maybe."

Bella knew he wasn't convinced. Their former teacher had wondered about their future as a couple—a nonexistent future. Saying as much would only cause discomfort. After all, they were both moving on, so she focused on driving and said no more.

***

During the rest of the trip back to Moreley, they spoke very little. When Jax suggested taking her home, Bella offered to go to the office with him so she could transcribe her notes. Of course, her real interest was in finding out what the others had learned.

Nolen was alone at the front counter when they entered. He smiled and greeted them with his usual cheerfulness.

After helping Bella with her wrap and removing his jacket and cap, Jax turned to his deputy again. "Is Richard in my office?"

"No, he and Mrs. Jenkins. I mean Jenny. Anyhow, they went back to the boardinghouse."

"Is he talking with Windsor?" Jax asked quickly.

Nolen shook his head. "Mr. Windsor isn't back yet. Mrs. Eddington said he may have decided to stay in Cincinnati longer. Sometimes, he does. The senior constable asked if he could look in Mr. Windsor's room. Mrs. Eddington wasn't so sure at first, but he said he'd done such searches in the past and it was perfectly fine."

"It is, although I'm sure Windsor will be upset," Jax said before turning to Bella. "I'm going over to see if they found anything important. Do you want to type your notes or come with me?"

She readily accepted. "I'd like to go with you." This was a golden opportunity to learn more, and Bella wasn't going to let it slide by.

***

Within moments, they were on their way back to the boardinghouse. After greeting the owners, Jax and Bella went to the third-floor suite. In the alcove off a small sitting room, they found Richard and Jenny poring over papers. "Anything important here?" Jax asked.

The older man shrugged. "He has correspondence from his sister. The last letter came shortly after the German invasion. She and the boy planned to escape Louvain. She must have gotten it out through England before the city was completely destroyed. She wrote about her husband's death and about atrocities in other towns." He handed the short pile to Jax. "It's nothing we haven't all heard or read, but her first-hand account is chilling."

Jax quickly scanned the last missive. "You're right. I don't agree with Windsor's prejudice toward German-Americans, but this had to upset him terribly."

"There are also letters from his British relatives," Jenny informed them. "We already knew he lost cousins, but the family's letters are heartbreaking."

Jax stared down at the papers. "I still don't think he would commit vandalism, let alone murder. Bella and I both had Mr. Windsor as a teacher, and that would be completely out of character."

"Do you know if Schwarz ever bullied Garlan?" Jenny asked.

Bella and Jax exchanged a glance before she replied, "No one has mentioned it, but I wouldn't be surprised if he had." She continued with a summary of additional information about the Belgian boy.

"I already decided to have Nolen talk to the other boys involved," Jax added.

"A good idea," Richard said. "We definitely need to talk with Windsor and Dubois." "I hoped that would be today," Jax said with a weary sigh. "I wish we had a way to contact him."

"Mrs. Eddington said Windsor is a very private man, and he never gave her any details about his family in Cincinnati," Jenny said, "so she doesn't know how to contact him there."

"I'm not surprised. Even though he and Miss Lavigne communicate regularly, she knew nothing about his anti-German activities," Jax told them before revealing the French teacher's comments.

Jenny and Richard looked at one another. Then, he turned back to Jax. "That's interesting. Is there any way Windsor would have known about Gus attacking and later abusing Helene?"

"Mademoiselle Lavigne didn't think so," Bella put in before expanding on what the woman had told them. "He lived in the boardinghouse, so he might have overheard their conversations at times. Although Mr. Windsor couldn't have killed Gus, he may have shared some of his feelings with his nephew." Her attention moved to Jax. Exhaustion lined his face, so she made another observation. "If so, combined with Garlan witnessing the argument in Boxwood last spring, it might add up to a motive."

Jenkins nodded. "At least we know Windsor should be back soon, if he still plans to be at the dinner. I'd like to learn more about his issues with Schwarz and about Garlan's reaction to the spring run-in."

Jax was silent for a moment before he answered. "They've had a long history of bad feelings, but not many people knew about Windsor's anti-German activities."

The older man ran a hand through his thick gun-metal gray hair. "I wonder why Schwarz and Meyers didn't talk about it with others."

A shrug moved Jax's shoulders. "Gus and Werner only came to town occasionally. They'd mostly go to Boxwood instead."

"As Mr. Fike said, people wouldn't have liked one of the teachers being involved in the movement. Being pro-Allies is different," Bella said.

"Yes, it is," Jax agreed. "But none of that helps us single out a solid suspect."

Jenkins clapped Jax's shoulder. "Son, we've made a lot of progress. Getting down to a few suspects in as many days is an accomplishment. I'm sorry some are fellow soldiers."

"Finding and arresting the killer is my job, and I'll do it no matter how I feel about it," Jax replied before looking at Bella. "We got information about Gus and Helene's marriage this afternoon, and we discussed some other ideas that could have played into the murder."

Jenkins' gray brows rose a fraction. "Perhaps we should go over everything at dinner. The café is closed until the New Year, but I'd like to buy supper for all of us. Is there another restaurant nearby? We could talk afterward."

"Boxwood Diner is open." Jax turned to Bella. "Do you need to get back to Ballantyne? I know you told Mac you'd be gone most of the afternoon, but this will cut into your evening."

The look of concern on Jax's face made Bella smile. "I don't mind spending my evening on the case, but we could go at Ballantyne. There's ham left from Christmas Eve dinner, and I can make potatoes to go with it. Plus, there are canned snap beans in the pantry. Someone gave Mac several jars last fall. It won't be a fancy meal, but we'd be comfortable and private."

Richard and Jenny Jenkins smiled and offered their thanks, but Jax frowned. "What about Curt and Carl? We can hardly tell them not to eat with us."

"They went to Boxwood. When I called earlier, Mac said Curt asked to borrow the Model T so Carl could go along.

They planned to see Wyatt and eat dinner at the diner there," Bella replied. "If they get home before you leave, you could talk with Curt again."

Jax agreed. "If it isn't too much trouble for you, eating at Ballantyne sounds fine." He looked at the others for confirmation.

The men nodded, and Jenny said, "If you'll let me help, it seems like a lovely idea."

***

Dinner was more than fine, and everyone told Bella so. Once the meal was over and Mac went to his room, she suggested the group retire to the library. Wood and kindling were in the grate, so she turned to Jax. "Would you mind starting a fire? It's chilly in here."

"Of course not," he told her before turning to the task.

The Jenkinses seated themselves on one of the sofas flanking the hearth while Nolen took one of the large chairs facing it, which left Bella and Jax to share the other sofa. She laid a notepad in her lap and glanced around the group. "I can take notes."

"That would be pleasant," Jenny told her. "Then, I can sit back and relax." A smile wreathed her pretty face.

Her husband chuckled. "You can sit back, my dear, but we'll want your opinion, so don't relax too much."

"Where do you think we should start, Richard?" Jax asked.

The older man replied, "You're in charge, so where do you think we should begin?"

A rueful smile tugged at one corner of Jax's mouth. "We should review all of the potential suspects and rate them according to motive, means, and opportunity." He pulled a notepad out of his pocket. "I can go over what we have and maybe you can add whatever information we uncover as we talk, Bella."

"I certainly can," she agreed.

"Great," Jax said. "Let's look at them individually. Although Wyatt has a motorbike and a pistol, I've put him at the end of the list, since he has little motive."

"I think you're right," Nolen said. "Wyatt hardly knows Gus. When I was in Boxwood, I asked if anyone ever saw the two of them talking. No one had."

Richard nodded. "Then, we can probably eliminate him unless none of the others pan out."

Jax nodded. "As for Harold, he disliked Gus because of his attitude toward veterans, and he was upset when the man married Helene."

When he paused, Bella observed, "We know Harold and Helene were smitten, at least to some extent, and we know the girl in France may have reminded Harold of her. I feel like he has more of a motive than Curt."

"I agree with you, Arabella," Jenny put in. "The French teacher said Harold was broken-hearted when Helene married Gus, and she went to see him when he got home, didn't she?"

Bella nodded. "She's been to see him at least twice when Gus was away, but neither Helene nor Harold mentioned courting years ago. She didn't want Jax confronting Harold, though. In fact, she said not to accuse him."

Richard put his elbows on his knees and leaned forward. "I doubt if either will admit to being smitten since they may think they're protecting each other."

"You're probably right, dear," Jenny added.

A frown furrowed Jax's brow. "We know a handgun was used, and we're pretty sure the killer had a motorcycle. There's got to be a clear clue to lead us to the right person. Nolen checked with folks living on the main road but some were gone. Maybe you can try again tomorrow. You can borrow my car."

The younger man grinned and nodded in affirmation. "Sure."

Richard absently tapped his fingers on the sofa arm. "Harold would be taking a big chance by leaving the station. Even if he only planned to let the horses out, he would have been gone at least fifteen minutes. More than one customer could have stopped during that time."

"I agree," Jax said, "but he says no one came in until nine. Curt has no alibi, and he surmised why Helene married Gus. He also mentioned disliking Schwarz for years since the man bullied Carl. Their more recent run-ins add weight to his possible guilt, especially the argument on the twenty-third. Curt swears he didn't kill Gus, but almost anyone would deny guilt."

The Jenkinses and Nolen agreed that Curt remained a suspect, but Bella sat silent until her lack of response was noticed. "What are your thoughts, Arabella?" Jenny asked.

"I'm probably biased, but I don't think Curt did it. I especially don't believe he harmed any of the animals on Schwarz's farm or at the Meyer place. He loves animals. He always has. Besides, his pistol butt isn't banged up like Harold's is."

"The killer could have used a hammer on the lock," Jax pointed out. "Or some other heavy object. Even a rock."

"I suppose," Bella murmured.

"It's possible the person who killed the animals and destroyed property earlier isn't the killer," Jenkins observed. "It could be two different people."

"That's true," Bella said, but she finally acceded. "If we're keeping Harold as a potential suspect, we have to keep Curt, too."

"I think that's wise for now," Jax said. "As for Mr. Windsor, he couldn't have killed Gus, but we don't know about Garlan yet." There was unanimous agreement on the observation. "Nolen, were you able to talk with any of the boys who fought with the boy?"

"A couple quit school and moved to the city, but I talked to Johnny Hughes and Rob Landon. Johnny said Garlan jumped him one day after school. Rob came to his aid. We already know both were hurt pretty bad," the deputy replied. "By the time Rob came along, Johnny was on the ground and not able to fight back. Then, Garlan turned on Rob and beat him, too."

"Dubois attacked the boy for no apparent reason?" Richard inquired in a troubled voice.

"According to Johnny, that's exactly what happened. Rob bent over to help Johnny, and Garlan went after him. He admitted to teasing Garlan a few times, but he swore he never started a fight," Nolen said. "When I talked to Landon, he insisted he only wanted to stop Garlan after Hughes was hurt."

"As a warning?" Jax asked.

Nolen nodded in agreement. "Rob has a reputation as being tough, but he still seemed upset over the fight with Dubois. Both Rob and Johnny said Garlan always started the fights. They never went after him individually or together like Garlan claimed."

Murmurs of dismay went through the group before Jax spoke. "What about the bicycles? Did they know anything?"

"They suspect Garlan, but their only proof was him laughing over the bikes being destroyed." Nolen chewed on his lower lip. "Even though it's their word against Dubois, I believe them."

"Gut feelings can be helpful," Richard said as a reminder.

"I hope Windsor and Dubois are back soon," Jax added. "Louis Thomley is important because of his guns, too. I really want to get the murder solved before the funeral." Wanted and needed to get it solved. But would they?

***

Shortly after the Jenkinses and Nolen left, the Molitor brothers returned to Ballantyne. Curt looked uneasy, so Jax tried for a casual approach. "Would you mind talking for a few minutes? Bella and I learned some things today that I'd like to go over with you."

Curt hesitated a moment before agreeing. "Of course."

Jax looked at Bella. "Is it all right if we use the library?"

"Certainly, and I can take notes for you."

"That's not necessary. It's just a casual conversation, not an interview." Jax said, looking away as her smile disappeared.

"All right." Her tone was at odds with the comment.

Jax sighed. He'd address her obvious dismay at some point, but he had reason for wanting to talk with Curt alone. Once they were seated in front of the crackling fire, Jax leaned back in his chair. He didn't plan to take notes. Instead, he'd have to file all of the information in the back of his mind and jot it down later.

"Bella and I spoke with Miss Lavigne this afternoon. You must remember her. She taught French in Moreley."

"I never took French, but everyone knew her," Curt replied. "She was real nice."

"We heard from her and others that Harold was very upset when Helene married Gus," Jax said.

"He was." Curt stared into the fire for several moments. "More than once, even in France, Harold asked me why she married him. After he found that French girl, he wondered if Gus had attacked Helene. He seemed set on the idea. I couldn't tell him what I knew." Curt put his hands over his face as if trying to block out the memories.

The gesture echoed inside Jax, who felt as distressed as Curt looked. Was his former sergeant a murderer? The possibility had his gut clenching in dread. "Have you and Harold talked about Helene recently?"

His troubled gaze lifted. "When I got back, Harold told me she stopped at the station after he got home and again last summer. Gus was real sick in July, so she went to town for medicine. I got gas right after she left, and Harold said how unhappy Helene was. How unhappy she'd been for a long time. He was furious. I tried to settle him down, but he said she deserved a better man than Gus Schwarz."

"I can't argue with that." Fresh apprehension gripped Jax. Neither Helene nor Harold had mentioned an additional meeting. "And that was last summer?"

"Yes, it was. Does that matter?"

A moment passed before Jax responded. He couldn't tell Curt everything, so he carefully weighed his words. "Probably not. Have you heard anything about his disputes with Anthony Windsor?" he asked, but his mind was still whirling with the knowledge that Helene had stopped to see Harold more than twice, and neither had admitted it.

A half-shrug moved one of Curt's shoulders. "Mr. Windsor talked a lot about us getting in the war long before we did. Schwarz got mad, but my ma said he were always giving Windsor trouble. Gus played pranks for years, even after he left school."

Jax nodded. Fike had revealed much the same information. "Do you know anything about Mr. Windsor being involved in anti-German activities?"

A look of confusion blanketed Curt's face. "Nothing like that happened here."

"He's from Cincinnati and goes back summers and holidays. A lot of problems took place there."

"Don't know what he did when he wasn't in Moreley. When I got home, Mr. Windsor said he was glad to see me back safe and sound. I said I wasn't sure how sound I was. He said how awful those Huns were. That's the word he used."

His brow furrowed in concentration. "He got pretty riled up."

Jax tucked the piece of information away for future reference. "Have you spoken with Garlan much?"

Curt shook his head. "No, he's not much for talk, but I understand. He saw some bad things as a boy."

"I know."

A frown puckered Curt's brow. "We talked about motorcycles once. Garlan bought Eric Eddington's old one. He was having trouble with it when I saw him in town, and he asked me if I'd take a look. I got it going, but suggested Harold do a better check."

"When was that?"

"Early last summer or late last spring. Not very long after I got home. Harold fixed it up good, but it was hard-used so I think Garlan only rides it to jobs outside town."

"I see." Jax paused briefly. "Did he mention anything about the war when you were helping him?"

Curt, his forehead furrowing in concentration, hesitated for several moments. "He said his father got killed during the invasion. Garlan wished the war had lasted longer. Wanted to fight the Huns to get even for his folks and friends." Dismay flashed in his eyes. "At the time, it didn't seem like an odd thing for a boy like him to say..." His voice trailed off.

Jax felt Curt's concern ripple through him. "No, it doesn't, but was he really angry, or was it more of a passing comment?"

"He didn't even speak with much emotion." Once again, he looked pensive. "You don't think Garlan could have killed

Schwarz, do you? Even though he wanted to fight, the boy's so quiet."

The adage *still waters run deep* came to Jax's mind. "I don't know, Curt. I haven't seen much of Garlan, but you're right about him being quiet."

"Do you still have a lot of suspects?"

Jax nodded. "Not many, and we're all working hard to pare them down to one, but I want to make sure we arrest the right person." More and more, Jax thought the man in front of him was not a solid suspect. He needed to prove it, though.

"I know you will," Curt replied. "You always do the right thing, lieutenant."

The last assertion made Jax cringe. He hadn't always done what was right and his best friend had died as a result.

***

When Jax and Curt went to the kitchen, they found Carl and Bella sitting at the table. "Bella, could I talk to you in the other room?" Jax asked when she failed to acknowledge him. She gave a curt nod and followed him to the front desk. Since Bella still said nothing, Jax went on, his voice a low whisper. "I didn't ask you to take notes because I knew Curt was uncomfortable when he spoke about Gus taking advantage of Helene. I thought he might be more open if I talked with him alone, and he was. I can't go over everything right now, but come to the office tomorrow morning. We can review the information then." Even as he spoke, Jax knew he was being foolish. He should let her be angry with him because that would maintain distance, needed distance. After the case was over, he wouldn't have any reason to see her on a regular basis. Then, staying away and aloof would be easier, he assured himself.

"You seem to be leaning toward Harold as the primary suspect," she murmured.

"I don't want Harold to be the killer," Jax admitted, "but so much of the evidence points to him. I can't ignore it."

Bella chewed on her lower lip. "I know, but there's still Garlan Dubois to consider. He could have taken Mr. Thomley's pistol, left the farm, and gone back without anyone knowing. If he did, you might see that it's as battered as Harold's."

"Maybe so," Jax murmured. "Maybe so." But *maybes* wouldn't solve the case.

***

The next morning, Bella headed to Moreley after breakfast. When she arrived at the constable's office, Jax was at the counter. "Good morning," she greeted him with a smile and went to stand near the stove. She put her hands out to soak up the warmth. "It's cold."

"Yes, it is," he replied, offering a half-smile in return. "I brought a thermos of coffee from home. How about a cup?"

"Thanks, but I'm already feeling better. The Ford's side curtains don't help a lot when it's so chilly."

He nodded. "I haven't got the stove in my office going yet, so we should talk out here."

"Sounds fine," Bella replied, narrowing her gaze on him. His blonde hair looked like he'd run his fingers through it more than once, but it was the drawn expression on his face telegraphing exhaustion. "Did you sleep at all?"

Jax shook his head. "Not a lot. I kept going over everything again and again. Unfortunately, it didn't do much good."

"Perhaps talking with Mr. Windsor will. Some of what we've learned already is surprising, but he may reveal a crucial clue."

A shrug lifted one of his shoulders. "Curt didn't have a lot to add about Windsor, although he knew more about Dubois."

Bella's interest was immediately engaged. "What?"

Jax summed up the discussion before finishing with "What do you think?"

"Many youngsters would say, and have said, the same thing as Garlan. You know a lot of American boys lied about their ages and volunteered. Anxious to be soldiers and fight for their country."

"You're right," Jax agreed, "but something about the phrase *get even* bothers me."

Bella clasped her hands in front of her as she marshalled her thoughts. "It does me, too, especially since he was evidently calm instead of emotional when he said it."

A long, low breath escaped Jax. "He's very quiet, but he's hurt at least two boys really badly."

Bella pulled one of the hard chairs closer to the stove and sat down. "Garlan must know about Windsor's anti-German activities, and he witnessed one altercation between his uncle and Gus."

"I talked to the constable in Boxwood a few minutes ago. He knew nothing about it. Fike said Nick didn't know, either, so I placed a call to the Toledo Police Department. Nick was in a meeting, but I left a message. Annabelle will ring me when the call comes through." He pulled his watch out and frowned. "It's been over an hour."

A rueful smile played across Bella's lips. "If you were an operator, you'd realize that an hour for a long-distance call is not bad. I could explain all of the steps and the number of people involved."

Jax chuckled as he held up both hands as if to ward off the description. "I bow to your greater knowledge, and I am very appreciative of the operators' efforts. It's just that I'm anxious to get more details."

Her expression grew serious. "We all are. What we've discovered about Garlan makes me really wonder. We've already discussed the atrocities in Belgium and how that affected people. This is a young boy who lost both of his parents, saw others die, and witnessed his hometown being burned and looted. It stands to reason he'd hold a lot of anger. But how much does it affect him? Enough to kill? And why kill Schwarz?"

"I don't disagree. Besides, Garlan lived with family in England for a time. He may have heard anti-German sentiments from them." Jax chewed on his lower lip. "Maybe Nick will shine some light on the situation. If not, Mr. Windsor and Garlan should be back today. One way or another, I hope to know more soon."

Nolen came in as Jax was speaking. After exchanging greetings, Jax ushered Bella into his office and got a fire going.

Chapter Twenty-Five

Several minutes later, Nolen tapped on the door to Jax's office. "Nick is on the phone."

"Thanks, Nolen. I'll be right there." Jax looked at Bella as he got to his feet. "I guess we'll find out what he knows, if anything, about Garlan."

Bella followed Jax to the main office. While she could only hear one side of the conversation, curiosity made waiting at the table impossible. After the usual pleasantries, Jax got to the point by outlining the events of Christmas Eve morning and asking about the spring confrontation between Windsor and Schwarz. Several moments of silence passed while he listened to Nick's reply. Finally, Jax said, "That's interesting." Again, he listened before responding with "I see. Thanks for the information and your time, Nick."

Although the conversation couldn't have taken more than ten minutes, Bella felt as if an eternity had passed while she waited. A glance at Nolen revealed he felt as anxious as she did. Jax had barely gotten the ear piece back on the hook when she could delay no longer. "What did Nick tell you?"

A sigh escaped Jax as he leaned against the counter. "He hadn't heard about the trouble in Boxwood last spring, but there was an incident between Garlan and Gus a few weeks later."

"What happened?" Bella asked.

Jax folded his arms across his chest. "It started because Gus and Garlan had a near collision outside of town. Garlan had just gotten his motorcycle back from Harold, and he was going for a joy ride. Gus was coming into town. He claimed Garlan almost hit him and tried to force him off the road. The kid raced back to town with Schwarz following him. They argued in front of the boardinghouse. Windsor heard and came out. He and Gus exchanged some pretty nasty words." He pinched the bridge of his nose between his thumb and forefinger. "Gus brought up Anthony's anti-German sentiments, and Windsor responded by accusing Schwarz of being anti-American."

"How did Nick know all this?" Bella asked.

"The Eddingtons were gone, but Mrs. Adams had called him about a possible prowler on her property," Jax replied, "so Nick was outside looking around when they all were in front of Eddingtons' place."

A rueful smile pulled up one corner of Nolen's mouth. "It's a good thing Mrs. Adams calls about prowlers on a regular basis."

Jax nodded. "In this case, it was because Nick got there shortly after Anthony went out to see about the ruckus."

"What else did Nick have to say?" Bella inquired. So far, none of the revelations changed the case at all.

Jax's nostrils flared with a sharp intake of breath. "About the time Nick got to them, Garlan was calling Gus a typical Hun and accusing him of being cruel and hateful. He said Gus was just like the man who had murdered his mother."

The horrifying images elicited by Jax's response made Bella gasp. A shiver rippled through her. Several moments passed before she could calm herself enough to speak again. "Did Garlan witness her death?"

"Evidently," Jax replied. "At that point, Mr. Windsor took Garlan into the house and asked Nick to give the boy as few minutes to settle down before asking any more questions. Nick agreed, of course."

"What did Schwarz say?" Nolen, who was still behind the counter, asked. "Was he at all sympathetic to Garlan?"

Jax shook his head. "No, not at all. Nick said Gus went on ranting about people hating Germans and how the Belgians were as bad as folks here. Nick tried to calm him down and ended up saying there was nothing he could do about Gus' claim that Garlan tried to hit him, or about Garlan's claim, for that matter. It was one's word against the other."

"It doesn't make sense that Garlan would try to hit a truck with a motorcycle," Nolen put in.

"No, it doesn't. I'm afraid Gus would have used any excuse to chase Garlan, simply because of his ongoing issues with Windsor."

For a moment, Bella chewed on her lower lip. "I think so, too." She clasped her hands together and mulled over what Nick had shared. "Besides, if Gus reminded Garlan of the man who killed his mother, he might have tried to force the truck into a ditch. That would have made Gus furious so, as you say, he probably would have reacted by chasing the motorcycle."

"That sounds reasonable. This isn't final proof, but I'm even more anxious to talk with Anthony and Garlan." Jax frowned as he glanced at his pocket watch. "The funeral is later today, and I'm worried about the Schwarz cousins deciding to take matters into their own hands."

"So, you think Garlan is a strong suspect," Bella suggested.

"Knowing the boy had a motive—a stronger one than we already knew—is important," Jax replied. "On top of that, he may have had opportunity since he was staying at the Thomley place. He could easily have left before dawn without Louis knowing. And he could have taken a gun if they weren't locked away. That's something we still need to find out."

Nolen nodded. "Mr. Thomley is pretty hard-of-hearing. He wouldn't have known if Garlan left and came back."

Sadness filled Bella. All of the suspects commanded sympathy for one reason or another. "I understood why Garlan would be angry before, and now, I understand how his pain could have become rage. None of that excuses him, but how awful if his grief and loss turned into vengeance."

"Revenge and anger have been the primary motives for every suspect," Jax pointed out. "They still are, no matter who the killer is."

A soft sigh escaped Bella. "I know it sounds crazy, but I guess I don't want it to be Garlan any more than Harold or Curt or Wyatt."

"Me, either," Nolen added.

Jax's strained expression softened. "In other words, none of us wants the killer to be someone we know, but it's always been highly unlikely that a stranger happened along, let the horses out, and killed Gus when he went to look for them."

"I can't argue with that," Bella said in a solemn voice.

***

Jenny and Richard arrived at the constable's office shortly after Jax spoke with Nick Nicholson. He revealed the conversation to the pair immediately. The married couple exchanged a knowing look.

"We also have some interesting news," the senior constable said. "I told you we'd go out this morning and see if the Thomleys were home, and they were. The son was concerned because his father's pistol is missing, the one he bought from Owen."

A frown furrowed Jax's brow. "Did Louis say when he first noticed it was gone?"

"He didn't notice it. His son looked for the weapon when he arrived and couldn't find it. Louis doesn't recall when he last saw it," Richard replied.

"Combined with what we already know, that's very disturbing," Jax observed, "and it definitely makes Garlan a top suspect to me."

"I agree with you," the senior constable said. "I have a couple of friends in the Cincinnati Police Department, so I can contact them if Windsor doesn't get back soon. They might be able to locate him and encourage him to come back." He pulled his pocket watch out. "It's only ten o'clock, so unless Windsor and Dubois left very early, they probably won't be here for another couple of hours."

"If they come today." Bella felt increasingly uncertain. If Garlan was the killer, would his uncle avoid bringing him back?

Jax nodded. "If they aren't here today, calling your friends in Cincinnati is a good idea."

"We can wait and see," Richard said.

"Eric Eddington said he'd call as soon as they return," Nolen told the group.

"Thanks," Jax said. "Until then, we'll have to wait it out. In the meantime, you can make the regular rounds. Then, go out the main road again and see if you can find anyone who wasn't home last time. It would help if someone saw a motorcycle on Christmas Eve morning and could identify the rider."

Nolen nodded before heading out the door.

"Jenny and I can drive out to the Thomley farm again," Richard offered. "The son was turning the place upside down looking for the gun when we left. Maybe he's found it. That wouldn't clear Garlan, but I'd like to know if the boy is armed or not."

"So would I," Jax said in a solemn tone. "While you're out there, I'll wait here in case Eric calls." With luck, that would be soon.

***

Jax went about his usual office activities after the others left. Watching him, Bella felt as edgy as he looked, but she focused on typing the notes taken in longhand and shorthand. Despite being busy, time hung heavily for her. The sooner the case was solved, the better.

When the Jenkinses returned, Bella hurried to the outer office where Jax was behind the counter. Richard immediately answered the question on her mind. "The son looked everywhere and hasn't found the pistol. He's convinced it was stolen."

Nolen returned as the senior constable was speaking. After the deputy removed his jacket, Jax focused on him. "Did anyone see a motorcycle the other morning?"

The deputy shrugged. "The Monroes' dog got out, and they were looking for him when they saw a motorcycle go by. That was around quarter to seven. They couldn't tell who was on it. Too dark."

As the color drained from Jax's face, Bella knew he was fighting for control. Despite Garlan now being scrutinized, Jax had to be worried that his former sergeant was guilty. Harold had a strong motive to kill Gus, along with means and opportunity. Of course, Curt had also been on the road about that time.

"There's still no way for us to focus on one person," Richard said.

"I hope talking with Windsor and Dubois will change that," Jax observed. "And I hope we can talk with them soon."

***

Within the hour, Eric Eddington called to say uncle and nephew had returned. "Anthony and Garlan will be here shortly," Jax said after hanging up.

"Good news," Richard said. "After you interview them, we should be able to either identify young Dubois as our top suspect or rule him out."

"I think they need to be interviewed separately," Jax said.

"I agree," the senior constable put in. "Perhaps you and I can do the interviews. While we speak with Mr. Windsor, Garlan can sit out here with Nolen. One of the ladies can take notes. Perhaps the other could go to the bakery for some cookies or such. Coffee and a treat can help put people at ease."

Bella didn't want to be relegated to running an errand, but she hesitated to speak. Jenny was more experienced, and she was Richard's wife. Bella was simply an interested citizen. As silent moments ticked away, she wished Jax would suggest she take notes. When he didn't, her spirits plummeted.

Finally, Jenny broke the quiet. "I could use a walk so, if it's all right with Bella, I'll go to the bakery."

As Bella met the older woman's gaze, Jenny offered a conspiratorial smile. "That sounds fine." She managed to keep her tone even, but Bella matched the smile with one of her own. Jax's expression didn't change, which kept her relief in check. His ambivalence about her help was discouraging.

"When they get here, we need to check the automobile to see if the pistol might be in it," Jax said to Richard. "Eric said they hadn't had a chance to unload anything."

"A good idea," the senior constable agreed.

"What if Garlan has the pistol on him?" Bella asked, sudden fear gripping her. If the boy had killed Schwarz, what would stop him from killing again?

"We'll search him, Arabella," Richard said.

Relief filled her until Jax spoke again.

"You might as well go into my office and wait there. I'll bring Windsor in when they get here. Just remember that I'm asking the questions."

His gruff tone and clear order grated on Bella's nerves, but she nodded and went into the cramped room. Within a short time, Jax ushered the teacher in. Richard entered behind them, and the three men joined her at the table.

"Good afternoon, Mr. Windsor," Bella greeted the man. When Jax turned a fierce expression on her, she lifted her chin a fraction. Clearly, he didn't want her talking to the man, but she had only offered the barest of salutations. Bella fought the urge to give Jax a piece of her mind. He'd never been bossy or overbearing with her. Why was he so high-handed now? Bella had no idea. However, she didn't like it at all.

"As I told you on the telephone, we've spoken with everyone who had trouble with Gus Schwarz in the past year or so," Jax began.

"Yes, I understand," Windsor told him. "As you must know already, my issues with Gus date back a number of years. He was very poorly behaved as a pupil, and he made my first year of teaching a sore trial. He continued to harass me for years afterward."

"Yes, we're aware of that." Jax leaned his elbows on the creaky table. "I also know you were very adamant that our country should have gone to war much sooner, which put you at odds with Gus, as well."

"It did," Windsor admitted. A long sigh escaped him. "I might have been too outspoken, but I lost family members early. My sister and brother-in-law who lived in Belgium, and two British cousins who died at the Somme. I know Schwarz was born here, but he boasted about his German roots. I'm sure it was to upset me and anyone else who supported American involvement. I'll admit I took the bait far too often."

The man's strained tone and tense expression telegraphed real regret. Bella's heart went out to him and to anyone who had suffered losses in the Great War. While she'd always been sympathetic to others, her empathy was hard-won through personal grief and sorrow.

"How did Garlan feel about moving here?" Richard asked. "That must have been difficult for him."

The teacher bowed his head before replying. "Many things have been hard for him. Garlan was barely twelve when the Germans invaded Belgium. His father hurried to the front, so my sister and nephew were left in Louvain." He swallowed convulsively.

"We know what happened in Louvain," Jax said in a soft voice. "We've heard your sister and Garlan escaped to the countryside as soon as they could."

Windsor lifted his gaze to meet Jax's. "They tried to escape after the town was burned and civilians were slaughtered. My sister hid Garlan because they were being pursued. The Germans probably found out her husband was a Belgian officer. Anyhow, she was killed, and Garlan was found by family friends who were leaving the city. They got him to my cousins in England. He stayed there until I was able to make arrangements for him to join me."

The variation in the story wasn't particularly surprising to Jax, but it opened a new avenue. "Do you know how long Garlan was alone or what happened to him when he was?"

Windsor bowed his head as a harsh breath escaped him. "My sister hid the boy, but he saw her attacked and murdered by a German officer. I don't know how the friends found him because he didn't venture far from her body." Anguish filled his voice. "When Garlan first got to England, he barely spoke at all. He wasn't much better when he arrived here. If you have been around him at all, you know how reserved and anxious he is."

Jax swallowed hard over the lump of emotion choking him. No child should have experienced what Garlan had. "Yes, I do," he agreed. He hadn't seen much of the boy, but Windsor's description rang true. And little wonder. "Is that why you took him out of school?" Fike had suggested fighting was the main reason. Would Windsor admit Garlan started the fights?

"Partly, but he was very far behind. He didn't go to school in Belgium after the invasion, and his English wasn't good enough to attend in Britain. It had improved by the time he came to me, and it's much better now, but he struggled in classes with youngsters his own age, and I didn't want to add any issues by placing him in a lower grade."

"That's understandable," Richard observed.

Jax agreed, but it didn't address what Fike had told them. "He didn't have arguments with other boys?"

Windsor stiffened. "Some of them teased him because they didn't understand what he endured."

Something in the man's defensive tone bothered Jax, but the words weren't much different from Fike's assertions, so he let it go. "That had to be difficult." More than difficult, he was sure, but Jax had to focus on the investigation, not his sympathy for the Belgian boy.

"Yes, it was," Anthony admitted. "And it was another reason I took him out of regular classes. I've been able to tutor him."

"And he was able to work from what we've heard." Richard made the observation casually.

"At odd jobs," the teacher confirmed. "He does better with only a few people at a time."

"We've also heard Garlan had a confrontation with Gus," Jax suggested. He knew the introduction of that event was abrupt, but he wanted candid comments from the teacher. So far, that hadn't happened.

Windsor ran one hand through his thinning hair. As he did, he looked at a point past Jax's shoulder. "Gus almost ran over him. Garlan was on his motorcycle, and Schwarz was in his truck. As you might imagine, it frightened the boy."

Jax maintained a calm demeanor and made a casual observation. "I see how it would have, but his reaction was quite strong, wasn't it?"

When the teacher looked back at Jax, his gaze was cold. "I don't think it was too strong."

"Didn't he refer to Gus as a typical Hun?" Jax asked, his voice was still composed.

Windsor sighed. "He shouldn't have used that word, but the boy heard it in Belgium and in England. People use it here, too. As a former soldier, you must know there were very hard feelings toward the Germans and, mostly, for good reason."

Jax didn't directly address the latter remark. "Anti-German sentiment was rife in your hometown."

Windsor's nostrils flared with a sharp intake of breath. "What are you suggesting, Jackson?"

Jax didn't miss the use of his full given name, the one Windsor had used years back. But Jax wasn't a kid now, he was the constable. "Nothing in particular, Anthony. I was simply making an observation."

"Nothing that happened in Cincinnati relates to Garlan, or to this case."

The teacher lifted his head, so it appeared that he was looking down his nose. The gesture reminded Jax of when he'd been in the older man's class. Back then, he'd been intimidated, but he wasn't now. "Events are often related," was his mild observation.

The other man narrowed his gaze. "Not in this case."

Since Jax knew arguing was futile, he moved on. "I've already spoken to the Eddingtons about Christmas Eve morning. They both said you were there until around ten at least, and you stopped at the post office on your way out of town. Is that right?"

"Yes." Windsor acted as if the single word was torn from him.

"What time did Garlan get back from the Thomley place?" Once again, Anthony stiffened. When several moments passed without a reply, Jax knew Windsor was wondering what the Eddingtons had said. As the silence lengthened, the teacher shifted restlessly in his chair, but Jax said nothing more. Instead, he bided his time and glanced from Richard, who waited patiently, to Bella, whose expression was thoughtful. Jax wished he could ask what each was thinking.

Finally, Windsor answered Jax. "I'm not sure of the time, but we were on the road by eleven, as I've said."

Bella went back to her note-taking, and Jax returned his attention to Anthony. "Thank you for your time, Mr. Windsor." He rose, but the other man stayed in his chair.

"I'd like to be here when you speak with Garlan." All haughtiness was gone, and only entreaty was evident. "He's still anxious at times, and I know he feels very nervous when speaking to anyone in authority, especially someone in uniform."

The plea, although understandable, didn't move Jax. "I'm sorry, but that's not possible." He paused for a moment. "I have a sweater I can put over my uniform shirt, though. And Bella can ask some of the questions." Out of the corner of his eye, he saw her start in surprise, but Jax kept his attention on Windsor. "We'll try to make it as brief and as casual as possible."

A sigh left the teacher. "All right." He rose and left the room without a backward glance.

Once he was gone, Richard turned to Jax. "I think having both of us question the boy could cause uneasiness. We want him to be comfortable enough to talk openly, if that's possible. I'll wait in the outer office. Perhaps, I can calm down Mr. Windsor a bit. Jenny should be back with the treats which might help, as well."

Once Richard was gone, Jax removed his uniform jacket, got the wool roll neck sweater from his desk, and pulled it over his shirt before turning to Bella. "Before I get Garlan, we need to spend a few minutes going over what has to be asked. Since it's just the two of us, I need you to chime in, at times. I'll give you a nod, okay?"

His suggestion surprised her, but she immediately agreed. "Of course. Just let me know what you want me to say."

He nodded before outlining some questions for her to pose. "We'll play it by ear. If you think of anything that seems important or requires follow-up, go ahead and ask."

"Fine."

Jax left the office and returned with Garlan. The boy, pale and wan, looked tense. When he glanced at her, Bella offered what she hoped was a reassuring smile. "Hello, Garlan. I don't know if you remember me, but my name is Arabella Stewart, and we met in the post office the other day."

He nodded. "Yes, I remember." His voice was barely audible.

"Please sit down, Garlan," Jax put in. "Miss Stewart is here to take notes and ask a few questions. We won't keep you long."

Bella noted that Jax kept his tone soft and soothing, almost like he was talking to a frightened child or a skittish dog. His effort to cover his uniform, along with his willingness to let her question the boy, indicated a level of sensitivity common in the old Jax, the one she'd known since childhood. The one who could make her forget what had happened in France. But that Jax never appeared for long, and she wouldn't harbor hope he ever would.

Once the boy was seated, Jax nodded to Bella.

"I'm sure Constable Hastings told you that we've spoken with a number of people who had problems with Mr. Schwarz," she began. When Garlan nodded, she continued.

"We heard you and he almost had an accident earlier in the year. Is that right?"

The boy's dark eyes appeared huge and haunted in his ashen face. He had looked much the same in the post office, though, so Bella wasn't at all sure his appearance now was meaningful. Over five years might have passed since the German invasion of Belgium but, to those who experienced it, she doubted if the memories had faded.

"Yes, I took a ride outside town. He tried to run over me."

The words were without inflection, but his hands clasped and unclasped as he spoke. "That must have been frightening," she suggested.

"Yes."

The single word reply didn't provide any insight so Bella looked back at Jax who nodded again. "What did you do after he tried to run over you?"

Briefly, his hands stilled. Then, Garlan began to clasp and unclasp them again. "I yelled at him."

"What did you say?"

His gaze skittered away from hers. "I don't remember."

Bella felt certain that was a lie, but she was afraid to call him on it. Increasing the boy's anxiety wouldn't help. "Do you recall him following you back to the boardinghouse?"

"Yes."

She gripped the pencil tighter as she mentally reviewed the questions suggested by Jax. "What was said then?"

"I don't remember. I was scared of that man, and Uncle said for me to go inside."

Emotion kindled in his dark gaze, but Bella was unable to discern the source—fear, anxiety, sadness, memories? It was impossible to tell. "What did your uncle say when he finished talking to Mr. Schwarz?"

"He said I should stay away from his farm or any place near it. He said if I saw the man in town, I should walk the other way."

The more Garlan talked, the more Bella realized his English was quite good.

"Did your uncle tell you why you should do that?" she asked.

"Because Schwarz is a bad man. He's hurt people."

Bella glanced at Jax whose wary expression matched her feelings. Windsor had asserted he took care not to mention his own anger or grief, and Eric Eddington said the same.

"Did you do as he suggested?" Jax put in.

"Yes, sir, I did. Schwarz was big and mean."

"So, you didn't see him face-to-face after the incident?" Jax asked.

Garlan shook his head. "Like I told you, Uncle said to avoid him, and I did."

"That was wise," Bella added, but she wasn't sure the boy was telling the truth. She wasn't sure Windsor had, either.

"Yes, ma'am."

"Your uncle told us the two of you left to visit family after ten o'clock on Christmas Eve morning," Jax observed, moving on.

"About then."

"What time did you leave the Thomley place?" Jax inquired.

A moment passed before Garlan replied. "Close to nine o'clock, I think."

Jax again glanced at Bella, a signal that he wanted her to ask the final question although she tried to make it sound more like a statement. Upsetting the boy wouldn't help. "And you were there all morning until you left for town?"

Again, Garlan's hands stilled. "All morning."

The two words were not convincing, but Bella wasn't sure why. Did she—deep inside—want the boy to be guilty so neither Curt nor Harold was?

"You had your motorcycle with you," Jax suggested.

"Yes." Again, the boy provided a one-word answer.

"What chores did you do for Mr. Thomley?" he asked.

The young Belgian stared at Jax for a moment. "Outside chores. Feeding the animals mostly. No crops right now, but I helped around the house, too."

"I see," Jax observed in a mild tone. "So, you could go any place on the property."

Garlan simply nodded.

"Did you ever see any guns in the house or barn?" Again, Jax kept his voice calm.

The youngster's eyes widened before he glanced away.

When Dubois didn't answer, Bella spoke. "Most farmers have a shotgun at least, and we've heard Mr. Thomley bought a pistol a few months ago."

The boy's hazel eyes met hers before lowering to the table. "If he has any, they must be put away."

Bella and Jax exchanged a long look before he said, "Thank you, Garlan." He got to his feet.

Garlan looked up at Jax. "Can I leave now?" For the first time, the boy showed animation.

"Yes. We may want to speak to you and your uncle again, but you're both free to go," Jax told him.

Garlan said nothing as he got up and left the office. Once he was gone, Jax looked at Bella. "What did you think?"

"I don't know what to think," she said in complete honesty. "We don't have enough to make Garlan the sole suspect, but we can't eliminate him, either. What about you? What are your thoughts?"

"About the same as yours." Jax ran one hand over his face. "I can't eliminate Garlan, but I can't eliminate Harold or Curt, either."

Richard and Jenny appeared at the door. "Are we interrupting?" the senior constable asked.

"Not at all," Jax replied. "Come in and sit down. We can go over these last two interviews. I'd like your opinions and Nolen's, too."

Chapter Twenty-Six

Once the group gathered at the table, Jax outlined what he and Bella had learned from Dubois. "Neither interview provided a real indication of who killed Schwarz," he said in summary.

"Not factually," Richard agreed, "but did either of you get a gut feeling from the boy?"

Jax rubbed his shoulder. "I lean toward Garlan as the killer, but I'm not as unbiased as I should be. Harold was my sergeant, and Curt was Matt's."

"Understandable," the senior constable replied. "What about you, Arabella? Did you have any strong feelings about what either Windsor or Dubois said?"

"I'm probably not impartial, either," she began. "But it wasn't what Garlan said that bothered me so much, it was the way he acted. He showed almost no emotion about anything until Jax said he could leave. Not only that, the boy gave one-word answers to the most important questions, and he claimed he didn't remember much about his run-in with Schwarz, which seems unlikely." She paused for a moment. "It felt like he had rehearsed his replies, but Eric called as soon as Garlan and Mr. Windsor got back. Then, they came right over here. That didn't give them much time to go over answers to possible questions."

"It gave Windsor time to advise the boy to say he didn't remember anything about his run-in with Gus," Jax pointed out. He looked at Richard. "What do you think?"

"That's quite likely," the older man replied, "and it's not a good sign."

"Do you think Mr. Windsor suspects, or even knows, that Garlan killed Schwarz?" Jenny asked. "If so, they might have reviewed what to do and say on the way back from Cincinnati in case you wanted to talk to them."

"I agree," Bella observed. "Garlan said Mr. Thomley keeps his guns locked up, but he looked upset when we asked about it, and we know one is missing."

Anxiety played along Jax's nerve ends. "Overall, the boy was stiff and nervous. If he has the gun and the Schwarz cousins confront him and his uncle, I'm afraid it won't end well. They're as eager to blame former soldiers as Gus was, but they'd quickly turn their sights on someone else, if it comes to that."

"The funeral is starting at three o'clock, so they won't have much time today," Nolen said, his tone somber.

"You're right. I think we can count on them not doing a lot until tomorrow," Richard said.

"Bella, will you call Curt and tell him to stay at Ballantyne for now? Explain why." Anxiety roughened Jax's voice.

"Of course," Bella felt her heart turn over. Although Richard thought the Schwarzes would wait until the next day to act, she was worried about Mac, Curt, and Carl. What if the cousins went to Ballantyne for a confrontation? She hurried to the outer office to use the telephone.

"Nolen, go over to the garage and talk to Harold. Tell him the situation and suggest his brother open the station with him tomorrow," Jax told his deputy. "He might want to stay at his brother's place tonight."

The younger man stood up. "I'll go right now."

"Perhaps Jenny and I should attend the funeral," Richard suggested. "I imagine the cousins will spend the rest of the day with Helene. If she invites people back to the house after the service, we'll go along."

Jax frowned. "I don't know that a lot of folks will be at his funeral, but it's a good idea for you two to go."

The couple was about to leave as Bella returned. "Curt went to Boxwood to help Wyatt work on his grandparents' old house. It's been vacant for a while, but Wyatt wants to live out there. There's no telephone, but Mac will keep Curt at Ballantyne when he gets back."

"Curt will have to go by the Schwarz place on his way home," Jax said in a troubled tone. "Nolen, after you talk to Harold and his brother, would you drive over to where Wyatt's grandparents lived?"

"Sure," the deputy replied.

"Good, you can take my car. Curt needs to be warned right away." After Nolen was gone, Jax turned to Bella. "I know you drove into town yourself, but I'd like you to wait until Nolen gets back. Then, just to be on the safe side, he can follow you to Ballantyne in my car."

His sincerity made Bella agree right away. "Of course. I can type the notes from these last two interviews while I wait."

***

Jax tried to do some paperwork at the front counter, but restlessness and anxiety plagued him so he finally went back to his office. Bella looked up from her typing when he entered the room. "Do you need something in your desk?" she asked.

He shook his head as he took the chair across from her. "No, I'm having trouble concentrating."

"So am I." She paused for a moment. "I'm guessing you didn't find the pistol since you didn't mention it to Windsor or Dubois."

"No, we didn't. It wasn't on Garlan or any place in the vehicle. Since it wasn't in their rooms, either, I don't know where else to look."

"Not finding it seems like a bad sign. It could be any place by now," Bella replied. She ran one forefinger back-and-forth across the typewriter keys. "I know we don't have enough evidence, but I think Garlan killed Gus."

With one hand, Jax massaged his shoulder. "I agree with you about Garlan, and I think Jenny is right about Windsor knowing. I keep going back to the confrontation between Gus and Anthony with Garlan as a witness. The vandalism started shortly after that, and I'm willing to bet every incident occurred when the kid was doing odd jobs for people outside town. If we don't turn up any other solid evidence, we'll have to look into the dates of the vandalism and his whereabouts."

"That's very possible," Bella agreed. "We know Mr. Windsor lied about Garlan not starting trouble with classmates. He made it sound like other boys picked on him and he just took it. Why didn't you confront him?"

"I was trying not to confront either one of them. I didn't want to give away too much because we can't arrest Garlan yet. The kid could run if he gets worried. If he has access to the gun, he could hurt someone else." He pinched the bridge of his nose in an effort to quell the headache starting to build. "He still might."

"Do you really think so?"

"It's a possibility, especially if the Schwarzes confront them. We can't account for Thomley's pistol, but Garlan could have hidden it some place." Jax slumped back in his chair. "If so, he could also go get it."

"He might have thrown it away," Bella pointed out. "As far as the Schwarz cousins, Richard said they aren't likely to do much until tomorrow."

"No, but I'm still on edge. We can't be sure Garlan is the killer." Weariness and frustration underscored each word.

"I understand," Bella murmured. "I know you need hard facts, but another thing that's been bothering me is Garlan's English. Earlier, Mr. Windsor indicated the boy's poor grasp of it was part of the reason for taking him out of school. Garlan has a definite accent, but he speaks quite well and seems to understand everything, too. He's only been in this country a year, and that's a lot of progress. Not impossible to become fluent in that time, and I know it's a minor point, but why lie?"

Jax sighed. "You're right. Windsor never admitted Garlan might have started any fights, so he had to have another excuse to take the boy out of school." He shook his head. "I hate waiting for something else to happen, especially when it could be something bad. I called and asked Eric to let me know if Windsor and Dubois leave the boardinghouse."

"You've done everything you could, Jax. Run down each clue, talked to every possible witness, and looked for the weapon. For now, all we can do is wait."

"Waiting is the hardest part," he murmured.

***

The wait was not long. Shortly after three-thirty, the phone rang. Bella followed Jax into the outer office and listened to his end of the brief conversation. "All right. Thanks for calling. I'm on my way."

"What happened?" she asked.

"There's a fire at the Schwarz place. That was Jeff Jefferson. He and the volunteer firemen will be on their way soon. I said I'd be right out, but I'll have to borrow your Ford since Nolen has the Chummy."

"I'll drive you," Bella said without hesitation.

The telephone ringing again interrupted the conversation. Jax grabbed it. After a moment, he said, "Yes. I know. Thanks for calling, though." After putting the earpiece back on the candlestick holder, he glanced at Bella. "That was Eric. He went out to their garage, and Garlan's motorbike is gone. He went to see if the boy was in the suite, but only Windsor was there taking a nap."

Before he could continue, she spoke. "Let me drive you. I promise to stay out of your way."

Jax looked like he was going to object, but instead, he nodded in agreement. "Let's go."

When they arrived, the fire wagon was on the scene, as were Jacob Jones and Oscar Werner. Jax jumped out of the car and headed toward them. "Do you know how it started?" he asked Jacob.

The farmer frowned. "It had to be Garlan Dubois. I saw him leaving on his motorcycle as I was running over here. At least, he let the animals out, but I'm afraid the sheds Gus rebuilt after the last fire are a loss. We may be able to save the barn, but that's not for sure. I better get back to helping."

As Jones started to hurry away, Jax asked, "Which way did Garlan head?"

Jacob jerked his thumb to the east. "That old bike won't last long if he keeps driving it as fast as when he left here."

"Thanks." Jax rushed back to the Ford. "I need to take your car, Bella."

"I can still drive." Her hands remained firmly fixed on the steering wheel.

Again, Jax wanted to argue, but getting her out of the car would be a challenge, and they didn't have time to argue. "Let's go." He had the passenger door open when Richard Jenkins and Anthony Windsor pulled into the yard.

"I heard about the fire as we were leaving the funeral," Jenkins said. "When I dropped Jenny off at the station, Windsor was there so he came along."

Jax quickly told them what Jacob had said.

"We'll be right behind you," the senior constable replied.

Once Jax was seated, Bella went to the main road and headed east. Jenkins and Windsor followed.

"When we catch up with Garlan, you need to stay in the car," Jax said to Bella. "Since he started another fire, it's hard to say what he might do next."

Bella resented the advice, especially since Jax had wanted to leave her behind entirely. She didn't like being dismissed or commanded. Especially not by him. Especially not when they'd been working well together, and she'd done nothing to merit a lecture.

Several seconds of silence slipped away before he spoke again. "Remember, we never found Louis Thomley's pistol. I don't want to worry about you getting shot while we try to settle the kid down."

Worry about you. The three words echoed in her mind. Early on, Jax had said he didn't want her to be hurt, and not because another murder would cause unnecessary complications. Her anger ebbed. His anxiety was sensible. "I'll stay back, but you, Richard, and Mr. Windsor need to be careful."

"Richard and I are armed, but we'll be cautious." Jax continued to stare straight ahead, as did Bella. They had only gone a few miles when they saw Garlan's motorcycle on the side of the road. "Stop here. I don't want to get too close to him yet."

Bella steered to the shoulder, and Richard pulled up behind them.

Garlan stood, gun in hand, next to his motorcycle. A shiver rippled through her. "He does have the pistol."

"I'm not surprised. We're just barely in range here. Keep the side curtains closed and lie on the seat." Jax's voice held a hard edge, but his gaze revealed real worry.

Bella didn't want to be a distraction, which shaped her response. "I will." Once he got out, she hunched down but pulled back the side curtain a few inches. Although she was relegated to the car, she wanted to hear what was being said. When she thought Jax was away from the vehicle, Bella lifted her head and peeked out to observe the scene.

Anthony Windsor turned to the lawmen. "Please let me talk to him. He may be willing to surrender."

The words carried to where Bella waited, as did Jax's reply. "All right, but if it looks like you're in danger, we move in."

Windsor nodded as he turned toward his nephew. "Garlan, listen to me. Please. You need to put the gun down."

The boy shook his head. "No. I escaped once, and I can escape again."

His voice was tremulous, but the words scared Bella. What did he mean *escape again?* Did Garlan know where he was or who was facing him? Did he think Richard and Jax were German soldiers? The possibility scalded her soul.

"You don't need to escape now," his uncle said in a soothing tone. "You're not in Belgium. You're in America, and you're safe."

Garlan continued to shake his head. As he did, the hand holding the gun swung back and forth. Even from her vantage point, Bella could see the boy's terror and confusion.

"No. They killed my father and my friends. They burned our town and killed my mother." His voice broke.

When he wiped at his cheeks with his free hand, Bella knew he must be crying and she blinked back tears of her own. As Jax turned to Richard and the pair exchange quiet words, her heart pounded in her ears. The thundering only intensified as Jax moved forward. He stopped when Garlan called out, "Stop or I'll shoot."

Jax froze in his tracks. "All right."

Bella's hands tightened on the steering wheel until her knuckles showed white. Jax was too close to Garlan for comfort.

"Toss your guns down," the youngster ordered.

"Garlan, these men won't hurt you," his uncle assured him.

"Then, they can throw away their guns."

Richard and Jax once again spoke in low tones before doing as ordered. A sick, sinking sensation filled Bella as she watched. Unarmed, the pair was completely vulnerable.

"Get down. On the ground," Garlan called. "All of you." Slowly but surely, the two constables followed the order. When Windsor didn't, his nephew called out again. "You, too, Uncle."

"Garlan, I won't hurt you," the man replied. "I'm here to help you."

"You weren't there when my mother needed help." The boy's plaintiff tone was heart-wrenching. "Now, move."

Windsor complied, but Garlan's accusation frightened Bella because he evidently blamed his uncle for his mother's death. If he saw Windsor and the lawmen as his adversaries, Garlan might not hesitate to kill them. A shudder rippled through her. What could she do to help?

Abruptly, the roar of another motorcycle broke the silence. Bella turned to see Curt coming down the road. She knew when he noticed the group on the shoulder because he slowed down and steered to a stop less than twenty feet from Garlan. The knot in Bella's stomach tightened. What was Curt doing? Garlan swung the gun toward him and yelled again. "Stop!"

Curt's gaze went from the young Belgian to the three men lying on the ground. Surprise blanketed his face.

"Be careful. We think he killed Gus," Jax called out.

At that, Curt put his hands in the air. "Looks like you got trouble with your bike, Garlan. I could help. I did last spring."

For several moments, Garlan stared at Curt. Finally, he nodded. "My bike broke down."

The response stunned Bella, but Curt smiled and replied in an easy tone, "I'd be happy to look at it."

Again, the boy hesitated before agreeing. "Thank you. I'd like to get back on the road." Garlan looked at the other men. "They want to take me prisoner, but I didn't do anything wrong."

Curt glanced at the other men and back at the boy. "They only want to talk." His tone was calm and measured.

"Yes, that's right," Jax immediately agreed.

"I don't believe you," Garlan shot back. "You said I might have killed that German. I didn't mean to. I was just playing a prank like I did before. But he came out and saw me. Then, he came after me yelling and cursing and threatening. I escaped once, but he was too close and so big. He hurt a lot of people. I knew he'd hurt me, too."

"You had a gun with you," Jax pointed out, his voice as controlled as Curt's had been.

"Only for protection. I wasn't going to hurt anyone. Or the animals, either." Garlan aimed the gun at Jax as he spoke. "You don't know. You don't understand." The words came out in a rush, and his tone became almost hysterical. "I should have killed him sooner. He hurt a lot of people."

The repeated sentiment made Bella's insides knot. Jax was in close range of the pistol now, and Garlan was increasingly confused. Did he think Schwarz was the man who had murdered his mother?

"Let me see if I can get the bike running," Curt suggested. He was still standing a few feet away and observing the deteriorating situation.

The boy looked at him. After a minute, he nodded. "All right."

Curt covered the distance between his bike and Garlan's in only a moment. Bella's pulse accelerated as she watched. Garlan's instability made her fear he would turn on Curt at any moment, but he didn't. She couldn't hear what either of them said, but they exchanged words before the former sergeant began to work on the motorcycle. After a few minutes, Garlan focused solely on the bike. As he did, the hand holding his gun fell to his side. Bella felt sweat dampen her palms as her anxiety grew. Jax would most certainly try to disarm the boy, but could he do it without getting shot?

Garlan must have seen the constables start to get up because he turned back to them. As he did, the hand with the gun came up. Almost simultaneously, Curt reached for the boy's arm. Despite the distance between Garlan and her, Bella saw his expression go back to furious. His words didn't carry, but she saw him struggle with Curt for the weapon.

Jax, who had retrieved his own revolver, was on his feet and running toward them with Jenkins and Windsor right behind him.

Suddenly, a gunshot rang out. Bella moved to get a better view. Shock froze Curt's face as he reached for Garlan, who crumpled to the ground. As she watched in horror, Bella felt bile rise in her throat. Jax's warning forgotten, she threw the car door open and dashed toward the men. When she got to Jax's side, she saw Windsor drop to his knees beside Garlan. Curt followed suit. Both of them looked up with pale faces and distraught expressions.

"He's gone." Windsor's voice, hoarse and husky, was barely audible.

Curt bowed his head. "Sweet heaven. I was trying to get the gun away from him. I didn't want to shoot him or hurt him. I wanted to help." Shock and sorrow underlined every word.

Jax laid a hand on the former soldier's shoulder. "He shot himself, Curt, and I think he intended to."

"So, do I," Jenkins murmured.

When Jax turned his attention to Bella, he scowled. "I asked you to stay in the car."

She frowned back. He hadn't asked. He had ordered her, but she resisted pointing that out. In fact, Bella ignored his assertion completely. "What can I do to help?"

Jax, who still looked angry with her, didn't immediately respond but Richard did. "We need your town doctor and mortician to come out. If you notify them and then go to Jax's office, that would be very useful. I dropped Jenny off there, so she will be wondering what's happened. Nolen will, too, once he realizes he missed Curt."

"Of course," she replied.

"Perhaps you could take Mr. Windsor with you," Richard continued.

Bella touched Windsor's sleeve. "Let's go now. There's nothing that you can do here."

He blinked hard, but several tears splashed down his pale, lined face. "All right."

Although she felt Jax's penetrating gaze still on her, Bella led the older man to her car without a backward glance.

***

Neither Bella nor Anthony Windsor spoke on their way back to town. Once they turned on to Main Street, she glanced his way. Tears streaked the man's face, and his shoulders shook with repressed sobs. Sympathy squeezed her heart. "Why don't I take you to the boardinghouse, Mr. Windsor?"

He sniffled loudly. "The constables will want to talk with me, I suppose." His ragged voice was barely audible.

"They won't be back right away, and you need some time to yourself. Jax can call on you later."

"All right."

Once Bella had dropped off the teacher and alerted Doc Smedlay and George Forrester to what had happened, she headed to the constable's office. Nolen, worried since he hadn't found Curt, was as anxious to get the news as Jenny. Both were sad to hear it, and a cloud of gloom hung over the group. All of them had wanted the case solved, but not in such a tragic manner.

Almost two hours passed before Jax and Richard entered the constable's office. Both moved slowly as if some great, invisible burden weighed them down. Jenny went to her husband's side, and he put one arm around her shoulders. Envy spread through Bella, but she had no right to offer such comfort to Jax. Nor would he want it.

"Bella and I made a pot of coffee, and Mrs. Rogers sent some sandwiches over. We've eaten, but the two of you look like you could use some food," Jenny suggested.

"That sounds like a good idea. Why don't we all go in your office, Jax?" the older man asked. "I don't know about you, but I'm tired." He glanced at the others. "I'm guessing everyone is."

The group agreed and, in a few minutes, they were once again assembled at the battered table. Bella retrieved their notebook and a pencil. As she did, Jax glanced her way for the first time since he'd returned. "You don't have to take notes. You've done more than enough already."

She forced a smile. "I don't mind, and I might as well finish what I started."

"I suppose we should go over everything while it's still fresh in our minds," he said in a weary voice. "Richard and I stopped at the Schwarz farm on our way back to town. I was able to briefly speak with Helene. She's exhausted, but when the cousins said they planned to stay another week, she told them she'd be fine alone."

"Really?" Jenny asked. "From what all of you have said, she's a meek, mild lady."

"She was," Jax replied, "but after being under Gus' control for years, she may be fed up."

"The Schwarz men didn't look happy, but Harold, Jacob, and several others who were still cleaning up after the fire said they'll help, so her family need not worry," Richard added. "The cousins didn't argue."

"Good," Jenny said. "Maybe Helene will have a decent life now."

"I hope so," Bella put in. She glanced from Richard to Jax. "Were all of her outbuildings destroyed?"

"The sheds were, but the damage in the barn was minimal. Some work will need to be completed before she can put animals in it again. For now, Jacob and Oscar have taken them." Richard picked up his sandwich and began to eat.

"What about Mr. Windsor?" Nolen asked. "Are we going to talk with him again?"

Jax laid down his sandwich. "We already did."

"How is he doing?" Bella inquired.

"Devastated and remorseful. He filled in some details, so with what we had learned already, we'll be able to wrap the case up shortly." Jax paused for a moment. "Windsor didn't think Garlan had anything to do with Gus' murder until they were getting ready to come back. Then, the boy got very upset. He wanted to stay in Cincinnati. Evidently, he's been a lot more unstable than others knew. The fights and thefts were part of the issue, but Garlan not only stole and broke the bicycles, he smashed windows and such. Anthony was quick to pay for the damage, so nothing was reported. We also talked briefly with Louis Thomley. He feels very bad about not keeping his guns locked up. He also told us he buys eggs from the Schwarzes. Helene usually delivers them but, since she was sick, Gus did it on the twenty-third. Garlan was there then."

"Do you think that precipitated the murder?" Jenny asked.

"We'll never know for sure. Garlan and Gus spoke, but Louis didn't hear the exchange. He said Garlan was visibly upset afterward, so it seems like a possible cause," Richard replied.

"I'm sure it was a difficult situation, but Windsor should have done something more," Jenny suggested.

Jax nodded. "Anthony tried talking to the boy many times. They even went to a doctor in Toledo because Garlan had nightmares frequently. We'd heard that already, but he also talked a lot about the *Huns,* as he called them. He developed a particular hatred toward Gus Schwarz after the run-in last spring. He kept talking about it, according to Anthony. It was like he was stuck on the experience." Jax paused to take a sip of coffee but left his sandwich on the plate.

"Wasn't his uncle suspicious when the vandalism started last spring? That was shortly after Garlan got his motorcycle and started doing odd jobs," Jenny added.

Her husband frowned. "He said he had no idea, but neither Jax nor I completely believe him. There's no way to prove he had suspicions, though."

"He certainly feels terrible now," Jax put in. "Windsor didn't say he felt guilty, but his regret is quite obvious."

"That it is," Richard concurred. "I doubt if he completely understood how angry his nephew was."

"Even if he had, there's no reliable treatment for that sort of ordeal," Jenny said.

"No, there isn't," Bella agreed. "In fact, some of the treatment for shell-shock victims—and it sounds like Garlan's issue was similar—only makes them worse."

"A lot of the procedures are barbaric," Jax agreed, "so I can understand why Anthony tried to deal with the boy himself. I'm sure he feared Garlan being put in an asylum." A sigh left him. "We can't be sure, but Garlan must have left the Thomley place very early on Christmas Eve morning to go the Schwarz farm."

"That makes sense. Garlan admitted he went to set the horses loose," Bella observed. "Do you think he only went for that reason?"

"I do," Richard said.

"I agree," Jax put in. "Garlan was surely the vandal, so he went to the farm several times before then, and he didn't try to kill Gus on any of those occasions. Of course, Gus didn't catch him so there were no confrontations. I believe that was the difference this time."

"I wonder why Schwarz didn't take his shotgun with him when he followed Garlan," Nolen observed.

"That's another thing we'll probably never know for sure. He may have thought he could intimidate Garlan and overpower him," the senior constable replied. "Bullies can become arrogant."

"Garlan might not have pulled the gun out until Gus caught up with him," Bella said.

"That's quite possible. Gus never had to use a weapon to scare anyone in the past. As anxious and shy as Garlan was, Gus may not have considered the boy a real threat," Jax added.

"Very likely," Jenny said.

"What about Curt? Where is he?" Bella asked.

Jax slumped back in his chair. "Doc is taking a look at him. Curt was shattered by what happened. It wasn't his fault at all. In fact, he probably saved my life with his actions."

"And mine, as well," Richard added.

As her husband spoke, Jenny laid her hand over his. "I'm sorry the boy died, but I'm glad both of you are safe."

"I am, too," Jax said, "but I understand Curt's remorse. Garlan already suffered so much. It doesn't seem fair at all."

Bella felt the same way, but she had another concern. "Even if Garlan hadn't killed one of you, he would have been found guilty of murdering Gus Schwarz, don't you think? His past trauma wouldn't lessen his sentence would it?"

The senior constable shook his head. "No, I'm afraid not. He suffered significant damage as a child, but that was over five years ago, and the law would likely see him as a man, not a boy, now. He most likely would have been sentenced to death."

For several moments, the group fell silent. Finally, Jax spoke. "He would have been held in jail awaiting trial and then, awaiting execution. I'm not sure he could have withstood that. He seemed so confused and disoriented today."

"Do you think he might have been put in an asylum instead?" Nolen asked.

"Even if he was, spending the rest of his life in one of those places might have been worse than dying," Jenny murmured.

Her husband nodded. "I believe you're right, my dear."

"Will you need to do more interviews?" Bella asked.

"No, Jax will finish his report and submit it," Richard replied.

"We told Anthony we want to talk with him again before he leaves town, but just to tie up any loose ends," Jax put in.

"Leave town? He just got back," Bella observed.

"Yes, but he's returning to Cincinnati. He plans to call Mr. Fike and quit," Jax said.

"That may be for the best," the senior constable observed. "Once word gets out about the extent of Garlan's difficulties, and his guilt in the Schwarz murder, Windsor might be snubbed, at the very least."

"I think it's a wise decision to move," Jax agreed. "He has no family here and, although people are generally decent, he's likely to feel better in his hometown."

"I suppose so," Bella said. "It's a terrible situation all the way around."

"That it is." Jenny agreed.

Jax pulled his watch out. "I need to call the mayor and let him know what happened. And I told Doc I'd check on Curt." He glanced at Richard and Jenny. "I can't thank the two of you enough for your help. I don't know what we would have done without you."

The senior constable smiled. "This is a good team." His gaze swept around the entire table. "Before we head home, I'll speak with your mayor about Nolen."

That brought a big smile to the deputy's lips. "Thank you."

Bella closed the notebook and put away her pencil. "I can type up these last notes this evening."

"Thanks," Jax replied. "I'll come out later and pick them up."

With that, the group dispersed.

Chapter Twenty-Seven

Bella was finishing her transcription when the sound of a motorcycle interrupted her. Immediately, she went to the kitchen where Curt, his face ashen, was entering the back door. When he saw her, he suddenly stopped in his tracks.

"How are you feeling?" Bella asked.

He shook his head. "Okay, but..." His voice trailed off.

"You didn't shoot him, Curt. He shot himself. Jax said so."

"Maybe, but if I hadn't gone for his gun, he might be alive."

The anguish in his tone made Bella ache. "Alive to be jailed and probably executed," she said. "He was so fragile and disoriented. I can't imagine how he would have endured prison, and I don't know how Mr. Windsor would have dealt with Garlan being electrocuted. He already feels guilty for not dealing with the boy's issues in a better way."

Curt leaned against the counter and folded his arms across his chest. "Jax said the same, and I suppose you're both right. But to see him die. Saw too much of that in France."

Tears filled Bella's eyes, and she blinked quickly to clear them away. "I know you did," she whispered.

His gaze went to her face. "I'm sorry, Bella. Don't mean to remind you of Matt."

She offered a slight smile. "I think of him every day, Curt. Not the way he died, but the way he lived."

"Same with me." The former soldier's voice was almost inaudible.

Tears pricked Bella's eyes, but she blinked them away. "Try to remember how he was in life. That's what he'd want. That's what they'd all want."

He gave a sharp nod. "I'll try."

"Have you eaten anything?"

"Mrs. Smedlay fed me."

"Good. Why don't you get some rest now? It's been a long day."

"Yep, it has," he agreed before heading toward the suite he shared with his brother.

Bella returned to her typing. Within a short time, she completed the task and was neatly stacking the papers when footsteps sounded on the front porch. Once the door opened, she wasn't surprised to see Jax, who looked every bit as dispirited, dejected, and depleted as Curt.

"I just finished typing the notes," she told him. "Why don't you sit by the fire? I'll fix some coffee and a plate of cookies."

"Don't bother, Bella." His tone was as weary as his countenance.

"It's not a bother, and you look like you could use something to perk you up."

His lips softened but didn't quite form a smile. "It may be a while before I *perk up,* as you say, but some coffee would be good." Jax doffed his cap and went to sit by the crackling fire.

"I won't be long," she told him once he'd settled in one of the wing chairs. When she returned with the snack, he was fast asleep. Not wanting to disturb him, she went about preparing a very late dinner for Mac and Carl.

***

About thirty minutes later, a tap on the kitchen door preceded Jax's arrival. A dark flush stained his lean cheeks. "I'm sorry I fell asleep."

"You needed the rest."

A shrug lifted one shoulder. "I'll get the report and be on my way."

"There's no hurry. Dinner will be ready soon. You only ate part of your sandwich earlier."

He hesitated. "I should get back to the office."

Bella chewed on her lower lip. "I know you said it's hard to be here because Ballantyne brings back a lot of memories and lost dreams but..."

Jax cut her off. "It isn't just that, Bella." He twirled his cap in his hands. Being around her so much over the past few days had wreaked havoc with the barrier he'd put between them. Now, he wanted to be around her more. Much more. But Bella didn't know the truth about him, about what he'd done, about the role he'd played in Matt's death. Jax was too afraid and ashamed to tell her. She needed to focus on the future, not be drawn back into the past.

"If not that, why be in a hurry to leave?"

Jax bowed his head. "I appreciate the offer, Bella. I really do, but I need to finish up the report tonight and get it to the mayor. He's pleased the murder is solved, but he wants the details—in writing—as soon as possible."

"I see."

Her tone indicated she clearly did not see, but he wasn't letting her. He couldn't. For the past few days, he'd dropped his guard and let her get close to him again. It couldn't continue. "I don't want to lose my job and, even though Fike has relented, there are still people in town who find me lacking as a constable. There's a council meeting tomorrow. I'll be there, but I want the mayor and councilmen to have my report beforehand. There will be fewer questions that way. At least I hope so."

"That's understandable," she replied. "I'll get the typed notes for you."

When Bella brushed past him, Jax had to ball his hands into fists to keep from reaching for her. With a sigh, he trailed her into the lobby. He needed to escape as soon as possible. That was best for both of them.

When she returned and handed him the typed notes, Bella offered a tentative grin. "Here you go."

Jax tried to match her smile. "Thank you for all of your help, Bella. You made a real difference in getting this case solved, and I appreciate it."

For several moments, she studied his face. "If you have another big case, will you accept my help?" she finally asked with a slight smile.

The image of her getting out of the car and being exposed to possible gunfire flashed through his mind's eye. Ice cold fear had filled him then, and it did now. He'd been the cause of her brother's death, but he wouldn't be the cause of hers. Knowing she would balk if he chastised her, Jax simply said, "I doubt that will happen. After all, this was the first murder in Moreley. I hope we don't have any more." He forced a casual grin although he felt far from relaxed. Bella had always been fearless, which was not necessarily a good trait. If he ever investigated another homicide, Jax planned to keep her well away.

"I hope so, too, but I wondered."

Something in her tone and expression indicated she wondered about more than that. He hurriedly put his constable's cap on his head and turned toward the door. "I need to get on my way. Take care of yourself, Bella." Jax was halfway outside when she replied.

"You need to do the same."

Suddenly, he realized those were the exact words they had exchanged after the long weekend in Paris with Matt. Speaking his past response *I absolutely will, and I'll take care of your brother, too* was impossible. Remorse and regret were always with him, and they rose hard and strong. Mac had been right. There could have been more, much more, between Jax and Bella at one time, but not now. Not ever. He hadn't kept her brother safe. Quite the contrary. It had been his own failing that led to Matt's death which meant, in all good conscience, Jax could never make promises to Bella again. He couldn't reveal the truth, either. Not about why Matt was dead or about Alan Brewster. The former would hurt her too much, and the latter would wound Bella's best friend. Better to keep the secrets, and his distance.

When he looked back, Jax saw only sincerity in her expression. Perhaps, she'd forgotten their exchange in Paris. "Not much happens around Moreley, as a rule," he said with forced nonchalance.

A smile lifted her lips. "I'm hoping a lot more will go on once spring is here. Good things like more visitors and more business. Now that we know no soldiers were involved in the crimes, word should spread which will help."

Her optimism had him nodding. "I'm sure it will, and you're probably right about more folks coming here and to town. That will keep you and Mac busy."

"I think so. Now that the murder and vandalism are solved, I plan to do everything I can to ensure Ballantyne gets back to normal."

"That will take a lot of work," he pointed out.

"Yes, it will but I don't mind. It's what I want most of all, and I'm willing to do whatever it takes," she said in a firm voice. "Of course, I have Mac, Carl, and Curt to help so I'm not alone."

Briefly, Jax wished he could help. He wished he had a right and a reason to be part of Ballantyne again. But he didn't. His life had taken a completely different direction. "I know you'll succeed," he replied. "Now, I better be on my way." Once again, he turned toward the door but, this time, he walked into the swirling snow without a backward glance.

***

When the door clicked shut behind him, Bella sighed. During the past few days, the two of them had chatted easily at times. Not many times, but still, she'd thought the old Jax was emerging. But how could he be the same when, due to his wounds, he'd had to put his dreams aside? Sadness filled her. Sadness for her childhood friend and girlhood crush. Sadness for what might have been. She still wished they could maintain some camaraderie, but the war had clearly injured Jax in more than one way. Physical injuries were bad, but emotional scars were so much worse.

A sigh escaped her. Bella was still coping with her own sorrow, but she had an important goal. Saving Ballantyne was what mattered now, and that would take all of her effort and attention. Fighting her own battles was enough; she couldn't take on Jax's struggles, too. At least his job was no longer in a precarious state, and neither were Ballantyne or Moreley. All was not well, but it was better. Much better. For that, she was grateful.

Don't miss out!

Visit the website below and you can sign up to receive emails whenever D.S. Lang publishes a new book. There's no charge and no obligation.

https://books2read.com/r/B-A-JJPN-XHUMB

BOOKS 2 READ

Connecting independent readers to independent writers.

Also by D.S. Lang

The Hounded Hoopster
The Surly Secretary
The Doro Banyon Mysteries Books 1-3

Watch for more at https://www.dslangbooks.com.

About the Author

D.S. Lang, a native Ohioan, has been making up stories since she was a little girl, and she still is! Along the way, she studied English and social studies as an undergrad. After graduate school, she went on to teach government and American history in high school. She also taught English at the junior high, high school, and college levels. In addition, she has worked as a program coordinator, golf shop manager, and online tutor.

Now, she spends much of her time reading, researching, and writing. Most recently, she has delved into the Great War era and the years immediately after it. Her Arabella Stewart Historical Mystery Series was inspired by her Great Uncle Brice who served in the American Expeditionary Force during World War One, and by her love of historical mysteries. In her spare time, she loves to spend time with family and friends, including her dog Izzy.

For more about D.S. and upcoming books in this series, please see her website and sign up for her newsletter at www.dslangbooks.com

Read more at https://www.dslangbooks.com.

www.ingramcontent.com/pod-product-compliance
Lightning Source LLC
Chambersburg PA
CBHW051330020726
47501CB00007B/2009